The Old Showmen and the Old London Fairs

Thomas Frost

Copyright © 2018 Okitoks Press

All rights reserved.

ISBN: 198426186X

ISBN-13: 978-1984261861

Table of Contents

CHAPTER I..3
CHAPTER II...8
CHAPTER III..13
CHAPTER IV. 22
CHAPTER V. 33
CHAPTER VI. 48
CHAPTER VII. 58
CHAPTER VIII. 64
CHAPTER IX 69
CHAPTER X. 82
CHAPTER XI. 102

CHAPTER I.

Origin of Fairs—Charter Fairs at Winchester and Chester—Croydon Fairs—Fairs in the Metropolis—Origin of Bartholomew Fair—Disputes between the Priors and the Corporation—The Westminster Fairs—Southwark Fair—Stepney Fair—Ceremonies observed in opening Fairs—Walking the Fair at Wolverhampton—The Key of the Fair at Croydon—Proclamation of Bartholomew Fair.

There can be no doubt that the practice of holding annual fairs for the sale of various descriptions of merchandise is of very great antiquity. The necessity of periodical gatherings at certain places for the interchange of the various products of industry must have been felt as soon as our ancestors became sufficiently advanced in civilisation to desire articles which were not produced in every locality, and for which, owing to the sparseness of the scattered population, there was not a demand in any single town that would furnish the producers with an adequate inducement to limit their business to one place. Most kinds of agricultural produce might be conveyed to the markets held every week in all the towns, and there disposed of; but there were some commodities, such as wool, for example, the entire production of which was confined to one period of the year, while the demand for many descriptions of manufactured goods in any one locality was not sufficient to enable a dealer in them to obtain a livelihood, unless he carried his wares from one town to another. What, therefore, the great fair of Nishnei-Novgorod is at the present day, the annual fairs of the English towns were, on a less extensive scale, during the middle ages.

One of the most ancient, as well as the most important, of the fairs of this country was that held on St. Giles's Hill, near Winchester. It was chartered by William I., who granted the tolls to his cousin, William Walkelyn, Bishop of Winchester. Its duration was originally limited to one day, but William II. extended it to three days, Henry I. to eight, Stephen to fourteen, and Henry II. (according to Milner, or Henry III., as some authorities say) to sixteen. Portions of the tolls were, subsequently to the date of the first charter, assigned to the priory of St. Swithin, the abbey of Hyde, and the hospital of St. Mary Magdalene. On the eve of the festival of St. Giles, on which day the fair commenced, the mayor and bailiffs of Winchester surrendered the keys of the four gates of the city, and with them their privileges, to the officers of the Bishop; and a court called the Pavilion, composed of the Bishop's justiciaries, was invested with authority to try all causes during the fair. The jurisdiction of this court extended seven miles in every direction from St. Giles's Hill, and collectors were placed at all the avenues to the fair to gather the tolls upon the merchandise taken there for sale. All wares offered for sale within this circle, except in the fair, were forfeit to the Bishop; all the shops in the city were closed, and no business was transacted within the prescribed limits, otherwise than in the fair. It is probable, however, that most of the shopkeepers had stalls on the fair ground.

This fair was attended by merchants from all parts of England, and even from France and Flanders. Streets were formed for the sale of different commodities, and distinguished by them, as the drapery, the pottery, the spicery, the stannary, etc. The neighbouring monasteries had also their respective stations, which they held under the Bishop, and sometimes sublet for a term of years. Milner says that the fair began to decline, as a place of resort for merchants, in the reign of Henry VI., the stannary, that is, the street appointed for the sale of the products of the Cornish mines, being unoccupied. From this period its decline seems to have been rapid, owing probably to the commercial development which followed the extinction of feudalism; though it continued to be an annual mart of considerable local importance down to the present century.

The description of this fair will serve, in a great measure, for all the fairs of the middle ages. Some of them were famous marts for certain descriptions of produce, as, for examples, Abingdon and Hemel Hempstead for wool, Newbury and Royston for cheese, Guildford and Maidstone for hops, Croydon and Kingston summer fairs for cherries; others for manufactured goods of particular kinds, as St. Bartholomew's, in the metropolis, for cloth (hence the local name of Cloth Fair), and Buntingford for hardwares. More usually, the fair was an annual market, to which the farmers of the district took their cattle, and the merchants of the great towns their woollen and linen goods, their hardwares and earthenwares, and the silks, laces, furs, spices, etc., which they imported from the Continent. These, as at Winchester, were arranged in streets of booths, fringed with the stalls of the pedlars and the purveyors of refreshments, for the humbler frequenters of the fair. The farmers, the merchants, and the customers of both, resorted to the more commodious and better-provided tents, in which, as Lydgate wrote of Eastcheap in the fifteenth century,

"One cried ribs of beef, and many a pie;
Pewter pots they clattered on a heap;
There was harp, pipe, and minstrelsy."

Of equal antiquity with the great fair at Winchester were the Chester fairs, held on the festivals of St. John and St. Werburgh, the tolls of which were granted to the abbey of St. Werburgh by Hugh Lupus, second Earl of Chester and nephew of William I. There was a curious provision in this grant, that thieves and other offenders should enjoy immunity from arrest within the city during the three days that the fair lasted. Frequent disputes arose out of this grant between the abbots of St. Werburgh and the mayor and corporation of the city. In the reign of Edward IV., the abbot claimed to have the fair of St. John held before the gates of the abbey, and that no goods should be exposed for sale elsewhere during the fair; while the mayor and corporation contended for the right of the citizens to sell their goods as usual, anywhere within the city. The citizens carried the point in their favour, and the abbot was induced to agree that the houses belonging to the abbey in the neighbourhood of the fair should not be let for the display of goods until those of the citizens were occupied for that purpose. Disputes between the abbey and the city concerning the fair of St. Werburgh continued until 1513, when, by an award of Sir Charles Booth, the abbey was deprived of its interest in that fair.

Croydon Fair dated from 1276, when the interest of Archbishop Kilwardby obtained for the town the right of holding a fair during nine days, beginning on the vigil of St. Botolph, that is, on the 16th of May. In 1314, Archbishop Reynolds obtained for the town a similar grant for a fair on the vigil and morrow of St. Matthew's day; and in 1343, Archbishop Stratford obtained a grant of a fair on the feast of St. John the Baptist. The earliest of these fairs was the first to sink into insignificance; but the others survived to a very recent period in the sheep and cattle fair, held in latter times on the 2nd of October and the two following days, and the cherry fair, held on the 5th of July and the two following days. Whatever may have been the relative importance of these fairs in former times, the former, though held at the least genial season, was, for at least a century before it was discontinued, the most considerable fair in the neighbourhood of the metropolis; while the July fair lost the advantage of being held in the summer, through the contracted limits within which its component parts were pitched. These were the streets between High Street and Surrey Street, and included the latter, formerly called Butcher Row; and the only space large enough for anything of dimensions exceeding those of a stall for the sale of toys or gingerbread, was that at the back of the Corn Market, on which the cattle-market was formerly held.

The first fair established in the metropolis was that which, originally held within the precincts of the priory of St. Bartholomew, soon grew beyond its original limits, and at length came to be held on the spacious area of West Smithfield. The origin of the fair is not related by Maitland, Entick, Northouck, and other historians of the metropolis, who seem to have thought a fair too light a matter for their grave consideration; and more recent writers, who have made it the subject of special research, do not agree in their accounts of it. According to the report made by the city solicitor to the Markets Committee in 1840, "at the earliest periods in which history makes mention of this subject, there were two fairs, or markets, held on the spot where Bartholomew Fair is now held, or in its immediate vicinity. These two fairs were originally held for two entire days only, the fairs being proclaimed on the eve of St. Bartholomew, and continued during the day of St. Bartholomew and the next morrow; both these fairs, or markets, were instituted for the purposes of trade; one of them was granted to the prior of the Convent of St. Bartholomew, 'and was kept for the clothiers of England, and drapers of London, who had their booths and standings within the churchyard of the priory, closed in with walls and gates, and locked every night, and watched, for the safety of their goods and wares.' The other was granted to the City of London, and consisted of the standing of cattle, and stands and booths for goods, with pickage and stallage, and tolls and profits appertaining to fairs and markets in the field of West Smithfield."

Nearly twenty years after this report was made, and when the fair had ceased to exist, Mr. Henry Morley, searching among the Guildhall archives for information on the subject, found that the fair originated at an earlier date than had hitherto been supposed; and that the original charter was granted by Henry I. in 1133 to Prior Rayer, by whom the monastery of St. Bartholomew was founded. Rayer whose name was Latinised into Raherus, and has been Anglicised by modern writers into Rahere, was originally the King's jester, and a great favourite of his royal master, who, on his becoming an Augustine monk, and, founding the priory of St. Bartholomew, rewarded him with the grant of the rents and tolls arising out of the fair for the benefit of the brotherhood. The prior was so zealous for the good of the monastery that, perhaps also because he retained a hankering after the business of his former profession, he is said to have annually gone into the fair, and exhibited his skill as a juggler, giving the largesses which he received from the spectators to the treasury of the convent.

It was admitted by the report of 1840 that documents in the office of the City solicitor afforded evidence of conflicting opinions on the subject in former times; and it seems probable that the belief in the two charters attributed to Henry II. and the dual character of the fair had its origin in the disputes which arose from time to time, during the thirteenth, fourteenth, and fifteenth centuries, between the civic and monastic authorities as to the right to the tolls payable on goods carried into that portion of the fair which was held in Smithfield, beyond the precincts of the priory. The latter claimed these, on the ground of the grant of the fair; the City claimed them, on the ground that the land belonged to the corporation. The dispute was a natural one, whether Henry II. had granted the Smithfield tolls to the City or not; and there is evidence on record that it arose again and again, until the dissolution of monasteries at the Reformation finally settled it by disposing of one of the parties.

In 1295 a dispute arose between the prior of St. Bartholomew's and Ralph Sandwich, custos of the City, the former maintaining that, as the privileges of the City had become forfeited to the Crown, the tolls of the fair should be paid into the Exchequer. Edward I., who was then at Durham, ordered that the matter should be referred to his treasurer and the barons of the Exchequer; but, while the matter was pending, the disputants grew so warm that the City authorities arrested some of the monks, and confined them in the Tun prison, in Cornhill. They were released by command of the King, but thereupon nine citizens forced the Tun, and released all the other prisoners, by way of resenting the royal interference. The rioters were imprisoned in their turn and a fine of twenty thousand marks was imposed upon the City; but the civic authorities proposed a compromise, and, for a further payment of three thousand marks, Edward consented to pardon the offenders, and to restore and confirm the privileges of the City.

The right of the City to the rents and tolls of the portion of the fair held beyond the precincts of the priory was finally decided in 1445, when the Court of Aldermen appointed four persons as keepers of the fair, and of the Court of Pie-powder, a tribunal instituted for the summary settlement of all disputes arising in the fair, and deriving its name, it is supposed, from *pieds poudres*, because the litigants had their causes tried with the dust of the fair on their feet.

At the dissolution of monasteries, in the reign of Henry VIII., the tolls which had been payable to the priory of St. Bartholomew were sold to Sir John Rich, then Attorney-General; and the right to hold the fair was held by his descendants until 1830, when it was purchased of Lord Kensington by the Corporation of London, and held thereafter by the City chamberlain and the town clerk in trust, thus vesting the rights and interests in both fairs in the same body.

Westminster Fair, locally termed Magdalen's, was established in 1257, by a charter granted by Henry III. to the abbot and canons of St. Peter's, and was held on Tothill Fields, the site of which is now covered by the Westminster House of Correction and some neighbouring streets.

The three days to which it was originally limited, were extended by Edward III. to thirty-one; but the fair was never so well attended as St. Bartholomew's, and fell into disuse soon afterwards.

There was another fair held in the adjoining parish of St. James, the following amusing notice of which in Machyn's diary is the earliest I have been able to find:—

"The xxv. day of June, Saint James fayer by Westminster was so great that a man could not have a pygg for money; and the bear wiffes had nother meate nor drink before iiij of cloke in the same day. And the chese went very well away for 1*d. q.* the pounde. Besides the great and mighti armie of beggares and bandes that were there." Beyond the fact that it was postponed in 1603 on account of the plague, nothing more is recorded concerning this fair until 1664, in which year it was suppressed, "as considered to tend rather to the advantage of looseness and irregularity than to the substantial promoting of any good, common and beneficial to the people."

Southwark Fair, locally known as Lady Fair, was established in 1462 by a charter granted by Edward IV. to the City of London, in the following terms:—

"We have also granted to the said Mayor, Commonalty, and Citizens, and their successors for ever, that they shall and may have yearly one fair in the town aforesaid, for three days, that is to say, the 7th, 8th, 9th days of September, to be holden, together with a Court of Pie-Powders, and with all the liberties to such fairs appertaining: And that they may have and hold there at their said Courts, before their said Minister or deputy, during the said three days, from day to day, hour to hour, and from time to time, all occasions, plaints, and pleas of a Court of Pie-Powders, together with all summons, attachments, arrests, issues, fines, redemptions, and commodities, and other rights whatsoever, to the said Court of Pie-Powders in any way pertaining, without any impediment, let, or hindrance of Us, our heirs or successors, or other our officers and ministers soever."

This charter has sometimes been referred to as granting to the Corporation the right to hold a fair in West Smithfield, in addition to the fair the tolls of which were received by the priory of St. Bartholomew; but that "the town aforesaid" was Southwark is shown by a previous clause, in which it is stated that "to take away from henceforth and utterly to abolish all and all manner of causes, occasions, and matters whereupon opinions, ambiguities, varieties, controversies, and discussions may arise," the King "granted to the said Mayor and Commonalty of the said City who now be, and their successors, the Mayor and Commonalty and Citizens of that City for the time being and for ever, the town of Southwark, with its appurtenances."

The origin of Camberwell Fair is lost in the mist of ages. In the evidence adduced before a petty sessions held at Union Hall in 1823, on the subject of its suppression, it was said that the custom of holding it was mentioned in the 'Domesday Book,' but the statement seems to have been made upon insufficient grounds. It commenced on the 9th of August, and continued three weeks, ending on St. Giles's day; but, in modern times, was limited, like most other fairs, to three days. It seems to have been originally held in the parish churchyard, but this practice was terminated by a clause in the Statute of Winchester, passed in the thirteenth year of the reign of Edward I. It was then removed to the green, where it was held until its suppression. Peckham Fair seems to have been irregular, and merely supplementary to Camberwell Fair.

Stepney Fair was of less ancient date. In 1664 Charles II., at the instance of the Earl of Cleveland, then lord of the manor of Stepney, granted a patent for a weekly market at Ratcliff Cross, and an annual fair on Michaelmas day at Mile End Green, or any other places within the manor of Stepney. The keeping of the market and fair, with all the revenues arising from tolls, etc., was given by the same grant, at the Earl of Cleveland's request, to Sir William Smith and his heirs for ever. The right continued to vest in the baronet's descendants for several years, but long before the suppression of the fair it passed to the lord of the manor, which, in 1720, was sold by the representatives of Lady Wentworth to John Wicker, Esquire, of Horsham, in Sussex, whose son alienated it in 1754. It is now possessed by the Colebrooke family.

The ceremonies observed in opening fairs evince the importance which attached to them. On the eve of the "great fair" of Wolverhampton, held on the 9th of July, there was a procession of men in armour, preceded by musicians playing what was known as the "fair tune," and followed by the steward of the deanery manor and the peace-officers of the town. The custom is said to have originated with the fair, when Wolverhampton was as famous as a mart of the wool trade as it now is for its ironmongery, and merchants resorted to the fair, which formerly lasted fourteen days, from all parts of England. The necessity of an armed force for the maintenance of order during the fair in those days is not improbable. This custom of "walking the fair," as it was called, was discontinued in 1789, and has not since been revived.

The October fair at Croydon was opened as soon as midnight had sounded by the town clock, or, in earlier times, by that of the parish church; the ceremony consisting in the carrying of a key, called "the key of the fair," through its principal avenues. The booth-keepers were then at liberty to serve refreshments to such customers as might present themselves, generally the idlers who followed the bearer of the key; and long before daylight the field resounded with the bleating of sheep, the lowing of cattle, the barking of dogs, and the shouting of shepherds and drovers.

The metropolitan fair of St. Bartholomew was opened by a proclamation, which used to be read at the gate leading into Cloth Fair by the Lord Mayor's attorney, and repeated after him by a sheriff's officer, in the presence of the Lord Mayor, aldermen, and sheriffs. The procession then perambulated Smithfield, and returned to the Mansion House, where, in the afternoon, those of his lordship's household dined together at the swordbearer's table, and so concluded the ceremony.

CHAPTER II.

Amusements of the Fairs in the Middle Ages—Shows and Showmen of the Sixteenth Century—Banks and his Learned Horse—Bartholomew Fair in the time of Charles I.—Punch and Judy—Office of the Revels—Origin of Hocus Pocus—Suppression of Bartholomew Fair—London Shows during the Protectorate—A Turkish Rope-Dancer—Barbara Vanbeck, the Bearded Woman.

Numerous illuminations of manuscripts in the Harleian collection, many of which were reproduced in Strutt's work on the sports and pastimes of the English people, having established the fact that itinerant professors of the art of amusing were in the habit of tramping from town to town, and village to village, for at least two centuries before the Norman Conquest of this country, there can be no doubt that the fairs were so many foci of attraction for them at the times when they were respectively held. As we are told that the minstrels and glee-men flocked to the towns and villages which grew up under the protection of the baronial castles when the marriage of the lord, or the coming of age of the heir, furnished an occasion of popular revelry, and also when the many red-letter days of the mediæval calendar came round, we may be sure that they were not absent from Bartlemy fair even in its earliest years.

Glee-men was a term which included dancers, posturers, jugglers, tumblers, and exhibitors of trained performing monkeys and quadrupeds; and, the masculine including the feminine in this case, many of these performers were women and girls. The illuminations which have been referred to, and which constitute our chief authority as to the amusements of the fairs during the middle ages, introduce us to female posturers and tumblers, in the act of performing the various feats which have been the stock in trade of the acrobatic profession down to the present day. The jugglers exhibited the same feats with balls and knives as their representatives of the nineteenth century; what is professionally designated "the shower," in which the balls succeed each other rapidly, while describing a semi-circle from right to left, is shown in one of the Harleian illuminations.

Balancing feats were also exhibited, and in one of these curious illustrations of the sights which delighted our fair-going ancestors, the balancing of a cart-wheel is represented—a trick which might have been witnessed not many years ago in the streets of London, the performer being an elderly negro, said to have been the father of the well-known rope-dancer, George Christoff, who represented the Pompeian performer on the *corde elastique*, when Mr. Oxenford's version of *The Last Days of Pompeii* was produced at the Queen's Theatre.

Performing monkeys, bears, and horses appear in many of the mediæval illuminations, and were probably as popular agents of public amusement in the earliest years of Bartlemy fair as they can be shown, from other authorities, to have been in the sixteenth century. That monkeys were imported rather numerously for the amusement of the public, may be inferred from the fact of some Chancellor of the Exchequer of the middle ages having subjected them to an import duty. Their agility was displayed chiefly in vaulting over a chain or cord. Bears were taught to feign death, and to walk erect after their leader, who played some musical instrument. Horses were also taught to walk on their hind legs, and one drawing in the Harleian collection shows a horse in this attitude, engaged in a mimic fight with a man armed with sword and buckler.

All these performances seem to have been continued, by successive generations of performers, down to the time of Elizabeth. Reginald Scot, writing in 1584, gives a lengthy enumeration of the tricks of the jugglers who frequented the fairs of the latter part of the sixteenth century. Among them are most of the common tricks of the present day, and not the least remarkable is the decapitation feat, which many of my readers have probably seen performed by the famous wizards of modern times at the Egyptian Hall. Three hundred years ago, it was called the decollation of St. John the Baptist, and was performed upon a table, upon which stood a dish to receive the head. The table, the dish, and the knife used in the apparent decapitation were all contrived for the purpose, the table having two holes in it, one to enable the assistant who submitted to the operation to conceal his head, the other, corresponding to a hole in the dish, to receive the head of another confederate, who was concealed beneath the table, in a sitting position; while the knife had a semi-circular opening in the blade to fit the neck. Another knife, of the ordinary kind, was shown to the spectators, who were prevented by a sleight of hand trick from observing the substitution for it of the knife used in the trick. The engraving in Malcolm's work shows the man to be operated upon lying upon the table, apparently headless, while the head of the other assistant appears in the dish.

That *lusus naturæ*, and other natural curiosities, had begun to be exhibited by showmen in the reign of Elizabeth, may be inferred from the allusions to such exhibitions in *The Tempest*, when Caliban is discovered, and the mariners speculate upon his place in the scale of animal being. It seems also that the practice of displaying in front of the shows large pictures of the wonderful feats, or curious natural objects, to be seen within, prevailed in the sixteenth century, and probably long before; for it is distinctly alluded to in a passage in Jonson's play of *The Alchymist*, in which the master of the servant who has filled the house with searchers for the philosopher's stone, says,

"What should my knave advance
To draw this company? He hung out no banners
Of a strange calf with five legs to be seen,
Or a huge lobster with six claws."

Some further glimpses of the Bartlemy fair shows of the Elizabethan period are afforded in the induction or prologue to another play of Jonson's, namely, the comedy of *Bartholomew Fair*, acted in 1614. "He," says the dramatist, speaking of himself, "has ne'er a sword and buckler-man in his fair; nor a juggler with a well-educated ape to come over the chain for the King of England, and back again for the Prince, and sit still on his haunches for the Pope and the King of Spain." The sword and buckler-man probably means a performer who took part in such a mimic combat of man and horse, as is represented in the illumination which has been referred to. The monkey whose Protestant proclivities are noted in the latter part of the passage is mentioned in a poem of Davenant's, presently to be quoted.

We cannot suppose absent from the metropolitan fairs the celebrated performing horse, Morocco, and his instructor, of whom Sir Walter Raleigh says, "If Banks had lived in older times, he would have shamed all the enchanters in the world; for whosoever was most famous among them could never master or instruct any beast as he did." That Shakspeare witnessed the performances of Morocco, which combined arithmetical calculations with saltatory exercises, is shown by the allusion in *Love's Labour Lost*, when Moth puzzles Armado with arithmetical questions, and says, "The dancing horse will tell you." Sir Kenelm Digby states that the animal "would restore a glove to the due owner after the master had whispered the man's name in his ear; and would tell the just number of pence in any piece of silver coin newly showed him by his master."

Banks quitted England for the Continent with his horse in 1608, and De Melleray, who witnessed the performance of the animal in the Rue St. Jacques, in Paris, says that Morocco could not only tell the number of francs in a crown, but knew that the crown was depreciated at that time, and knew the exact amount of the depreciation. From Paris, Banks travelled with his learned horse to Orleans, where the fame which they had acquired brought him under the imputation of being a sorcerer, and he had a narrow escape of being burned at a stake in that character. Bishop Morton says that he cleared himself by commanding his horse to "seek out one in the press of the people who had a crucifix on his hat; which done, he bade him kneel down unto it, and not this only, but also to rise up again, and to kiss it. 'And now, gentlemen,' (quoth he), 'I think my horse hath acquitted both me and himself;' and so his adversaries rested satisfied; conceiving (as it might seem) that the devil had no power to come near the cross."

We next hear of Banks and his horse at Frankfort-on-the-Maine, where Bishop Morton saw them, and heard from the former the story of his narrow escape at Orleans. Their further wanderings cannot be traced; and, though it has been inferred, from a passage in a burlesque poem by Jonson, that Banks was burned as a sorcerer, the grounds which the poet had for assigning such a dreadful end for the famous horse-charmer are unknown, and may have been no more than an imperfect recollection of what he had heard of the Orleans story.

A hare which played the tabor is alluded to by Jonson in the comedy before mentioned; and this performance also was not unknown to earlier times, one of the illuminations copied by Strutt showing it to have been exhibited in the fifteenth century. When Jonson wrote his comedy, the amusing classes, encouraged by popular favour, were raising their heads again, after the sore discouragement of the Vagrancy Act of Elizabeth's reign, which scheduled jugglers and minstrels with strolling thieves, gipsy fortune-tellers, and itinerant beggars. Elizabeth's tastes seem to have inclined more to bull-baiting and bear-baiting than to dancing and minstrelsy, juggling and tumbling; and, besides this, there was a broad line drawn in those days, and even down to the reign of George III., as will be hereafter noticed, between the upper ten thousand and the masses, as to the amusements which might or ought to be permitted to the former and denied to the latter.

In the succeeding reign the operation of the Vagrancy Act was powerfully aided by the rise of the Puritans, who regarded all amusements as worldly vanities and snares of the Evil One, and indulgence in them as a coquetting with sin. As yet they lacked the power to suppress the fairs and close the theatres, though their will was good to whip and imprison all such inciters to sin and agents of Satan as they conceived minstrels, actors, and showmen to be; and Bartholomew Fair showed no diminution of popular patronage even in the reign of Charles I.

"Hither," says the author of a scarce pamphlet, printed in 1641, "resort people of all sorts and conditions. Christchurch cloisters are now hung full of pictures. It is remarkable, and worth your observation, to behold and hear the strange sights and confused sounds in the fair. Here, a knave in a fool's coat, with a trumpet sounding, or on a drum beating, invites you to see his puppets. There, a rogue like a wild woodman, or in an antic shape like an incubus, desires your company to view his motion; on the other side, hocus pocus, with three yards of tape or ribbon in his hand, showing his art of legerdemain, to the admiration and astonishment of a company of cockoloaches. Amongst these, you shall see a gray goosecap (as wise as the rest), with a 'What do ye lack?' in his mouth, stand in his booth shaking a rattle, or scraping on a fiddle, with which children are so taken, that they presently cry out for these fopperies: and all these together make such a distracted noise, that you would think Babel were not comparable to it.

"Here there are also your gamesters in action: some turning of a whimsey, others throwing for pewter, who can quickly dissolve a round shilling into a three-halfpenny saucer. Long Lane at this time looks very fair, and puts out her best clothes, with the wrong side outward, so turned for their better turning off; and Cloth Fair is now in great request: well fare the ale-houses therein, yet better may a man fare (but at a dearer rate) in the pig-market, alias pasty-nook, or pie-corner, where pigs are all hours of the day on the stalls, piping hot, and would cry, (if they could speak,) 'Come, eat me!'"

The puppets and "motions" alluded to in the foregoing description were beginning to be a very favourite spectacle, and none of the puppet plays of the period were more popular than the serio-comic drama of *Punch and Judy*, attributed to Silvio Florillo, an Italian comic dramatist of the time. According to the original version of the story, which has undergone various changes, some of which have been made within the memory of the existing generation, Punch, in a paroxysm of jealousy, destroys his infant child, upon which Judy, in revenge, belabours him with a cudgel. The exasperated hunchback seizes another stick, beats his wife to death, and throws from the window the two corpses, which attracts the notice of a constable, who enters the house to arrest the murderer. Punch flies, but is arrested by an officer of the Inquisition, and lodged in prison; but contrives to escape by bribing the gaoler. His subsequent encounters with a dog, a doctor, a skeleton, and a demon are said to be an allegory, intended to convey the triumph of humanity over ennui, disease, death, and the devil; but, as there is nothing allegorical in the former portion of the story, this seems doubtful.

The allegory was soon lost sight of, if it was ever intended, and the latter part of the story has long been that which excites the most risibility. As usually represented in this country during the last fifty years, and probably for a much longer period, Punch does not bribe the gaoler, but evades execution for his crimes by strangling the hangman with his own noose. Who has not observed the delight, venting itself in screams of laughter, with which young and old witness the comical little wretch's fight with the constable, the wicked leer with which he induces the hangman to put his neck in the noose by way of instruction, and the impish chuckling in which he indulges while strangling his last victim? The crowd laughs at all this in the same spirit as the audience at a theatre applauds furiously while a policeman is bonneted and otherwise maltreated in a pantomime or burlesque. The tightness of the matrimonial noose, it is to be feared, materially influences the feeling with which the murder of a faithless wife is regarded by those whose poverty shuts out the prospect of divorce. And Punch is such a droll, diverting vagabond, that even those who have witnessed his crimes are irresistibly seduced into laughter by his grotesque antics and his cynical bursts of merriment, which render him such a strange combination of the demon and the buffoon.

The earliest notices of the representation in London of 'Punch's Moral Drama,' as an old comic song calls it, occur in the overseer's books of St. Martin's in the Fields for 1666 and 1667, in which are four entries of sums, ranging from twenty-two shillings and sixpence to fifty-two shillings and sixpence, as "Rec. of Punchinello, ye Italian popet player, for his booth at Charing Cross."

Hocus pocus, used in the Bartholomew Fair pamphlet as a generic term for conjurors, is derived from the assumed name of one of the craft, of whom Ady, in 'A Candle in the Dark,' wrote as follows:—

"I will speak of one man more excelling in that craft than others, that went about in King James's time, and long since, who called himself the King's Majestie's most excellent Hocus Pocus; and so was he called because at playing every trick he used to say, *Hocus pocus tontus talontus, vade celeriter jubeo*—a dark composition of words to blind the eyes of the beholders."

All these professors of the various arts of popular entertainment had, at this period, to pay an annual licence duty to the Master of the Revels, whose office was created by Henry VIII. in 1546. Its jurisdiction extended over all wandering minstrels and every one who blew a trumpet publicly, except "the King's players." The seal of the office, used under five sovereigns, was engraved on wood, and was formerly in the possession of the late Francis Douce, by whose permission it was engraved for Chalmers's 'Apology for the Believers in the Shakspeare MSS.,' and subsequently for Smith's 'Ancient Topography of London.' The legend round it was, "SIGILL : OFFIC : JOCOR : MASCAR : ET REVELL : DNIS REG." The Long Parliament abolished the office, which, indeed, would have been a sinecure under the Puritan rule, for in 1647 the entertainers of the people were forbidden to exercise their vocation, the theatres were closed, the May-poles removed, and the fairs shorn of all their wonted amusements, and reduced to the status of annual markets.

There is, in the library of the British Museum, a doggrel ballad, printed as a broadsheet, called *The Dagonizing of Bartholomew Fair*, which describes, with coarse humour, the grossness of which may be attributed in part to the mingled resentment and contempt which underlies it, the measures taken by the civic authorities for the removal from the fair of the showmen who had pitched there, in spite of the determination of the Lord Mayor and the Court of Aldermen, to suppress with the utmost rigour everything which could move to laughter or minister to wonder. Among these are mentioned a fire-eating conjuror, a "Jack Pudding," and "wonders made of wax," being the earliest notice of a wax-work exhibition which I have been able to discover.

Whether the itinerant traders who were wont to set up their stalls in the fairs of Smithfield, and Westminster, and Southwark, found it worth their while to do so during the thirteen years of the banishment of shows, there is nothing to show; but we are not without evidence that the showmen were able to follow their vocation without the fairs. Evelyn, who was a lover of strange sights, records in his diary that, in 1654,—"I saw a tame lion play familiarly with a lamb; he was a huge beast, and I thrust my hand into his mouth, and found his tongue rough, like a cat's; also a sheep with six legs, which made use of five of them to walk; and a goose that had four legs, two crops, and as many vents."

Three years later, two other entries are made, concerning shows which he witnessed. First we have, "June 18th. At Greenwich I saw a sort of cat, brought from the East Indies, shaped and snouted much like the Egyptian racoon, in the body like a monkey, and so footed; the ears and tail like a cat, only the tail much longer, and the skin variously ringed with black and white; with the tail it wound up its body like a serpent, and so got up into trees, and with it wrap its whole body round. Its hair was woolly like a lamb; it was exceedingly nimble, gentle, and purred as does the cat." This animal was probably a monkey of the species called by Cuvier, the toque; it is a native of the western regions of India, and one of the most amusing, as well as the most common, of the simial tenants of modern menageries.

"August 15th. Going to London with some company, we stept in to see a famous rope-dancer, called *The Turk*. I saw even to astonishment the agility with which he performed; he walked barefooted, taking hold by his toes only of a rope almost perpendicular, and without so much as touching it with his hands; he danced blindfold on the high rope, and with a boy of twelve years old tied to one of his feet about twenty feet beneath him, dangling as he danced, yet he moved as nimbly as if it had been but a feather. Lastly he stood on his head, on the top of a very high mast, danced on a small rope that was very slack, and finally flew down the perpendicular on his breast, his head foremost, his legs and arms extended, with divers other activities.

"I saw the hairy woman, twenty years old, whom I had before seen when a child. She was born at Augsburg, in Germany. Her very eyebrows were combed upwards, and all her forehead as thick and even as grows on any woman's head, neatly dressed; a very long lock of hair out of each ear; she had also a most prolix beard, and moustachios, with long locks growing on the middle of her nose, like an Iceland dog exactly, the colour of a bright brown, fine as well-dressed flax. She was now married, and told me she had one child that was not hairy, nor were any of her parents or relations. She was very well shaped, and played well on the harpsichord."

This extraordinary creature must have been more than twenty years of age when Evelyn saw her, for the engraved portrait described by Granger bears the following inscription:—"Barbara Vanbeck, wife to Michael Vanbeck, born at Augsburg, in High Germany; daughter of Balthasar and Anne Ursler. Aged 29. A.D. 1651. R. Gaywood f. London."

Another engraved portrait, in the collection of the Earl of Bute, represents her playing the harpsichord, and has a Dutch inscription, with the words—"Isaac Brunn delin. et sc. 1653." One of Gaywood's prints, which, in Granger's time, was in the possession of Fredericks, the bookseller, at Bath, had the following memorandum written under the inscription:—"This woman I saw in Ratcliffe Highway in 1668, and was satisfied she was a woman. John Bulfinch." Granger describes her from the portraits, as follows:—"The face and hands of this woman are represented hairy all over. Her aspect resembles that of a monkey. She has a very long and large spreading beard, the hair of which hangs loose and flowing like the hair of the head. She is playing on the organ. Vanbeck married this frightful creature on purpose to carry her about for a show."

CHAPTER III.

Strolling Players in the Seventeenth Century—Southwark Fair—Bartholomew Fair—Pepys and the Monkeys—Polichinello—Jacob Hall, the Rope-Dancer—Another Bearded Woman—Richardson, the Fire-Eater—The Cheshire Dwarf—Killigrew and the Strollers—Fair on the Thames—The Irish Giant—A Dutch Rope-Dancer—Music Booths—Joseph Clark, the Posturer—William Philips, the Zany—William Stokes, the Vaulter—A Show in Threadneedle Street.

The period of the Protectorate was one of suffering and depression for the entertaining classes, who were driven into obscure taverns and back streets by the severity with which the anti-recreation edicts of the Long Parliament were enforced, and even then were in constant danger of Bridewell and the whipping-post. Performances took place occasionally at the Red Bull theatre, in St. John Street, West Smithfield, when the actors were able to bribe the subordinate officials at Whitehall to connive at the infraction of the law; but sometimes the fact became known to some higher authority who had not been bribed, or whose connivance could not be procured, and then the performance was interrupted by a party of soldiers, and the actors marched off to Bridewell, where they might esteem themselves fortunate if they escaped a whipping as well as a month's imprisonment as idle vagabonds.

Unable to exercise their vocation in London, the actors travelled into the country, and gave dramatic performances in barns and at fairs, in places where the rigour of the law was diminished, or the edicts rendered of no avail, by the magistrates' want of sympathy with the pleasure-abolishing mania, and the readiness of the majority of the inhabitants to assist at violations of the Acts. In one of his wanderings about the country, Cox, the comedian, shod a horse with so much dexterity, in the drama that was being represented, that the village blacksmith offered him employment in his forge at a rate of remuneration exceeding by a shilling a week the ordinary wages of the craft. The story is a good illustration of the realistic tendencies of the theatre two hundred years ago, especially as the practice which then prevailed of apprenticeship to the stage renders it improbable that Cox had ever learned the art of shoeing a horse with a view to practising it as a craftsman.

The provincial perambulations of actors did not, however, owe their beginning to the edicts of the Long Parliament, there being evidence that companies of strolling players existed contemporaneously with the theatres in which Burbage played Richard III. and Shakespeare the Ghost in *Hamlet*. In a prologue which was written for some London apprentices when they played *The Hog hath lost his Pearl* in 1614, their want of skill in acting and elocution is honestly admitted in the following lines—

"We are not half so skilled as strolling players,
Who could not please here as at country fairs."

In the household book of the Clifford family, quoted by Dr. Whitaker in his 'History of Craven,' there is an entry in 1633 of the payment of one pound to "certain itinerant players," who seem to have given a private representation, for which they were thus munificently remunerated; and two years later, an entry occurs of the payment of the same amount to "a certain company of roguish players who represented *A New Way to pay Old Debts*," the adjective being used, probably to distinguish this company, as being unlicensed or unrecognized, from the strolling players who had permission to call themselves by the name of some nobleman, and to wear his livery. The Earl of Leicester maintained such a company, and several other nobles of that period did the same, the actors being known as my Lord Leicester's company, or as the case might be, and being allowed to perform elsewhere when their services were not required by their patron.

The depressed condition of actors at this period is amusingly illustrated by the story of Griffin and Goodman occupying the same chamber, and having but one decent shirt between them, which they wore in turn,—a destitution of linen surpassed only by that which is said to have characterised the ragged regiment of Sir John Falstaff, who had only half a shirt among them all. The single shirt of the two actors was the occasion of a quarrel and a separation between them, one of the twain having worn it out of his turn, under the temptation of an assignation with a lady. What became of the shirt upon the separation of their respective interests in it, we are not told.

The restoration of monarchy and the Stuarts was followed immediately by the re-opening of the theatres and the resumption of the old popular amusements at fairs. Actors held up their heads again; the showmen hung out their pictured cloths in Smithfield and on the Bowling Green in Southwark; the fiddlers and the ballad-singers re-appeared in the streets and in houses of public entertainment. Charles II. entered London, amidst the jubilations of the multitude, on the 29th of May, 1660; and on the 13th of September following, Evelyn wrote in his diary as follows:—

"I saw in Southwark, at St. Margaret's Fair, monkeys and apes dance, and do other feats of activity, on the high rope; they were gallantly clad *à la monde*, went upright, saluted the company, bowing and pulling off their hats; they saluted one another with as good a grace as if instructed by a dancing master; they turned heels over head with a basket having eggs in it, without breaking any; also, with lighted candles in their hands, and on their heads, without extinguishing them, and with vessels of water without spilling a drop. I also saw an Italian wench dance and perform all the tricks on the high rope to admiration; all the Court went to see her. Likewise, here was a man who took up a piece of iron cannon of about 400 lb. weight with the hair of his head only."

Evelyn and Pepys have left no record of the presence of shows at Bartholomew Fair in the first year of the Restoration, nor does the collection of Bartholomew Fair *notabilia* in the library of the British Museum furnish any indication of them; but Pepys tells us that on the 31st of August, in the following year, he went "to Bartholomew Fair, and there met with my Ladies Jemima and Paulina, with Mr. Pickering and Mademoiselle, at seeing the monkeys dance, which was much to see, when they could be brought to do it, but it troubled me to sit among such nasty company." Few years seem to have passed without a visit to Bartholomew Fair on the part of the gossiping old diarist. In 1663 he writes, under date the 7th of September, "To Bartholomew Fair, where I met Mr. Pickering, and he and I went to see the monkeys at the Dutch house, which is far beyond the other that my wife and I saw the other day; and thence to see the dancing on the ropes, which was very poor and tedious."

In the following year two visits to this fair are recorded in Pepys' diary, as follows:—

"Sept. 2. To Bartholomew Fair, and our boy with us, and there showed him the dancing on ropes, and several others the best shows." "Sept. 7. With Creed walked to Bartholomew Fair,—this being the last day, and there I saw the best dancing on ropes that I think I ever saw in my life." In the two following years the fairs and other amusements of London were interrupted by the plague, to the serious loss and detriment of the entertaining classes. Punch and other puppets were the only amusements of 1665 and 1666; and Pepys records that, on the 22nd of August in the latter year—the year of the great fire,—he and his wife went in a coach to Moorfields, "and there saw Polichinello, which pleases me mightily."

In 1667 the fear of the plague had passed away, and the public again patronised the theatres and other places of amusement. "To Polichinello," writes Pepys on the 8th of April, "and there had three times more sport than at the play, and so home." To compensate himself for having missed Bartholomew Fair two years running on account of the plague, he now went three times. "Went twice round Bartholomew Fair," he writes in his diary on the 28th of August, "which I was glad to see again, after two years missing it by the plague." "30th. To Bartholomew Fair, to walk up and down, and there, among other things, found my Lady Castlemaine at a puppet-play, *Patient Grizill*, and the street full of people expecting her coming out." "Sept. 4. With my wife and Mr. Hewer to Bartholomew Fair, and there saw Polichinello."

The fair probably offered better and more various amusements every year, for Pepys records five visits in 1668, when we first hear of the celebrated rope-dancer, Jacob Hall. "August 27. With my wife and W. Batelier and Deb.; carried them to Bartholomew Fair, where we saw the dancing of the ropes, and nothing else, it being late." "29. Met my wife in a coach, and took her and Mercer and Deb. to Bartholomew Fair; and there did see a ridiculous obscene little stage-play called *Marry Andrey* , a foolish thing, but seen by everybody: and so to Jacob Hall's dancing of the ropes, a thing worth seeing, and mightily followed." "Sept. 1. To Bartholomew Fair, and there saw several sights; among others, the mare that tells money and many things to admiration, and among others come to me, when she was bid to go to him of the company that most loved to kiss a pretty wench in a corner. And this did cost me 12*d.* to the horse, which I had flung him before, and did give me occasion to kiss a mighty *belle fille*, that was exceeding plain, but *fort belle*." "4. At noon my wife, and Deb. and Mercer, and W. Hewer and I, to the fair, and there at the old house, did eat a pig, and was pretty merry, but saw no sights, my wife having a mind to see the play of *Bartholomew Fair* with puppets." "7. With my Lord Brouncker (who was this day in unusual manner merry, I believe with drink,) Minnes, and W. Pen to Bartholomew Fair; and there saw the dancing mare again, which to-day I found to act much worse than the other day, she forgetting many things, which her master beat her for, and was mightily vexed; and then the dancing of the ropes, and also a little stage play, which was very ridiculous."

Perhaps a better illustration of the difference between the manners and amusements of the seventeenth century and those of the nineteenth could not be found than that which is afforded by the contrast between the picture drawn by Pepys and the fancy sketch which the reader may draw for himself by giving the figures introduced the names of persons now living. Let the scene be Greenwich Fair, as we all remember it, and the incidents the Secretary to the Admiralty, accompanied by his wife and her maid, going there in his carriage; stopping on the way to witness the vagaries of Punch; meeting the Mistress of the Robes at a marionette performance in a tent; and afterwards, as we shall presently find Pepys doing, drinking in a public-house with a rope-dancer, reputed to be the paramour of a lady of rank, whom our supposed secretary may have met the evening before at Buckingham Palace.

Pepys relates that he went, in the same year, "to Southwark Fair, very dirty, and there saw the puppet-show of Whittington, which was pretty to see; and how that idle thing do work upon people that see it, and even myself too! And thence to Jacob Hall's dancing of the ropes, where I saw such action as I never saw before, and mightily worth seeing; and here took acquaintance with a fellow that carried me to a tavern, whither come the music of this booth, and bye and bye Jacob Hall himself, with whom I had a mind to speak, to hear whether he had ever any mischief by falls in his time. He told me, 'Yes, many, but never to the breaking of a limb;' he seems a mighty strong man. So giving them a bottle or two of wine, I away with Payne, the waterman. He, seeking me at the play, did get a link to light me, and so light me to the Bear, where Bland, my waterman, waited for me with gold and other things he kept for me, to the value of £40 and more, which I had about me, for fear of my pockets being cut. So by link-light through the bridge, it being mighty dark, but still weather, and so home." Jacob Hall was as famous for his handsome face and symmetrical form as for his skill and grace on the rope. He is said to have shared with Harte, the actor, the favours of Nell Gwynne, and afterwards to have been a pensioned favourite of the profligate Countess of Castlemaine. His portrait in Grammont's 'Memoirs' was engraved from an unnamed picture by Van Oost, first said to represent the famous rope-dancer by Ames, in 1748.

A passage in one of Davenant's poems affords some information concerning the character of the shows which formed the attraction of the fairs at this period,

"Now vaulter good, and dancing lass
On rope, and man that cries, Hey, pass!
And tumbler young that needs but stoop,
Lay head to heel, to creep through hoop;
And man in chimney hid to dress
Puppet that acts our old Queen Bess,
And man that, while the puppets play,
Through nose expoundeth what they say;
And white oat-eater that does dwell
In stable small at sign of Bell,
That lifts up hoof to show the pranks
Taught by magician styled Banks;
And ape led captive still in chain
Till he renounce the Pope and Spain;
All these on hoof now trudge from town,
To cheat poor turnip-eating clown."

The preceding chapter will have rendered the allusions intelligible to the reader of the present day.

Among the shows of this period was another bearded woman, whom Pepys saw in Holborn, towards the end of 1668. "She is a little plain woman," he writes, "a Dane; her name, Ursula Dyan; about forty years old; her voice like a little girl's; with a beard as much as any man I ever saw, black almost, and grizzly; it began to grow at about seven years old, and was shaved not above seven months ago, and is now so big as any man's almost that I ever saw; I say, bushy and thick. It was a strange sight to me, I confess, and what pleased me mightily." There was a female giant, too, of whom Evelyn says, under date the 13th of February, 1669, "I went to see a tall gigantic woman, who measured six feet ten inches at twenty-one years old, born in the Low Countries."

Salamandering feats are not so pleasant to witness as the performances of the acrobat and the gymnast, but they create wonder, and, probably, were wondered at more two hundred years ago than at the present time, when the scientific principles on which their success depends are better understood. The earliest performer of the feats which made Girardelli and Chabert famous half a century ago seems to have been Richardson, of whom the following account is given by Evelyn, who witnessed his performance in 1672:—

"I took leave of my Lady Sunderland, who was going to Paris to my lord, now ambassador there. She made me stay dinner at Leicester House, and afterwards sent for Richardson, the famous fire-eater. He devoured brimstone on glowing coals before us, chewing and swallowing them; he melted a beer-glass and eat it quite up; then, taking a live coal on his tongue, he put on it a raw oyster, the coal was blown on with bellows till it flamed and sparkled in his mouth, and so remained till the oyster gaped and was quite boiled. Then he melted pitch and wax with sulphur, which he drank down as it flamed; I saw it flaming in his mouth, a good while; he also took up a thick piece of iron, such as laundresses use to put in their smoothing-boxes, when it was fiery hot, held it between his teeth, then in his hands and threw it about like a stone; but this I observed he cared not to do very long; then he stood on a small pot, and, bending his body, took a glowing iron with his mouth from between his feet without touching the pot or ground with his hands; with divers other prodigious feats."

There are few notices of the London fairs in contemporary memoirs and journals, and as few advertisements of showmen have been preserved by collectors of such literary curiosities, between the last visit to Southwark Fair recorded by Pepys and the period of the Revolution. The public mind was agitated during this time by plots and rumours of plots, by State trials and Tower Hill executions, which alternately excited men to rage and chilled them with horror. Giants and dwarfs, and monstrosities of all kinds, seem to have been more run after, under the influence of these events, than puppets and players. Take the following as an example, an announcement which was printed in 1677:—

"At Mr. Croomes, at the signe of the Shoe and Slap neer the Hospital-gate, in West Smithfield, is to be seen *The Wonder of Nature*, viz., A girl about sixteen years of age, born in Cheshire, and not much above eighteen inches long, having shed the teeth seven several times, and not a perfect bone in any part of her, onely the head, yet she hath all her senses to admiration, and discourses, reads very well, sings, whistles, and all very pleasant to hear. God save the King!"

The office of Master of the Revels, which had been held by Thomas Killigrew, the Court jester, was conferred, at his death, upon his son, who leased the licensing of ballad-singers to a bookseller named Clarke, as appears from the following announcement, which was inserted in the *London Gazette* in 1682:—

"Whereas Mr. John Clarke, of London, bookseller, did rent of Charles Killigrew, Esq., the licensing of all ballad-singers for five years; which time is expired at Lady Day next. These are, therefore, to give notice to all ballad-singers, that take out licenses at the office of the revels, at Whitehall, for singing and selling of ballads and small books, according to an ancient custom. And all persons concerned are hereby desired to take notice of, and to suppress, all mountebanks, rope-dancers, prize-players, ballad-singers, and such as make show of motions and strange sights, that have not a license in red and black letters, under the hand and seal of the said Charles Killigrew, Esq., Master of the Revels to his Majesty."

The only entertainment of which I have found an announcement for this year is the following:—"At Mr. Saffry's, a Dutch-woman's Booth, over against the Greyhound Inn, in West Smithfield, during the time of the fair, will be acted the incomparable Entertainment call'd The Irish Evidence, with the Humours of Teige. With a Variety of Dances. By the first Newmarket Company." Further glimpses of the fair are afforded, however, by the offer of a reward for "the three horses stolen by James Rudderford, a mountebank, and Jeremiah March, his clown;" and the announcement that, "The German Woman that danc'd where the Italian Tumbler kept his Booth, being over against the Swan Tavern, by Hosier Lane end in Bartholomew Fair, is run away from her Mistress, the Fifth of this instant; She is of a Brownish complexion, with Brown Hair, and between 17 and 18 years of Age; if any person whatsoever can bring Tidings to one Mr. Hone's, at the Duke of Albemarle's Head, at the end of Duck Lane, so that her Mistress may have her again, they shall be rewarded to their own content."

In the winter of 1683-4, an addition was temporarily made to the London fairs by the opportunity which the freezing of the Thames afforded for holding a fair on the ice. The river became frozen on the 23rd of December, and on the first day of 1684 the ice was so thick between the bridges that long rows of booths were erected for the sale of refreshments to the thousands of persons who congregated upon it. Evelyn, who visited the strange scene more than once, saw "people and tents selling all sort of wares, as in the City." The frost becoming more intense when it had endured a month, the sports of horse-racing and bull-baiting were presented on the ice; and sledges and skaters were seen gliding swiftly in every direction, with, as Evelyn relates, "puppet-plays and interludes, tippling, and other lewd places." The ice was so thick that the booths and stalls remained even when thaw had commenced, but the water soon rendered it disagreeable to walk upon, and long cracks warned the purveyors of recreation and refection to retreat to the land. The fair ended on the 5th of February.

It was during the continuance of this seventeenth century Frost Fair that Evelyn saw a human salamander, when he dined at Sir Stephen Fox's, and "after dinner came a fellow who eat live charcoal, glowingly ignited, quenching them in his mouth, and then champing and swallowing them down. There was a dog also which seemed to do many rational actions." The last sentence is rather obscure; the writer probably intended to convey that the animal performed many actions which seemed rational.

During the Southwark Fair of the following year, there was a giant exhibited at the Catherine Wheel Inn, a famous hostelry down to our own time. Printers had not yet corrected the irregular spelling of the preceding century, as appears from the following announcement:—"The Gyant, or the Miracle of Nature, being that so much admired young man, aged nineteen years last June, 1684. Born in Ireland, of such a prodigious height and bigness, and every way proportionable, the like hath not been seen since the memory of man. He hath been several times shown at Court, and his Majesty was pleased to walk under his arm, and he is grown very much since; he now reaches ten foot and a half, fathomes near eight foot, spans fifteen inches; And is believed to be as big as one of the Gyants in Guild-Hall. He is to be seen at the Sign of the Catherine Wheel in Southwark Fair. *Vivat Rex.*"

There was probably also to be seen at this fair the Dutch woman of whom an author quoted by Strutt says that, "when she first danced and vaulted on the rope in London, the spectators beheld her with pleasure mixed with pain, as she seemed every moment in danger of breaking her neck." About this time, there was introduced at the London fairs, an entertainment resembling that now given in the music-halls, in which vocal and instrumental music was alternated with rope-dancing and tumbling. The shows in which these performances were given were called music-booths, though the musical element was far from predominating. The musical portion of the entertainment was not of the highest order, if we may trust the judgment of Ward, the author of the *London Spy*, who says that he "had rather have heard an old barber ring Whittington's bells upon the cittern than all the music these houses afforded."

Such dramatic performances as were given in the booths at this time seem to have been, in a great measure, confined to the puppet-plays so often mentioned in the memoirs and diaries of the period. Granger mentions one Philips, who, in the reign of James II., "was some time fiddler to a puppet-show; in which capacity, he held many a dialogue with Punch, in much the same strain as he did afterwards with the mountebank doctor, his master, upon the stage. This Zany, being regularly educated, had the advantage of his brethren." Besides the serio-comic drama of Punch and Judy, many popular stories were represented by the puppets of those days, which set forth the fortunes of Dick Whittington and the sorrows of Griselda, the vagaries of Merry Andrew and the humours of Bartholomew Fair, as delineated by the pen of Ben Jonson. It is a noteworthy circumstance, as showing the estimation in which the Smithfield Fair was held by the upper and middle classes at this period, and for more than half a century afterwards, that the summer season of the patent theatres, which closed at that time, always concluded with a representation of Jonson's now forgotten comedy.

A slight general view of Bartholomew Fair in 1685, with some equally slight and curious moralising on the subject, is presented by Sir Robert Southwell, in a letter addressed to his son, the Honourable Edward Southwell, who was then in London with his tutor, Mr. Webster.

"I think it not now," says Sir Robert, "so proper to quote you verses out of Persius, or to talk of Cæsar and Euclid, as to consider the great theatre of Bartholomew Fair, where I doubt not but you often resort, and 'twere not amiss if you cou'd convert that tumult into a profitable book. You wou'd certainly see the garboil there to more advantage if Mr. Webster and you wou'd read, or cou'd see acted, the play of Ben Jonson, call'd Bartholomew Fair: for then afterwards going to the spot, you wou'd note if things and humours were the same to day, as they were fifty years ago, and take pattern of the observations which a man of sense may raise out of matters that seem even ridiculous. Take then with you the impressions of that play, and in addition thereunto, I shou'd think it not amiss if you then got up into some high window, in order to survey the whole pit at once. I fancy then you will say, *Totus mundus agit histrionem*, and then you wou'd note into how many various shapes human nature throws itself, in order to buy cheap and sell dear, for all is but traffick and commerce, some to give, some to take, and all is by exchange, to make the entertainment complete.

"The main importance of this fair is not so much for merchandize, and the supplying what people really want; but as a sort of Bacchanalia, to gratifie the multitude in their wandering and irregular thoughts. Here you see the rope-dancers gett their living meerly by hazarding of their lives, and why men will pay money and take pleasure to see such dangers, is of seperate and philosophical consideration. You have others who are acting fools, drunkards, and madmen, but for the same wages which they might get by honest labour, and live with credit besides.

"Others, if born in any monstrous shape, or have children that are such, here they celebrate their misery, and by getting of money, forget how odious they are made. When you see the toy-shops, and the strange variety of things, much more impertinent than hobby-horses or gloves of gingerbread, you must know there are customers for all these matters, and it wou'd be a pleasing sight cou'd we see painted a true figure of all these impertinent minds and their fantastick passions, who come trudging hither, only for such things. 'Tis out of this credulous crowd that the ballad-singers attrackt an assembly, who listen and admire, while their confederate pickpockets are diving and fishing for their prey.

"'Tis from those of this number who are more refined, that the mountebank obtains audience and credit, and it were a good bargain if such customers had nothing for their money but words, but they are best content to pay for druggs, and medicines, which commonly doe them hurt. There is one corner of this Elizium field devoted to the eating of pig, and the surfeits that attend it. The fruits of the season are everywhere scatter'd about, and those who eat imprudently do but hasten to the physitian or the churchyard."

In 1697, William Philips, the zany or Jack Pudding mentioned by Granger, was arrested and publicly whipped for perpetrating, in Bartholomew Fair, a jest on the repressive tendencies of the Government, which has been preserved by Prior in a poem. It seems that he made his appearance on the exterior platform of the show at which he was engaged, with a tongue in his left hand and a black pudding in his right. Professing to have learned an important secret, by which he hoped to profit, he communicated it to the mountebank, as related by Prior, as follows:—

"Be of your patron's mind whate'er he says;
Sleep very much, think little, and talk less:
Mind neither good nor bad, nor right nor wrong;
But eat your pudding, slave, and hold your tongue."

Mr. Morley conjectures that this Philips was the W. Phillips who wrote the tragedy of the *Revengeful Queen*, published in 1698, and who was supposed to be the author of another, *Alcamenes and Menelippa*, and of a farce called *Britons, Strike Home*, which was acted in a booth in Bartholomew Fair. But worth more than all these plays would now be, if it could be discovered, the book published in 1688, of which, only the title-page is preserved in the Harleian collection, viz., 'The Comical History of the famous Merry Andrew, W. Phill., Giving an Account of his Pleasant Humours, Various Adventures, Cheats, Frolicks, and Cunning Designs, both in City and Country.'

The circus was an entertainment as yet unknown. The only equestrian performances were of the kind given by Banks, and repeated, as we learn from Davenant and Pepys, by performers who came after him, of whom there was a regular succession down to the time of Philip Astley. The first entertainer who introduced horses into vaulting acts seems to have been William Stokes, a famous vaulter of the reigns of the latter Stuarts. He was the author of a manual of the art of vaulting, which was published at Oxford in 1652, and contains several engravings, showing him in the act of vaulting over a horse, over two horses, and leaping upon them, in one alighting in the saddle, and in another upon the bare back of the horse, *à la Bradbury*.

Another of the great show characters of this period was Joseph Clark, the posturer, who according to a notice of him in the Transactions of the Royal Philosophical Society, "had such an absolute command of all his muscles and joints that he could disjoint almost his whole body." His performance seems to have consisted chiefly in the imitation of every kind of human deformity; and he is said to have imposed so completely upon Molins, a famous surgeon of that period, as to be dismissed by him as an incurable cripple. His portrait in Tempest's collection represents him in the act of shouldering his leg, an antic which is imitated by a monkey.

Clark was the "whimsical fellow, commonly known by the name of the Posture-master," mentioned by Addison in the 'Guardian,' No. 102. He was the son of a distiller in Shoe Lane, who designed him for the medical profession, but a brief experience with John Coniers, an apothecary in Fleet Street, not pleasing him, he was apprenticed to a mercer in Bishopsgate Street. Trade suited him no better than medicine, it would seem, for he afterwards went to Paris, in the retinue of the Duke of Buckingham, and there first displayed his powers as a posturer. He died in 1690, at his house in Pall Mall, and was buried in the church of St. Martin-in-the-Fields. Many portraits of him, in different attitudes, are extant in the British Museum.

Monstrosities have always been profitable subjects for exhibition. Shakespeare tells us, and may be presumed to have intended the remark to convey his impression of the tendency of his own generation, that people would give more to see a dead Indian than to relieve a lame beggar; and the profits of the exhibition of Julia Pastrana and the so-called Kostroma people show that the public interest in such monstrosities remains unabated. But what would "City men" say to such an exhibition in Threadneedle Street? I take the following announcement from a newspaper of June, 1698:—

"At Moncrieff's Coffee-house, in Threadneedle Street, near the Royal Exchange, is exposed to view, for sixpence a piece, a Monster that lately died there, being Humane upwards and bruit downwards, wonderful to behold: the like was never seen in England before, the skin is so exactly stuffed that the whole lineaments and proportion of the Monster are as plain to be seen as when it was alive. And a very fine Civet Cat, spotted like a Leopard, and is now alive, that was brought from Africa with it. They are exposed to view from eight in the morning to eight at night."

At the King's Head, in West Smithfield, there was this year exhibited "a little Scotch Man, which has been admired by all that have yet seen him, he being but two Foot and six Inches high; and is near upon 60 years of Age. He was marry'd several years, and had Issue by his Wife, two sons (one of which is with him now). He Sings and Dances with his son, and has had the Honour to be shewn before several Persons of Note at their Houses, as far as they have yet travelled. He formerly kept a Writing school; and discourses of the Scriptures, and of many Eminent Histories, very wisely; and gives great satisfaction to all spectators; and if need requires, there are several Persons in this town, that will justifie that they were his Schollars, and see him Marry'd."

In the same year, David Cornwell exhibited, at the Ram's Head, in Fenchurch Street, a singular lad, advertised as "the Bold Grimace Spaniard," who was said to have "liv'd 15 years among wild creatures in the Mountains, and is reasonably suppos'd to have been taken out of his cradle an Infant, by some savage Beast, and wonderfully preserv'd, till some Comedians accidentally pass'd through those parts, and perceiving him to be of Human Race, pursu'd him to his Cave, where they caught him in a Net. They found something wonderful in his Nature, and took him with them in their Travels through *Spain* and *Italy*. He performs the following surprising grimaces, viz., He lolls out his Tongue a foot long, turns his eyes in and out at the same time; contracts his Face as small as an Apple; extends his Mouth six inches, and turns it into the shape of a Bird's Beak, and his eyes like to an Owl's; turns his mouth into the Form of a Hat cock'd up three ways; and also frames it in the manner of a four-square Buckle; licks his Nose with his Tongue, like a Cow; rolls one Eyebrow two inches up, the other two down; changes his face to such an astonishing Degree, as to appear like a Corpse long bury'd. Altho' bred wild so long, yet by travelling with the aforesaid Comedians 18 years, he can sing wonderfully fine, and accompanies his voice with a thorow Bass on the Lute. His former natural Estrangement from human conversation oblig'd *Mr. Cornwell* to bring a Jackanapes over with him for his Companion, in whom he takes great Delight and Satisfaction."

How many of these show creatures were impostors, and how many genuine eccentricities of human nature, it is impossible to say. Barnum's revelations have made us sceptical. But the numerous advertisements of this kind in the newspapers of the period show that the passion for monstrosities was as strongly developed in the latter half of the seventeenth century as at the present day.

Barnes and Appleby's booth for tumbling and rope-dancing appears from the following advertisement, extracted from a newspaper of 1699, to have attended Bartholomew Fair the previous year:—

"At Mr. Barnes's and Mr. Appleby's Booth, between the Crown Tavern and the Hospital Gate, over against the Cross Daggers, next to Miller's Droll Booth, in West Smithfield, where the English and Dutch Flaggs, with Barnes's and the two German Maidens' pictures, will hang out, during the time of Bartholomew Fair, will be seen the most excellent and incomparable performances in Dancing on the Slack Rope, Walking on the Slack Rope, Vaulting and Tumbling on the Stage, by these five, the most famous Companies in the Universe, viz., The English, Irish, High German, French, and Morocco, now united. The Two German Maidens, who exceeded all mankind in their performances, are within this twelvemonth improved to a Miracle."

In this year I find the following advertisement of a music booth, which must have been one of the earliest established:—

"Thomas Dale, Drawer at the Crown Tavern at Aldgate, keepeth the Turk's Head *Musick Booth*, in Smithfield Rounds, over against the *Greyhound* Inn during the time of *Bartholomew Fair*, Where is a Glass of good Wine, Mum, Syder, Beer, Ale, and all other Sorts of Liquors, to be Sold; and where you will likewise be entertained with good Musick, Singing, and Dancing. You will see a Scaramouch Dance, the Italian Punch's Dance, the Quarter Staff, the Antick, the Countryman and Countrywoman's Dance, and the Merry Cuckolds of Hogsden.

"Also a young Man that dances an Entry, Salabrand, and Jigg, and a Woman that dances with Six Naked Rapiers, that we Challenge the whole Fair to do the like. There is likewise a Young Woman that Dances with Fourteen Glasses on the Backs and Palms of her Hands, and turns round with them above an Hundred Times as fast as a Windmill turns; and another Young Man that Dances a Jigg incomparably well, to the Admiration of all Spectators. *Vivat Rex.*"

James Miles, who announced himself as from Sadler's Wells, kept the Gun music-booth in the fair, and announced nineteen dances, among which were "a dance of three bullies and three Quakers;" a cripples' dance by six persons with wooden legs and crutches, "in imitation of a jovial crew;" a dance with swords, and on a ladder, by a young woman, "with that variety that she challenges all her sex to do the like;" and a new entertainment, "between a Scaramouch, a Harlequin, and a Punchinello, in imitation of bilking a reckoning." We shall meet with James Miles again in the next chapter and century.

CHAPTER IV.

Attempts to Suppress the Shows at Bartholomew Fair—A remarkable Dutch Boy—Theatrical Booths at the London Fairs—Penkethman, the Comedian—May Fair—Barnes and Finley—Lady Mary—Doggett, the Comedian—Simpson, the Vaulter—Clench, the Whistler—A Show at Charing Cross—Another Performing Horse—Powell and Crawley, the Puppet-Showmen—Miles's Music-Booth—Settle and Mrs. Mynn—Southwark Fair—Mrs. Horton, the Actress—Bullock and Leigh—Penkethman and Pack—Boheme, the Actor—Suppression of May Fair—Woodward, the Comedian—A Female Hercules—Tiddy-dol, the Gingerbread Vendor.

So early as the close of the seventeenth century, one hundred and fifty years before the fair was abolished, we find endeavours being made, in emulation of the Puritans, to banish every kind of amusement from Bartholomew Fair, and limit it to the purposes of an annual market. In 1700, the Lord Mayor and Court of Aldermen resolved that no booths should be permitted to be erected in Smithfield that year; but on the 6th of August it was announced that "the lessees of West Smithfield having on Friday last represented to a Court of Aldermen at Guildhall, that it would be highly injurious to them to have the erection of all booths there totally prohibited, the right honourable Lord Mayor and the Court of Aldermen have, on consideration of the premises, granted licence to erect some booths during the time of Bartholomew Fair now approaching; but none are permitted for music-booths, or any that may be means to promote debauchery." And, on the 23rd, when the Lord Mayor went on horseback to proclaim the fair, he ordered two music-booths to be taken down immediately.

On the 4th of June, in the following year, the grand jury made a presentment to the following effect:—"Whereas we have seen a printed order of the Lord Mayor and Court of Aldermen, the 25th June, 1700, to prevent the great profaneness, vice, and debauchery, so frequently used and practised in Bartholomew Fair, by strictly charging and commanding all persons concerned in the said fair, and in the sheds and booths to be erected and built therein or places adjacent, that they do not let, set, or hire, or use any booth, shed, stall, or other erection whatsoever to be used or employed for interludes, stage-plays, comedies, gaming-places, lotteries, or music meetings: and as we are informed the present Lord Mayor and Court of Aldermen have passed another order to the same effect on the 3rd instant, we take this occasion to return our most hearty thanks for their religious care and great zeal in this matter; we esteeming a renewing of their former practices at the Fair a continuing one of the chiefest nurseries of vice next to the play-houses; therefore earnestly desire that the said orders may be vigorously prosecuted, and that this honourable Court would endeavour that the said fair may be employed to those good ends and purposes it was at first designed."

This presentment deserves, and will repay, the most attentive consideration of those who would know the real character of the amusements presented at the London fairs, and the motives and aims of those who endeavoured to suppress them. The grand jury profess to be actuated by a desire to diminish profanity, vice, and debauchery; and, if this had been their real and sole object, nothing could have been more laudable. But, like those who would suppress the liquor traffic in order to prevent drunkenness, they confounded the use with the abuse of the thing which they condemned, and sought to deprive the masses of every kind of amusement, because some persons could not participate therein without indulging in vicious and debasing pleasures. It might have been supposed that Bartholomew Fair was pre-eminently a means and occasion of vice and debauchery, and that its continuance was incompatible with the maintenance of public order and the due guardianship of public morals, if the grand jury had not coupled with their condemnation an expression of their opinion that it was not so bad as the theatres. In that sentence is disclosed the real motive and aim of those who sought the suppression of the amusements of the people at the London Fairs.

That the morals and manners of that age were of a low standard is undeniable; but they would have been worse if the fairs had been abolished, and the theatres closed, as the fanatics of the day willed. Men and women cannot be made pious or virtuous by the prohibition of theatres, concerts, and balls, any more than they can be rendered temperate by suppressing the public sale of beer, wine, and spirits. Naturally, a virtuous man, without being a straight-laced opponent of "cakes and ale," would have seen, in walking through a fair, much that he would deplore, and desire to amend; but such a man would have the same reflections inspired by a visit to a theatre or a music-hall, or any other amusement of the present day. He would not, however, if he was sensible as well as virtuous, conclude from what he saw and heard that all public amusements ought to be prohibited. To suppress places of popular entertainment because some persons abuse them would be like destroying a garden because a snail crawls over the foliage, or an earwig lurks in the flowers.

The London fairs were attended this year by a remarkable Dutch boy, about eight or nine years of age, whose eyes presented markings of the iris in which sharp-sighted persons, aided perhaps by a considerable development of the organ of wonder, read certain Latin and Hebrew words. In one eye, the observer read, or was persuaded that he could read, the words *Deus meus*; in the other, in Hebrew characters, the word *Elohim*. The boy's parents, by whom he was exhibited, affirmed that his eyes had presented these remarkable peculiarities from his birth. Great numbers of persons, including the most eminent physiologists and physicians of the day, went to see him; and the learned, who examined his eyes with great attention, were as far from solving the mystery as the crowd of ordinary sight-seers. Some of them regarded the case as an imposture, but they were unable to suggest any means by which such a fraud could be accomplished. Others regarded it as "almost" supernatural, a qualification not very easy to understand. The supposed characters were probably natural, and only to be seen as Roman and Hebrew letters by imaginative persons, or those who viewed them with the eye of faith. Whatever their nature, the boy's sight was not affected by them in the slightest degree.

The theatrical booths attending the London fairs began at this time to be more numerous, and to present an entertainment of a better character than had hitherto been seen. The elder Penkethman appears to have been the first actor of good position on the stage who set the example of performing in a temporary canvas theatre during the fairs, and it was soon followed by the leading actors and actresses of the royal theatres. In a dialogue on the state of the stage, published in 1702, and attributed to Gildon, Critick calls Penkethman "the flower of Bartholomew Fair, and the idol of the rabble; a fellow that overdoes everything, and spoils many a part with his own stuff." He had then been ten years on the stage, having made his first appearance at Drury Lane in 1692, as the tailor, a small part in *The Volunteers*. Four years later, we find him playing, at the same theatre, such parts as Snap in *Love's Last Shift*, Dr. Pulse in *The Lost Lover*, and Nick Froth in *The Cornish Comedy*.

What the author of the pamphlet just quoted says of this actor receives confirmation and illustration from an anecdote told of him, in connection with the first representation of Farquhar's *Recruiting Officer* at Drury Lane in 1706. Penkethman, who played Thomas Appletree, one of the rustic recruits, when asked his name by Wilks, to whom the part of Captain Plume was assigned, replied, "Why, don't you know my name, Bob? I thought every fool knew that."

"Thomas Appletree," whispered Wilks, assuming the office of prompter.

"Thomas Appletree!" exclaimed Penkethman, aloud. "Thomas Devil! My name is Will Penkethman." Then, turning to the gallery, he addressed one of the audience thus:— "Hark you, friend; don't you know my name?"

"Yes, Master Pinkey," responded the occupant of a front seat in the gallery. "We know it very well."

The theatre was soon in an uproar: the audience at first laughed at the folly of Penkethman and the evident distress of Wilks; but the joke soon grew tiresome, and they began to hiss. Penkethman saw his mistake, and speedily changed displeasure into applause by crying out, with a loud nasal twang, and a countenance as ludicrously melancholy as he could make it, "Adzooks! I fear I am wrong!"

Barnes, the rope-dancer, had at this time lost his former partner, Appleby, and taken into partnership an acrobat named Finley. They advertised their show in 1701 at Bartholomew Fair as, "Her Majesty's Company of Rope Dancers." They had two

German girls "lately arrived from France;" and it was announced that "the famous Mr. Barnes, of whose performances this kingdom is so sensible, Dances with 2 Children at his feet, and with Boots and Spurs. Mrs. Finley, distinguished by the name of Lady Mary for her incomparable Dancing, has much improved herself since the last Fair. You will likewise be entertained with such variety of Tumbling by Mr. Finley and his Company, as was never seen in the Fair before. Note, that for the conveniency of the Gentry, there is a back-door in Smithfield Rounds."

They were not without rivals, though the absence of names from the following advertisement renders it probable that the "famous company" calculated upon larger gains from anonymous boasting than they could hope for from the announcement of their names:—

"At the Great Booth over against the Hospital Gate in Bartholomew Fair, will be seen the Famous Company of Rope Dancers, they being the Greatest Performers of Men, Women, and Children that can be found beyond the Seas, so that the world cannot parallel them for Dancing on the Low Rope, Vaulting on the High Rope, and for Walking on the Slack and Sloaping Ropes, out-doing all others to that degree, that it has highly recommended them, both in Bartholomew Fair and May Fair last, to all the best persons of Quality in England. And by all are owned to be the only amazing Wonders of the World in every thing they do: It is there you will see the Italian Scaramouch dancing on the Rope, with a Wheel-barrow before him, with two Children and a Dog in it, and with a Duck on his Head who sings to the Company, and causes much Laughter. The whole entertainment will be so extremely fine and diverting, as never was done by any but this Company alone."

Doggett, whom Cibber calls the most natural actor of the day, and whose name is associated with the coat and badge rowed for annually, on the 1st of August, by London watermen's apprentices, was here this year, with a theatrical booth, erected at the end of Hosier Lane, where was presented, as the advertisements tell us, "A New Droll call'd the Distressed Virgin or *the Unnatural Parents*. Being a True History of the *Fair Maid of the West*, or the Loving Sisters. With the Comical Travels of *Poor Trusty*, in Search of his *Master's Daughter*, and his Encounter with *Three Witches*. Also variety of *Comick Dances and Songs, with Scenes and Machines never seen before. Vivat Regina*." Doggett was at this time manager of Drury Lane.

Miller, the actor, also had a theatrical booth in the fair, and made the following announcement:—

"Never acted before. At *Miller's Booth*, over against *the Cross Daggers*, near the *Crown Tavern*, during the time of *Bartholomew Fair*, will be presented an Excellent New Droll, call'd The Tempest, or *the Distressed Lovers*. With the *English Hero* and the *Island Princess*, and the Comical Humours of the Inchanted *Scotchman*; or *Jockey* and the *Three Witches*. Showing how a Nobleman of England was cast away upon the Indian Shore, and in his Travel found the Princess of the Country, with whom he fell in Love, and after many Dangers and Perils, was married to her; and his faithful Scotchman, who was saved with him, travelling through Woods, fell in among Witches, when between 'em is abundance of comical Diversions. There in the Tempest is Neptune, with his Triton in his Chariot drawn with Sea Horses and Mair Maids singing. With variety of Entertainment, performed by the best Masters; the Particulars would be too tedious to be inserted here. *Vivat Regina*."

The similarity of the chief incidents in the dramas presented by Doggett and Miller is striking. In both we have the troubles of the lovers, the comical adventures of a man-servant, and the encounter with witches. We shall find these incidents reproduced again and again, with variations, and under different titles, in the plays set before Bartholomew audiences of the eighteenth century.

May Fair first assumed importance this year, when the multiplication of shows of all kinds caused it to assume dimensions which had not hitherto distinguished it. It was held on the north side of Piccadilly, in Shepherd's Market, White Horse Street, Shepherd's Court, Sun Court, Market Court, an open space westward, extending to Tyburn Lane (now Park Lane), Chapel Street, Shepherd Street, Market Street, Hertford Street, and Carrington Street. The ground-floor of the market-house, usually occupied by butchers' stalls, was appropriated during the fair to the sale of toys and gingerbread; and the upper portion was converted into a theatre. The open space westward was covered with the booths of jugglers, fencers, and boxers, the stands of mountebanks, swings, round-abouts, etc., while the sides of the streets were occupied by sausage stalls and gambling tables. The first-floor windows were also, in some instances, made to serve as the proscenia of puppet shows.

I have been able to trace only two shows to this fair in 1702, namely Barnes and Finley's and Miller's, which stood opposite to the former, and presented "an excellent droll called *Crispin and Crispianus: or, A Shoemaker a Prince*; with the best machines, singing and dancing ever yet in the fair." A great concourse of people attended from all parts of the metropolis; an injudicious attempt on the part of the local authorities to exclude persons of immoral character, which has always been found impracticable in places of public amusement, resulted in a serious riot. Some young women being arrested by the constables on the allegation that they were prostitutes, they were rescued by a party of soldiers; and a conflict was begun, which extended as other constables came up, and the "rough" element took part with the rescuers of the incriminated women. One constable was killed, and three others dangerously wounded before the fight ended. The man by whose hand the constable fell contrived to escape; but a butcher who had been active in the affray was arrested, and convicted, and suffered the capital penalty at Tyburn.

In the following year, the fair was presented as a nuisance by the grand jury of Middlesex; but it continued to be held for several years afterwards. Barnes and Finley again had a show at Bartholomew Fair, to which the public were invited to "see my Lady Mary perform such steps on the dancing-rope as have never been seen before." The young lady thus designated, and whose performance attracted crowds of spectators to Barnes and Finley's show, was said to be the daughter of a Florentine noble, and had given up all for love by eloping with Finley. By the companion of her flight she was taught to dance upon the tight rope, and for a few years was an entertainer of considerable popularity; but, venturing to exhibit her agility and grace while *enceinte*, she lost her balance, fell from the rope, and died almost immediately after giving birth to a stillborn child.

Bullock and Simpson, the former an actor of some celebrity at Drury Lane, joined Penkethman this year in a show at Bartholomew Fair, in which *Jephtha's Rash Vow* was performed, Penkethman playing the part of Toby, and Bullock that of Ezekiel. Bullock is described in the pamphlet attributed to Gildon as "the best comedian who has trod the stage since Nokes and Leigh, and a fellow that has a very humble opinion of himself." So much modesty must have made him a *rara avis* among actors, who have, as a rule, a very exalted opinion of themselves. He had been six years on the stage at this time, having made his first appearance in 1696, at Drury Lane, as Sly in *Love's Last Shift*. His ability was soon recognised; and in the same year he played Sir Morgan Blunder in *The Younger Brother*, and Shuffle in *The Cornish Comedy*. Parker and Doggett also had a booth this year at the same fair, playing *Bateman; or, the Unhappy Marriage*, with the latter comedian in the part of Sparrow.

Penkethman at this time, from his salary as an actor at Drury Lane, his gains from attending Bartholomew and Southwark Fairs with his show, and the profits of the

Richmond Theatre, which he either owned or leased, was in the receipt of a considerable income. "He is the darling of Fortunatus," says Downes, writing in 1708, "and has gained more in theatres and fairs in twelve years than those who have tugged at the oar of acting these fifty." He did not retire from the stage, however, until 1724.

Some of the minor shows of this period must now be noticed. A bill of this time—the date cannot always be fixed—invites the visitors to Bartholomew Fair to witness "the wonderful performances of that most celebrated master Simpson, the famous vaulter, who being lately arrived from Italy, will show the world what vaulting is." The chroniclers of the period have not preserved any record, save this bill, of this not too modest performer. A more famous entertainer was Clench, a native of Barnet, whose advertisements state that he "imitates horses, huntsmen, and a pack of hounds, a doctor, an old woman, a drunken man, bells, the flute, and the organ, with three voices, by his own natural voice, to the greatest perfection," and that he was "the only man that could ever attain so great an art." He had a rival, however, in the whistling man, mentioned in the 'Spectator,' who was noted for imitating the notes of all kinds of birds. Clench attended all the fairs in and around London, and at other times gave his performance at the corner of Bartholomew Lane, behind the old Exchange.

To this period also belongs the following curious announcement of "a collection of strange and wonderful creatures from most parts of the world, all alive," to be seen over against the Mews Gate, Charing Cross, by her Majesty's permission.

"The first being a little *Black Man*, being but 3 foot high, and 32 years of age, straight and proportionable every way, who is distinguished by the Name of the *Black Prince*, and has been shewn before most Kings and Princes in Christendom. The next being his wife, the *Little Woman*, NOT 3 foot high, and 30 years of Age, straight and proportionable as any woman in the Land, which is commonly called the *Fairy Queen*; she gives general satisfaction to all that sees her, by Diverting them with Dancing, being big with Child. Likewise their little *Turkey Horse*, being but 2 foot odd inches high, and above 12 years of Age, that shews several diverting and surprising Actions, at the Word of Command. The least Man, Woman, and Horse that ever was seen in the World Alive. *The Horse being kept in a box.* The next being a strange Monstrous Female Creature that was taken in the woods in the Deserts of Æthiopia in Prester *John's* Country, in the remotest parts of Africa. The next is the noble *Picary*, which is very much admir'd by the Learned. The next being the noble *Jack-call*, the Lion's Provider, which hunts in the Forest for the Lion's Prey. Likewise a small *Egyptian Panther*, spotted like a *Leopard*. The next being a strange, monstrous creature, brought from the *Coast of Brazil*, having a Head like a Child, Legs and Arms very wonderful, with a Long Tail like a Serpent, wherewith he Feeds himself, as an *Elephant* doth with his Trunk. With several other Rarities too tedious to mention in this Bill.

"And as no such Collection was ever shewn in this Place before, we hope they will give you content and satisfaction, assuring you, that they are the greatest Rarities that ever was shewn alive in this Kingdom, and are to be seen from nine o'clock in the Morning, till 10 at Night, where true Attendance shall be given during our stay in this Place, which will be very short. *Long live the* Queen."

The proprietors of menageries and circuses are always amusing, if not very lucid, when they set forth in type the attractions of their shows. The owner of the rarities exhibited over against the Mews Gate in the reign of Queen Anne was no exception to the rule. The picary and the jack-call may be readily identified as the peccary and the jackal, but "a strange monstrous female creature" defies recognition, even with the addition that it was brought from Prester John's country. The Brazilian wonder may be classified with safety with the long-tailed monkeys, especially as another and shorter advertisement, in the 'Spectator,' describes it a little more explicitly as a satyr. It was, probably, a spider monkey, one variety of which is said, by Humboldt, to use its prehensile tail for the purpose of picking insects out of crevices.

The Harleian Collection contains the following announcement of a performing horse:—

"To be seen, at the Ship, upon Great Tower Hill, the finest taught horse in the world. He fetches and carries like a spaniel dog. If you hide a glove, a handkerchief, a door-key, a pewter basin, or so small a thing as a silver two-pence, he will seek about the room till he has found it; and then he will bring it to his master. He will also tell the number of spots on a card, and leap through a hoop; with a variety of other curious performances."

Powell, the famous puppet-showman mentioned in the 'Spectator,' in humorous contrast with the Italian Opera, never missed Bartholomew Fair, where, however, he had a rival in Crawley, two of whose bills have been preserved in the Harleian Collection. Pinkethman, another "motion-maker," as the exhibitors of these shows were called, and also mentioned in the 'Spectator,' introduced on his stage the divinities of Olympus ascending and descending to the sound of music. Strutt, who says that he saw something of the same kind at a country fair in 1760, thinks that the scenes and figures were painted upon a flat surface and cut out, like those of a boy's portable theatre, and that motion was imparted to them by clock-work. This he conjectures to have been the character also of the representation, with moving figures, of the camp before Lisle, which was exhibited, in the reign of Anne, in the Strand, opposite the Globe Tavern, near Hungerford Market.

One of the two bills of Crawley's show which have been preserved was issued for Bartholomew Fair, and the other for Southwark Fair. The former is as follows:—

"At Crawley's Booth, over against the Crown Tavern in Smithfield, during the time of Bartholomew Fair, will be presented a little opera, called the *Old Creation of the World*, yet newly revived; with the addition of *Noah's flood*; also several fountains playing water during the time of the play. The last scene does present Noah and his family coming out of the ark, with all the beasts two by two, and all the fowls of the air seen in a prospect sitting upon trees; likewise over the ark is seen the sun rising in a most glorious manner: moreover, a multitude of angels will be seen in a double rank, which presents a double prospect, one for the sun, the other for a palace, where will be seen six angels ringing of bells. Likewise machines descending from above, double, with Dives rising out of hell, and Lazarus seen in Abraham's bosom, besides several figures dancing jiggs, sarabands, and country dances, to the admiration of the spectators; with the merry conceits of *Squire Punch and Sir John Spendall*." This curious medley was "completed by an entertainment of singing, and dancing with several naked swords by a child of eight years of age." In the bill for Southwark Fair we find the addition of "the ball of little dogs," said to have come from Louvain, and to perform "by their cunning tricks wonders in the world of dancing. You shall see one of them named Marquis of Gaillerdain, whose dexterity is not to be compared; he dances with Madame Poucette his mistress and the rest of their company at the sound of instruments, all of them observing so well the cadence that they amaze everybody;" it is added that these celebrated performers had danced before Queen Anne and most of the nobility, and amazed everybody.

James Miles, who has been mentioned in the last chapter, promised the visitors, in a bill preserved in the Harleian Collection, that they should see "a young woman dance with the swords, and upon a ladder, surpassing all her sex." Nineteen different dances were performed in his show, among which he mentions a "wrestlers' dance" and vaulting upon the slack rope. Respecting this dancing with swords, Strutt says that he remembered seeing "at Flockton's, a much noted but very clumsy juggler, a girl about eighteen or twenty years of age, who came upon the stage with four naked swords, two in each hand; when the music played, she turned round with great swiftness, and formed a great variety of figures with the swords, holding them overhead, down by her sides, behind her, and occasionally she thrust them in her bosom. The dance generally continued ten or twelve minutes; and when it was finished, she stopped suddenly, without appearing to be in the least giddy from the constant reiteration of the same motion."

The ladder-dance was performed upon a light ladder, which the performer shifted from place to place, ascended and descended, without permitting it to fall. It was practised at Sadler's Wells at the commencement of the last century, and revived there in 1770. Strutt thought it originated in the stilt-dance, which appears, from an illumination of the reign of Henry III., to have been practised in the thirteenth century.

Mrs. Mynn appears as a Bartholomew Fair theatrical manageress in 1707, when Settle, then nearly sixty years of age, and in far from flourishing circumstances, adapted to her stage his spectacular drama of the *Siege of Troy*, which had been produced at Drury Lane six years previously. Settle, who was a good contriver of spectacles, though a bad dramatic poet, reduced it from five acts to three, striking out four or five of the *dramatis personæ*, cutting down the serious portions of the dialogue, and giving greater breadth as well as length to the comic incidents, without which no Bartholomew audience would have been satisfied. As acted in her theatrical booth, it was printed by Mrs. Mynn, with the following introduction:—

"*A Printed Publication of an* Entertainment *performed on a* Smithfield Stage, *which, how gay or richly soever set off, will hardly reach to a higher Title than the customary name of a* Droll, *may seem somewhat new. But as the present undertaking, the work of ten Months' preparation, is so extraordinary a Performance, that without Boast or Vanity we may modestly say, In the whole several Scenes, Movements, and* Machines, *it is no ways Inferiour even to any one* Opera *yet seen in either of* the Royal Theatres; *we are therefore under some sort of Necessity to make this Publication, thereby to give ev'n the meanest of our audience a full Light into all the Object they will there meet in this* Expensive Entertainment; *the* Proprietors *of which have adventur'd to make, under some small Hopes, That as they yearly see some of their happier Brethren Undertakers in the* Fair, *more cheaply obtain even the Engrost Smiles of the* Gentry *and* Quality *at so much an easier Price; so on the other side their own more costly Projection (though less Favourites) might possibly attain to that good Fortune, at least to attract a little share of the good graces of the more Honourable part of the Audience, and perhaps be able to purchase some of those smiles which elsewhere have been thus long the profuser Donation of particular Affection and Favour.*"

In the following year, Settle arranged for Mrs. Mynn the dramatic spectacle of *Whittington*, long famous at Bartholomew Fair, concluding with a mediæval Lord Mayor's cavalcade, in which nine different pageants were introduced.

In 1708, the first menagerie seems to have appeared at Bartholomew Fair, where it stood near the hospital gate, and attracted considerable attention. Sir Hans Sloane cannot be supposed to have missed such an opportunity of studying animals little known, as he is said to have constantly visited the fair for that purpose, and to have retained the services of a draughtsman for their representation.

The first menagerie in this country was undoubtedly that, which for several centuries, was maintained in the Tower of London, and the beginning of which may be traced to the presentation of three leopards to Henry III. by the Emperor of Germany, in allusion to the heraldic device of the former. Several royal orders are extant which show the progress made in the formation of the menagerie and furnish many interesting particulars concerning the animals. Two of these documents, addressed by Henry III. to the sheriffs of London, have reference to a white bear. The first, dated 1253, directs that fourpence a day should be allowed for the animal's subsistence; and the second, made in the following year, commands that, "for the keeper of our white bear, lately sent us from Norway, and which is in our Tower of London, ye cause to be had one muzzle and one iron chain, to hold that bear without the water, and one long and strong cord to hold the same bear when fishing in the river of Thames."

Other mandates, relating to an elephant, were issued in the same reign, in one of which it is directed, "that ye cause, without delay, to be built at our Tower of London, one house of forty feet long, and twenty feet deep, for our elephant; providing that it be so made and so strong that, when need be it may be fit and necessary for other uses." We learn from Matthew Paris that this animal was presented to Henry by the King of France. It was ten years old, and ten feet in height. It lived till the forty-first year of Henry's reign, in which year it is recorded that, for the maintenance of the elephant and its keeper, from Michaelmas to St. Valentine's Day, immediately before it died, the charge was nearly seventeen pounds—a considerable sum for those days.

Many additions were made to the Tower menagerie in the reign of Edward III.; and notably a lion and lioness, a leopard, and two wild cats. The office of keeper of the lions was created by Henry VI., with an allowance of sixpence a day for the keeper, and a like sum "for the maintenance of every lion or leopard now being in his custody, or that shall be in his custody hereafter." This office was continued until comparatively recent times, when it was abolished with the menagerie, a step which put an end likewise to the time-honoured hoax, said to have been practised upon country cousins, of going to the water side, below London Bridge, to see the lions washed.

The building appropriated to the keeping and exhibition of the animals was a wide semi-circular edifice, in which were constructed, at distances of a few feet apart, a number of arched "dens," divided into two or more compartments, and secured by strong iron bars. Opposite these cages was a gallery of corresponding form, with a low stone parapet, and approached from the back by a flight of steps. This was appropriated exclusively to the accommodation of the royal family, who witnessed from it the feeding of the beasts and the combats described by Mr. Ainsworth in the romance which made the older portions of the Tower familiar ground to so many readers.

The menagerie which appeared in Smithfield in 1708, and the ownership of which I have been unable to discover, was a very small concern; but with the showman's knowledge of the popular love of the marvellous, was announced as "a Collection of Strange and Wonderful Creatures," which included "the Noble *Casheware*, brought from the Island of Java in the East Indies, one of the strangest creatures in the Universe, being half a Bird, and half a Beast, reaches 16 Hands High from the Ground, his Head is like a Bird, and so is his Feet, he hath no hinder Claw, Wings, Tongue, nor Tail; his Body is like to the Body of a Deer; instead of Feathers, his fore-part is covered with Hair like an Ox, his hinder-part with a double Feather in one Quill; he Eats Iron, Steel, or Stones; he hath 2 Spears grows by his side."

There is now no difficulty in recognising this strange bird as the cassowary, the representative in the Indian islands of the ostrich. There was also a leopard from Lebanon, an eagle from Russia, a "posoun" (opossum ?) from Hispaniola, and, besides a "Great Mare of the Tartarian Breed," which "had the Honour to be show'd before Queen Anne, Prince George, and most of the Nobility," "a little black hairy *Monster*, bred in the *Desarts of Arabia*, a natural Ruff of Hair about his Face, walks upright, takes a Glass of Ale in his Hand and drinks it off; and doth several other things to admiration." This animal was probably a specimen of the maned colobus, a native of the forests of Sierra Leone, and called by Pennant the full-bottomed monkey, in allusion to the full-bottom periwig of his day.

A pamphlet was published in 1710, with the title, *The Wonders of England*, purporting to contain "Doggett and Penkethman's dialogue with Old Nick, on the suppression of Bartholomew Fair," and accounts of many strange and wonderful things; but it was a mere "catch-penny," as such productions of the Monmouth Street press were called, not containing a line about the suppression of the fair, and the title, as Hone observes, "like the showmen's painted cloths in the fair, pictures monsters not visible within."

The lesser sights of a fair in the first quarter of the eighteenth century are graphically delineated by Gay, in his character of the ballad singer, in "The Shepherd's Week," bringing before the mind's eye the stalls, the lotteries, the mountebanks, the tumblers, the rope-dancers, the raree-shows, the puppets, and "all the fun of the fair."

"How pedlers' stalls with glittering toys are laid,
The various fairings of the country maid.
Long silken laces hang upon the twine,
And rows of pins and amber bracelets shine;
How the tight lass knives, combs, and scissors spies,
And looks on thimbles with desiring eyes.
Of lotteries next with tuneful note he told,
Where silver spoons are won, and rings of gold.
The lads and lasses trudge the street along,
And all the fair is crowded in his song.
The mountebank now treads the stage, and sells
His pills, his balsams, and his ague-spells;
Now o'er and o'er the nimble tumbler springs,
And on the rope the venturous maiden swings;
Jack Pudding, in his party-coloured jacket,
Tosses the glove, and jokes at every packet.
Of raree-shows he sung, and Punch's feats,
Of pockets picked in crowds, and various cheats."

The theatrical booths, of which we have only casual notices or records during the seventeenth century and the first dozen years of the eighteenth, became an important feature of the London fairs about 1714, from which time those of Bartholomew and Southwark were regularly attended by many of the leading actors and actresses of Drury Lane, Covent Garden, the Haymarket, Lincoln's Inn Fields, and Goodman's Fields theatres, down to the middle of the century, excepting those years in which no theatrical booths were allowed to be put up in Smithfield. The theatrical companies which attended the fairs were not, however, drawn entirely from the London theatres. Three or four actors associated in the proprietorship and management, or were engaged by a popular favourite, and the rest of the company was recruited from provincial theatres, or from the strolling comedians of the country fairs.

The London fairs were not, therefore, neglected by metropolitan managers in quest of talent, who, by witnessing the performances in booths on Smithfield or Southwark Green, sometimes found and transferred to their own boards, actors and actresses who proved stars of the first magnitude. It was in Bartholomew Fair that Booth found Walker, the original representative of Captain Macheath, playing in the *Siege of Troy*; and in Southwark Fair, in 1714, that the same manager saw Mrs. Horton acting in *Cupid and Psyche*, and was so pleased with her impersonation that he immediately offered her an engagement at Drury Lane, where she appeared the following season as Melinda, in the *Recruiting Officer*. She made her first appearance in 1713, as Marcia in *Cato*, with a strolling company then performing at Windsor; and is said to have been one of the most beautiful women that ever trod the stage.

Penkethman's company played the *Constant Lovers* in Southwark Fair in the year that proved so fortunate for Mrs. Horton, the comedian himself playing Buzzard, and Bullock taking the part of Sir Timothy Littlewit. In the following year, as we learn from a newspaper paragraph "a great play-house" was erected in the middle of Smithfield for "the King's players," being "the largest ever built." In 1717 Bullock did not accompany

Penkethman, but set up a booth of his own, in conjunction with Leigh; while Penkethman formed a partnership with Pack, and produced the new "droll," *Twice Married and a Maid Still*, in which the former personated Old Merriwell; Pack, Tim; Quin, Vincent; Ryan, Peregrine; Spiller, Trusty; and Mrs. Spiller, Lucia. Penkethman's booth received the honour of a visit from the Prince of Wales. On the evening of the 13th of September, the popular favourite and several of the company were arrested on the stage by a party of constables, in the presence of a hundred and fifty of the nobility and gentry; but, pleading that they were "the King's servants," they were released without being subjected to the pains and penalties of vagrancy.

In 1719, Bullock's name appears alone as the proprietor of the theatrical booth set up in Birdcage Alley, for Southwark Fair, and in which the *Jew of Venice* was represented, with singing and dancing, and Harper's representation of the freaks and humours of a drunken man, which, having been greatly admired at Lincoln's Inn Fields, where he and Bullock were both then engaged, could not fail to delight a fair audience. It was in this year that Boheme made his first appearance, as Menelaus in the *Siege of Troy*, in a booth at Southwark, where he was seen and immediately engaged by the manager of Lincoln's Inn Fields, where he appeared the following season as Worcester in *Henry IV.*, and subsequently as the Ghost in *Hamlet*, York in *Richard II.*, Pisanio in *Cymbeline*, Brabantio in *Othello*, etc.

The theatres at this time were closed during the continuance of Bartholomew Fair, the concourse of all classes to that popular resort preventing them from obtaining remunerative audiences at that time, while the actors could obtain larger salaries in booths than they received at the theatres, and some realised large amounts by associating in the ownership of a booth. The Haymarket company presented the *Beggar's Opera*, at Bartholomew and Southwark Fairs in 1720; and Penkethman had his booth at both fairs, this year without a partner.

May Fair, which had long been falling into disrepute, now ceased to be held. It was presented by the grand jury of Middlesex four years successively as a nuisance; and the county magistrates then presented an address to the Crown, praying for its suppression by royal proclamation. Pennant, who says that he remembered the last May Fair, describes the locality as "covered with booths, temporary theatres, and every enticement to low pleasure." A more particular description was given in 1774, in a communication from Carter, the antiquary, to the "Gentleman's Magazine."

"A mountebank's stage," he tells us, "was erected opposite the Three Jolly Butchers public-house (on the east side of the market area, now the King's Arms). Here Woodward, the inimitable comedian and harlequin, made his first appearance as Merry Andrew; from these humble boards he soon after made his way to Covent Garden Theatre. Then there was 'beheading of puppets.' In a coal-shed attached to a grocer's shop (then Mr. Frith's, now Mr. Frampton's), one of these mock executions was exposed to the attending crowd. A shutter was fixed horizontally, on the edge of which, after many previous ceremonies, a puppet laid its head, and another puppet instantly chopped it off with an axe. In a circular stair-case window, at the north end of Sun Court, a similar performance took place by another set of puppets. In these representations, the late punishment of the Scottish chieftain (Lord Lovat) was alluded to, in order to gratify the feelings of southern loyalty, at the expense of that further north.

"In a fore one-pair room, on the west side of Sun Court, a Frenchman submitted to the curious the astonishing strength of the 'strong woman,' his wife. A blacksmith's anvil being procured from White Horse Street, with three of the men, they brought it up, and placed it on the floor. The woman was short, but most beautifully and delicately formed, and of a most lovely countenance. She first let down her hair (a light auburn), of a length descending to her knees, which she twisted round the projecting part of the anvil, and then, with seeming ease, lifted the ponderous weight some inches from the floor. After this, a bed was laid in the middle of the room; when, reclining on her back, and uncovering her bosom, the husband ordered the smiths to place thereon the anvil, and forge upon it a horse-shoe! This they obeyed, by taking from the fire a red-hot piece of iron, and with their forging hammers completing the shoe, with the same might and indifference as when in the shop at their constant labour. The prostrate fair one appeared to endure this with the utmost composure, talking and singing during the whole process; then, with an effort which to the bystanders seemed like some supernatural trial, cast the anvil from off her body, jumping up at the same moment with extreme gaiety, and without the least discomposure of her dress or person. That no trick or collusion could possibly be practised on the occasion was obvious, from the following evidence:—the audience stood promiscuously about the room, among whom were our family and friends; the smiths were utter strangers to the Frenchman, but known to us; therefore, the several efforts of strength must have proceeded from the natural and surprising power this foreign dame was possessed of. She next put her naked feet on a red-hot salamander, without receiving the least injury; but this is a feat familiar with us at this time.

"Here, too, was 'Tiddy-dol.' This celebrated vendor of gingerbread, from his eccentricity of character, and extensive dealings in his way, was always hailed as the king of itinerant tradesmen. In his person he was tall, well made, and his features handsome. He affected to dress like a person of rank; white gold-laced suit of clothes, laced ruffled shirt, laced hat and feather, white silk stockings, with the addition of a fine white apron. Among his harangues to gain customers, take this as a specimen:—'Mary, Mary, where are you *now*, Mary? I live, when at home, at the second house in Little Ball Street, two steps underground, with a wiscum, riscum, and a why-not. Walk in, ladies and gentlemen; my shop is on the second-floor backwards, with a brass knocker at the door. Here is your nice gingerbread, your spice gingerbread; it will melt in your mouth like a red-hot brick-bat, and rumble in your inside like Punch and his wheelbarrow.' He always finished his address by singing this fag-end of some popular ballad:—Ti-tid-dy, ti-ti, ti-tid-dy, ti-ti, ti-tid-dy, ti-ti, tid-dy, did-dy, dol-lol, ti-tid-dy, ti-tid-dy, ti-ti, tid-dy, tid-dy, dol. Hence arose his nick-name of 'Tiddy-dol.'"

In Hogarth's picture of the execution of the idle apprentice at Tyburn, Tiddy-dol is seen holding up a cake of gingerbread, and addressing the crowd in his peculiar style, his costume agreeing with the foregoing description. His proper name was Ford, and so well-known was he that, on his once being missed for a week from his usual stand in the Haymarket, on the unusual occasion of an excursion to a country fair, a "catch-penny" account of his alleged murder was sold in the streets by thousands. In 1721, as appears from a paragraph in the 'London Journal' of May 27th, "the ground on which May Fair formerly stood is marked out for a large square, and several fine streets and houses are to be built upon it."

CHAPTER V.

Bartholomew Fair Theatricals—Lee, the Theatrical Printer—Harper, the Comedian—Rayner and Pullen—Fielding, the Novelist, a Showman—Cibber's Booth—Hippisley, the Actor—Fire in Bartholomew Fair—Fawkes, the Conjuror—Royal Visit to Fielding's Booth—Yeates, the Showman—Mrs. Pritchard, the Actress—Southwark Fair—

Tottenham Court Fair—Ryan, the Actor—Hallam's Booth—Griffin, the Actor—Visit of the Prince of Wales to Bartholomew Fair—Laguerre's Booth—Heidegger—More Theatrical Booths—Their Suppression at Bartholomew Fair—Hogarth at Southwark Fair—Violante, the Rope-Dancer—Cadman, the Flying Man.

The success of the theatrical booths at the London fairs induced Lee, a theatrical printer in Blue Maid Alley, Southwark, and son-in-law of Mrs. Mynn, to set up one, which we first hear of at Bartholomew Fair in 1725, when the popular drama of the *Unnatural Parents* was represented in it. Lee subsequently took into partnership in his managerial speculation the popular comedian, Harper, in conjunction with whom he produced, in 1728, a musical drama with the strange title of the *Quakers' Opera*, which, as well as the subject, was suggested by the extraordinary popularity of Gay's *Beggars' Opera*, the plot being derived from the adventures of the notorious burglar made famous in our time by Mr. Ainsworth's romance of 'Jack Sheppard.' It was adapted for the fairs from a drama published in 1725 as *The Prison-breaker*, "as intended to be acted at the Theatre Royal, Lincoln's Inn Fields."

Fielding, the future novelist, appeared this year, and in several successive years, as a Bartholomew Fair showman, setting up a theatrical booth in George Yard. He was then in his twenty-third year, aristocratically connected and liberally educated, but almost destitute of pecuniary resources, though the son of a general and a judge's daughter, and the great grandson of an earl, while he was as gay as Sheridan and as careless as Goldsmith. On leaving Eton he had studied law two years at Leyden, but was obliged to return to England through the failure of the allowance which his father had promised, but was too improvident to supply. Finding himself without resources, and becoming acquainted with some of the company at the Haymarket, he found the means, in conjunction with Reynolds, the actor, to set up a theatrical booth in the locality mentioned, and afterwards, during Southwark Fair, at the lower end of Blue Maid Alley, on the green.

Fielding and Reynolds drew their company from the Haymarket, and produced the *Beggars' Opera*, with "all the songs and dances, set to music, as performed at the theatre in Lincoln's Inn Fields." Their advertisements for Southwark Fair inform the public that "there is a commodious passage for the quality and coaches through the Half Moon Inn, and care will be taken that there shall be lights, and people to conduct them to their places."

In the following year Fielding and Reynolds had separate shows, the former retaining the eligible site of George Yard for Bartholomew Fair, and producing Colley's *Beggars' Wedding*, an opera in imitation of Gay's, which had been originally acted in Dublin, and afterwards at the Haymarket.

Reynolds, one of the Haymarket company, set up his booth between the hospital gate and the Crown Tavern, and produced the same piece under the title of *Hunter*, that being the name of the principal character. He had the Haymarket band and scenery, with Ray, from Drury Lane, in the principal part, and Mrs. Nokes as Tippit. Both he and Fielding announced Hulett for Chaunter, the king of the beggars, and continued to do so during the fair; but the comedian could not have acted several times daily in both booths, and as he did not return to the Haymarket after the fair, but joined the Lincoln's Inn Fields company, he was probably secured by Fielding.

Bullock, who had now seceded from the Lincoln's Inn Fields company and joined the new establishment in Goodman's Fields, under the management of Odell, also appeared at Bartholomew Fair this year without a partner, producing *Dorastus and Faunia*, and an adaptation of Doggett's *Country Wake* with the new title of *Flora*, announcing it, in deference to the new taste, as being "after the manner of the *Beggars' Opera*." Rayner and Pullen's company performed, at the Black Boy Inn, near Hosier Lane, an adaptation of Gay's opera, the dashing highwayman being personated by Powell, Polly by Mrs. Rayner, and Lucy by Mrs. Pullen.

In 1730, Fielding had a partner in Oates, a Drury Lane comedian, and again erected his theatre in George Yard, which site was retained for him during the whole period of his Bartholomew Fair experience. They produced a new opera, called the *Generous Freemason*, which was written by William Rufus Chetwood, many years prompter at Drury Lane. Oates personated Sebastian, and Fielding took the part of Clerimont himself. Miss Oates was Maria. After the opera there were "several entertainments of dancing by Mons. de Luce, Mademoiselle de Lorme, and others, particularly the Wooden Shoe Dance, Perrot and Pierette, and the dance of the Black Joke."

Reynolds was there again, with the historical drama of *Scipio's Triumph* and the pantomime of *Harlequin's Contrivance*. Lee and Harper presented *Robin Hood*, and Penkethman and Giffard the historical drama of *Wat Tyler and Jack Straw*. Penkethman had retired from the stage in 1724, and it is doubtful whether he lent his name on this occasion to Giffard, who was then lessee of Goodman's Fields, or the latter had taken the younger Penkethman into partnership with him.

Among the minor shows this year was a collection of natural curiosities, advertised as follows:—

"These are to give notice to all Ladies, Gentlemen, and others. That at the end of Hosier Lane, in Smithfield, are to be seen, during the Time of the Fair, Two Rattle Snakes, one a very large size, and rattles that you may hear him at a quarter of a mile almost, and something of Musick, that grows on the tails thereof; of divers colours, forms, and shapes, with darts that they extend out of their mouths, about two inches long. They were taken on the Mountains of Leamea. A Fine Creature, of a small size, taken in Mocha, that burrows under ground. It is of divers colours, and very beautiful. The Teeth of a Dead Rattle Snake, to be seen and handled, with the Rattles. A Sea Snail, taken on the Coast of India. Also, the Horn of a Flying Buck. Together with a curious Collection of Animals and Insects from all Parts of the World. To be seen without Loss of Time."

Bullock did not appear as an individual manager in the following year, having associated himself with Cibber, Griffin, and Hallam. The theatrical booth of which they were joint proprietors stood near Hosier Lane, where the tragedy of *Tamerlane the Great* was presented, the hero being played by Hallam, and Bajazet by Cibber. The entertainment must have been longer than usual, for it comprised a comedy, *The Miser*, adapted from *L'Avare* of Molière, in which Griffin played Lovegold, and Bullock was Cabbage; and a pantomime or ballet, called a *Ridotto al fresco*. Miller, Mills, and Oates, whose theatre was over against the hospital gate, presented the *Banished General*, a romantic drama, playing the principal parts themselves.

Oates having joined Miller and Mills, Fielding had for partners this year Hippisley and Hall, the former of whom appeared at Bartholomew Fair for the first time. He kept a coffee-house in Newcastle Court, Strand, which was frequented by members of the theatrical profession. Chetwood wrote for them a romantic drama called *The Emperor of China*, in which the pathetic and the comic elements were blended in a manner to please fair audiences, whose sympathies were engaged by the sub-title, *Love in Distress and Virtue Rewarded*. Hippisley played Shallow, a Welsh squire on his travels; Hall, his servant, Robin Booby; young Penkethman, Sir Arthur Addleplot; and Mrs. Egleton, a chambermaid, Loveit.

A fire occurred this year in one of the smaller booths, and, though little damage was done, the alarm caused so much fright to the wife of Fawkes, the conjuror, whose show adjoined the booth in which the fire broke out, as to induce premature parturition. This is the only fire recorded as having occurred in Bartholomew Fair during the seven centuries of its existence.

I have found no Bartholomew Fair advertisement of Lee and Harper for this year; but at Southwark Fair, where their show stood on the bowling green, behind the Marshalsea Prison, they presented *Bateman*, with a variety of singing and dancing, and a pantomimic entertainment called the *Harlot's Progress*. A change of performance being found necessary, they presented the "celebrated droll" of *Jephtha's Rash Vow*, in which Harper played the strangely incongruous part of a Captain Bluster.

"To which," continues the advertisement, "will be added, a new Pantomime Opera (which the Town has lately been in Expectation to see perform'd) call'd

"The Fall of Phaeton. Wherein is shown the Rivalship of Phaeton and Epaphus; their Quarrel about Lybia, daughter to King Merops, which causes Phaeton to go to the Palace of the Sun, to know if Apollo is his father, and for Proof of it requires the Guidance of his Father's Chariot, which obtain'd, he ascends in the Chariot through the Air to light the World; in the Course the Horses proving unruly go out of their way and set the World on Fire; Jupiter descends on an Eagle, and with his Thunder-bolt strikes Phaeton out of the Chariot into the River Po.

"The whole intermix'd with Comic Scenes between Punch, Harlequin, Scaramouch, Pierrot, and Colombine.

"The Part of Jupiter by Mr. Hewet; Apollo, Mr. Hulett; Phaeton, Mr. Aston; Epaphus, Mr. Nichols; Lybia, Mrs. Spiller; Phathusa, Mrs. Williamson; Lampetia, Mrs. Canterel; Phebe, Mrs. Spellman; Clymena, Mrs. Fitzgerald.

"N.B. We shall begin at Ten in the Morning and continue Playing till Ten at Night.

"N.B. The true Book of the Droll is printed and sold by G. Lee in Bluemaid Alley, Southwark, and all others (not printed by him) are false."

Fawkes, the conjuror, whose show has been incidentally mentioned, located it, in the intervals between the fairs, in James Street, near the Haymarket, where he this year performed the marvellous flower trick, by which the conjuror, Stodare, made so much of his fame a few years ago at the Egyptian Hall. Fawkes had a partner, Pinchbeck, who was as clever a mechanist as the former was a conjuror; and no small portion of the attractiveness of the show was due to Pinchbeck's musical clock, his mechanical contrivance for moving pictures, and which he called the Venetian machine (something, probably, like the famous cyclorama of the Colosseum), and his "artificial view of the world," with dioramic effects. Feats of posturing were exhibited between Fawkes's conjuring tricks and the exhibition of Pinchbeck's ingenious mechanism.

In 1732, Fielding had Hippisley alone as a partner in his theatrical enterprise, and presented the historical drama of *The Fall of Essex*, followed by an adapted translation (his own work) of *Le Médecin malgré Lui* of Molière, under the title of *The Forced Physician*. The Prince and Princess of Wales visited Fielding's theatre on the 30th of August, and were so much pleased with the performances that they witnessed both plays a second time.

Lee and Harper presented this year the *Siege of Bethulia*, "containing the Ancient History of Judith and Holofernes, and the Comical Humours of Rustego and his man Terrible." Holofernes was represented by Mullart, Judith by Spiller (so say the advertisements; perhaps the prefix "Mrs." was inadvertently omitted by the printer), and Rustego by Harper. As this was the first year in which this curious play was acted by Lee and Harper's company, the earlier date of 1721, assigned to Setchel's print of Bartholomew Fair, is an obvious error, as the title of this play is therein represented on the front of Lee and Harper's show. It is not easy to understand how such an error can have obtained currency, it being further proclaimed by the introduction of a peep-show of the siege of Gibraltar, which occurred in 1728.

Setchel's print was a copy of one which adorned a fan fabricated for sale in the fair, and had appended to it a description, ascribed to Caulfield, the author of a collection of 'Remarkable Characters.' The authorship of the descriptive matter is doubtful, however, as it asserts the portrait of Fawkes to be the only one in existence; while Caulfield, in his brief notice of the conjuror, mentions another and more elaborate one. Lee and Harper's booth is conspicuously shown in the print, with a picture of the murder of Holofernes at the back of the exterior platform, on which are Mullart, and (I presume) Mrs. Spiller, dressed for Holofernes and Judith, and three others of the company, one in the garb of harlequin, another dancing, and the third blowing a trumpet. Judith is costumed in a head-dress of red and blue feathers, laced stomacher, white hanging sleeves, and a flounced crimson skirt; while Holofernes wears a flowing robe, edged with gold lace, a helmet and cuirass, and brown buskins.

Fawkes's show also occupies a conspicuous place with its pictured cloth, representing conjuring and tumbling feats, and Fawkes on the platform, doing a conjuring trick, while a harlequin draws attention to him, and a trumpeter bawls through his brazen instrument of torture an invitation to the spectators to "walk up!" Near this show is another with a picture of a woman dancing on the tight rope. The scene is filled up with the peep-show before mentioned, a swing of the four-carred kind, a toy-stall, a sausage-stall, and a gin-stall—one of those incentives to vice and disorder which were permitted to be present, perhaps "for the good of trade," when amusements were banished.

In 1733, Fielding and Hippisley's booth again stood in George Yard, where they presented the romantic drama of *Love and Jealousy*, and a ballad opera called *The Cure for Covetousness*, adapted by Fielding from *Les Fourberies de Scapin* of Molière. In this piece Mrs. Pritchard first won the popularity which secured her an engagement at Drury Lane for the ensuing season, as, though she had acted before at the Haymarket and Goodman's Fields, she attracted little attention until, in the character of Loveit, she sang with Salway the duet, "Sweet, if you love me, smiling turn," which was received with so much applause that Fielding and Hippisley had it printed, and distributed copies in the fair by thousands. Hippisley played Scapin in this opera, and Penkethman, announced as the "son of the late facetious Mr. William Penkethman," Old Gripe. There was dancing between the acts, and the *Ridotto al fresco* afterwards; and the advertisements add that, "to divert the audience during the filling of the booth, the famous Mr. Phillips will perform his surprising postures on the stage."

The newspapers of the time inform us that they had "crowded audiences," and that "a great number of the nobility intend to honour them with their presence," which they probably did. All classes then went to Bartholomew Fair, as in Pepys' time; the gentleman with the star on his coat in Setchel's print was said to be Sir Robert Walpole.

Cibber, Griffin, Bullock, and Hallam again appeared in partnership, and repeated the performances which they had found attractive in the preceding year. Cibber played Bajazet in the tragedy, and Mrs. Charke, his youngest daughter, Haly. This lady appeared subsequently on the scene as the proprietress of a puppet-show, and finally as the keeper of a sausage-stall. Griffin played Lovegold in the *Miser*, as he had done the preceding winter at Drury Lane; but none of the Drury actresses performed this year in the fairs, and Miss Raftor's part of Lappet was transferred to Mrs. Roberts.

Lee and Harper presented *Jephtha's Rash Vow*, in which Hulett appeared; and Miller, Mills, and Oates, the tragedy of *Jane Shore*, in which Miss Oates personated the heroine; her father, Tim Hampwell; and Chapman, Captain Blunderbuss. After the tragedy came a new mythological entertainment, called the *Garden of Venus*; and the advertisements state that, "To entertain the Company before the Opera begins, there will be a variety of

Rope-Dancing and Tumbling by the best Performers; particularly the famous Italian Woman, Mademoiselle De Reverant and her Daughter, who gave such universal satisfaction at the Publick Act at Oxford; the celebrated Signor Morosini, who never performed in the Fair before; Mons. Jano and others, and Tumbling by young River and Miss Derrum, a child of nine years old." De Reverant is not an Italian name, and it is to be hoped, for the sake of the lady's good name and the management's sense of decorum, that the prefix of Mademoiselle was an error of the printer. Jano was a performer at Sadler's Wells, and other places of amusement in the vicinity of the metropolis, where tea-gardens and music-rooms were now becoming numerous.

Tottenham Court fair, the origin of which I have been unable to trace, emerged from its obscurity this year, when Lee and Harper, in conjunction with a third partner named Petit, set up a show there, behind the King's Head, near the Hampstead Road. The entertainments were *Bateman* and the *Ridotto al fresco*. The fair began on the 4th of August.

Petit's name is not in the advertisements for Southwark Fair, where Lee and Harper gave the same performance as at Tottenham Court. A new aspirant to popular favour appeared this year on Southwark Green, namely, Yeates's theatrical booth, in which a ballad opera called *The Harlot's Progress* was performed, with "Yeates, junior's, incomparable dexterity of hand: also a new and glorious prospect, or a lively view of the installation of His Royal Highness the Prince of Orange.

"Note.—At a large room near his booth are to be seen, without any loss of time, two large ostriches, lately arrived from the Deserts of Arabia, being male and female."

Fawkes, the conjuror, was now dead, but Pinchbeck carried on the show, in conjunction with his late partner's son, and issued the following announcement:—

"This is to give notice, that Mr. Pinchbeck *and* Fawkes, *who have had the honour to perform before the Royal Family, and most of the Nobility and Gentry in the Kingdom with great applause, during the time of* Southwark Fair, *will divert the Publick with the following surprising Entertainments, at their great Theatrical Room, at the* Queen's Arms, *joining to the* Marshalsea Gate. First, the surprising Tumbler from Frankfort in Germany, who shows several astonishing things by the Art of Tumbling; the like never seen before since the memory of man. Secondly, the diverting and incomparable dexterity of hand, performed by Mr. Pinchbeck, who causes a tree to grow out of a flower-pot on the table, which blossoms and bears ripe fruit in a minute; also a man in a maze, or a perpetual motion, where he makes a little ball to run continually, which would last was it for seven years together only by the word of command. He has several tricks entirely new, which were never done by any other person than himself. Third, the famous little posture-master of nine years old, who shows several astonishing postures by activity of body, different from any other posture-master in Europe."

The fourth and fifth items of the programme were Pinchbeck's musical clock and the Venetian machine. The advertisement concludes with the announcement that "while the booth is filling, the little posture-master will divert the company with several wonders on the slack rope. Beginning every day at ten o'clock in the morning, and ending at ten at night." As Pinchbeck now performed the conjuring tricks for which his former partner had been famous, and the latter's son does not appear as a performer, it is probable that young Fawkes was merely a sleeping partner in the concern, his father having accumulated by the exercise of his profession, a capital of ten thousand pounds.

It was in this year that Highmore, actuated by the spirit which in recent times has prompted the prosecution of music-hall proprietors by theatrical managers, swore an information against Harper as an offender under the Vagrancy Act, which condemned strolling players to the same penalties as wandering ballad-singers and sturdy beggars.

Why, it may be asked, was Harper selected as the scape-goat of all the comedians who performed in the London fairs, and among whom were Cibber, Bullock, Hippisley, Hallam, Ryan, Laguerre, Chapman, Hall, and other leading actors of the theatres royal? There is no evidence of personal animosity against Harper on Highmore's part, but it is not much to the latter's credit that he was supposed to have selected for a victim a man who was thought to be timid enough to be frightened into submission.

Harper was arrested on the 12th November, and taken before a magistrate, by whom he was committed to Bridewell, as a vagrant, on evidence being given that he had performed at Bartholomew and Southwark Fairs, and also at Drury Lane. He appealed against the decision, and the cause was tried in the Court of King's Bench, before the Lord Chief Justice, on the 20th. Eminent counsel were retained on both sides, the prosecution insisting that the appellant had brought himself under the operation of the Vagrancy Act by "wandering from place to place" in the exercise of his vocation; and counsel for the appellant contending that, as Harper was a householder of Westminster and a freeholder of Surrey, it was ridiculous to represent him as a vagabond, or to pretend that he was likely to become chargeable as a pauper to the parish in which he resided. "My client," said his counsel, "is an honest man, who pays his debts, and injures no man, and is well esteemed by many gentlemen of good condition." The result was, that Harper was discharged on his own recognizances to be of good conduct, and left Westminster Hall amidst the acclamations of several hundreds of persons, whom his popularity had caused to assemble.

In the following year, the managerial arrangements for the fairs again received considerable modification. The partnership of Miller, Mills, and Oates was dissolved, and the last-named actor again joined Fielding, while Hippisley joined Bullock and Hallam, and Hall formed a new combination with Ryan, Laguerre, and Chapman. Harper's partnership with Lee was dissolved by the latter's death, and the fear of having his recognizances estreated seems to have prevented him from appearing at the fairs. Fielding and Oates presented *Don Carlos* and the ballad opera of *The Constant Lovers*, in which Oates played Ragout, his daughter Arabella, and Mrs. Pritchard, in grateful remembrance of her Bartholomew Fair triumph of the preceding year, Chloe.

Hippisley, Bullock, and Hallam presented *Fair Rosamond*, followed by *The Impostor*, in which Vizard was played by Hippisley, Balderdash by Bullock, and Solomon Smack by Hallam's son. During the last week of the fair, Hippisley gave, as an interlude, his diverting medley in the character of a drunken man, for which impersonation he was long as celebrated as Harper was for a similar representation.

Ryan, Laguerre, Chapman, and Hall gave what appears a long programme for a fair, and suggests more than the ordinary amount of "cutting down." The performances commenced with *Don John*, in which the libertine prince was played by Ryan, and Jacomo by Chapman. After the tragedy came a ballad opera, *The Barren Island*, in which Hall played the boatswain, Laguerre the gunner, and Penkethman the coxswain. The performances concluded with a farce, *The Farrier Nicked*, in which Laguerre was Merry, Penkethman the farrier's man, and Hall an ale-wife.

At Southwark Fair this year, Lee's booth, now conducted by his widow, stood in Axe and Bottle Yard, and presented the *Siege of Troy*, "which," says the advertisement, "in its decorations, machinery, and paintings, far exceeds anything of the like kind that ever was seen in the fairs before, the scenes and clothes being entirely new. All the parts to be performed to the best advantage, by persons from the theatres. The part of Paris by Mr. Hulett; King Menelaus, Mr. Roberts; Ulysses, Mr. Aston; Simon, Mr. Hind; Captain of the Guard, Mr. Mackenzie; Bustle the Cobler, Mr. Morgan; Butcher, Mr. Pearce; Taylor, Mr. Hicks; Cassandra, Mrs. Spiller; Venus, Mrs. Lacy; Helen, Mrs. Purden; Cobler's

Wife, Mrs. Morgan. With several Entertainments of Singing and Dancing by the best masters.

"N.B. There being a puppet-show in Mermaid Court, leading down to the Green, called *The Siege of Troy*; These are to forewarn the Publick, that they may not be imposed on by counterfeits, the only celebrated droll of that kind was first brought to perfection by the late famous Mrs. Mynns, and can only be performed by her daughter, Mrs. Lee."

Mrs. Lee seems to have had a formidable rival in another theatrical booth, which appeared anonymously, and from this circumstance, combined with the fact of its occupying the site on which Lee and Harper's canvas theatre had stood for several successive years, may not unreasonably be regarded as the venture of Harper. All I have found concerning it is the bill, which, as being a good specimen of the announcements issued by the proprietors of the theatrical booths attending the London fairs, is given entire.

"*At the Great* Theatrical Booth

On the Bowling-Green behind the Marshalsea, down Mermaid-Court next the Queen's-Arms Tavern, during the Time of Southwark Fair, (which began the 8th instant and ends the 21st), will be presented that diverting Droll call'd,

The True and Ancient History of
Maudlin, *the Merchant's Daughter* of Bristol,
AND
Her Constant Lover Antonio,

Who she follow'd into Italy, disguising herself in Man's Habit; shewing the Hardships she underwent by being Shipwreck'd on the coast of Algier, where she met her Lover, who was doom'd to be burnt at a Stake by the King of that Country, who fell in Love with her and proffer'd her his Crown, which she despised, and chose rather to share the Fate of her Antonio than renounce the Christian Religion to embrace that of their Impostor Prophet, Mahomet.

With the Comical Humours of
Roger, Antonio's Man,

And variety of Singing and Dancing between the Acts by Mr. Sandham, Mrs. Woodward, and Miss Sandham.

"Particularly, a new Dialogue to be sung by Mr. Excell and Mrs. Fitzgerald. Written by the Author of *Bacchus one day gaily striding*, &c. and a hornpipe by Mr. Taylor. To which will be added a new Entertainment (never perform'd before) called

The Intriguing Harlequin
OR
Any Wife better than None.
With Scenes, Machines, and other Decorations
proper to the Entertainment."

Pinchbeck and Fawkes had a booth this year on the Bowling Green, where the entertainments of the preceding year were repeated, the little posturer being again announced as only nine years of age. Pinchbeck had a shop in Fleet Street at this time, (mentioned in the thirty-fifth number of the 'Adventurer'), and, perhaps, an interest in the wax figures exhibited by Fawkes at the Old Tennis Court, as "the so much famed piece of machinery, consisting of large artificial wax figures five foot high, which have all the just motions and gestures of human life, and have been for several years shewn at Bath and Tunbridge Wells, and no where else, except this time two years at the Opera Room in the Haymarket; and by them will be presented the comical tragedy of *Tom Thumb*. With several scenes out of *The Tragedy of Tragedies*, and dancing between the acts. To which will be added, an entertainment of dancing called *The Necromancer: or, Harlequin Dr.*

Faustus, with the fairy song and dance. The clothes, scenes, and decorations are entirely new. The doors to be opened at four, and to begin at six o'clock. Pit 2s. 6d. Gallery 1s. Tickets to be had at Mr. Chenevix's toy-shop, over against Suffolk Street, Charing Cross; at the Tennis Court Coffee House; at Mr. Edward Pinchbeck's, at the Musical Clock in Fleet Street; at Mr. Smith's, a perfumer, at the Civet Cat in New Bond Street near Hanover Square; at the little man's fan-shop in St. James's Street."

Fawkes and Pinchbeck seem to have speculated in exhibitions and entertainments of various descriptions, for besides this marionette performance and the conjuring show, there seems to have been another show, which appeared at Bartholomew Fair this year, as their joint enterprise, and for which Fielding wrote a dramatic trifle called *The Humours of Covent Garden*. It was probably a performance of puppets, like that at the Old Tennis Court.

The licences granted by the Corporation for mountebanks, conjurors, and others, to exercise their avocations at Bartholomew Fair had hitherto extended to fourteen days; but in 1735 the Court of Aldermen resolved—"That Bartholomew Fair shall not exceed Bartholomew eve, Bartholomew day, and the next morrow, and shall be restricted to the sale of goods, wares, and merchandises, usually sold in fairs, and no acting shall be permitted therein." There were, therefore, no shows this year; and, as the Licensing Act had rendered all unlicensed entertainers liable to the pains and penalties of vagrancy, and Sir John Barnard was known to be determined to suppress all such "idle amusements" as dancing, singing, tumbling, juggling, and the like, the toymen, the vendors of gingerbread, the purveyors of sausages, and the gin-stalls had the fair to themselves.

There seems no evidence, however, that there was less disorder, or less indulgence in vice, in Bartholomew Fair this year than on former occasions. "Lady Holland's mob," as the concourse of roughs was called which anticipated the official proclamation of the fair by swarming through the streets adjacent to Smithfield on the previous night, assembled as usual, shouting, ringing bells, and breaking lamps, as had been the annual wont from the time of the Long Parliament, though the association of Lady Holland's name with these riotous proceedings is a mystery which I have not been able to unravel. Nor is there any reason for supposing that drunkenness was banished from the fair with the shows; for, though it is probable that a much smaller number of persons resorted to Smithfield, it is certain that gin-stalls constituted a greater temptation to excessive indulgence in alcoholic fluids, in the absence of all means of amusement, than the larger numbers that visited the shows were exposed to. The idea of promoting temperance by depriving the people of the choice between the public-house and the theatre or music-hall is the most absurd that has ever been conceived.

It was on the 15th of March, in this year, that Ryan, the comedian and Bartholomew Fair theatrical manager, was attacked at midnight, in Great Queen Street, by a footpad, who fired a pistol in his face, inflicting injuries which deprived him of consciousness, and then robbed him of his sword, which, however, was afterwards picked up in the street. Ryan was carried home, and attended by a surgeon, who found his jaws shattered, and several teeth dislodged. A performance was given at Covent Garden for his benefit on the 19th, when he had a crowded house, and the play was the *Provoked Husband*, with Hallam as Lord Townly, and the farce the *School for Women*, which was new, in the Robertsonian sense, being adapted from Molière. Hippisley played in it. The Prince of Wales was prevented by a prior engagement from attending, but he sent Ryan a hundred guineas. The wounded actor was unable to perform until the 25th of April, when he re-appeared as Bellair in a new comedy, Popple's *Double Deceit*, in which Sir William Courtlove was personated by Hippisley, Gayliffe by Hallam, and Jerry by Chapman.

Smithfield presented its wonted fair aspect on the eve of Bartholomew, 1736, the civic authorities having seen the error of their ways, and testified their sense thereof by again permitting shows to be erected. Hippisley joined Fielding this year, and they presented *Don Carlos* and the *Cheats of Scapin*, Mrs. Pritchard re-appearing in the character of Loveit. Hallam and Chapman joined in partnership, and produced *Fair Rosamond* and a ballad opera.

Fielding had at this time an income of two hundred a year, besides what he derived from translating and adapting French plays for the London stage, and the profits of his annual speculation in Smithfield. But, if he had had three times as much, he would have been always in debt, and occasionally in difficulties. Besides being careless and extravagant in his expenditure, he was generous to a fault. His pocket was at all times a bank upon which friendship or distress might draw. One illustration of this trait in his character I found in an old collection of anecdotes published in 1787. Some parochial taxes for his house in Beaufort Buildings, in the Strand, being unpaid, and repeated application for payment having been made in vain, he was at last informed by the collector that further procrastination would be productive of unpleasant consequences.

In this dilemma, Fielding, having no money, obtained ten or twelves guineas of Tonson, on account of some literary work which he had then in hand. He was returning to Beaufort Buildings, jingling his guineas, when he met in the Strand an Eton chum, whom he had not seen for several years. Question and answer followed quickly as the friends shook each other's hands with beaming eyes, and then they adjourned to a tavern, where Fielding ordered dinner, that they might talk over old times. Care was given to the winds, and the hours flew on unthought of, as the showman and his old schoolfellow partook of "the feast of reason, and the flow of soul." Fielding's friend was "hard up," and the fact was no sooner divulged than his purse received the greater part of the money for which the future novelist had pledged sheets of manuscript as yet unwritten.

It was past midnight when Fielding, raised by wine and friendship to the seventh heaven, reached home. In reply to the questions of his sister, who had anxiously awaited his coming, as to the cause of his long absence, he related his felicitous meeting with his former chum. "But, Harry," said Amelia, "the collector has called twice for the rates." Thus brought down to earth again, Fielding looked grave; it was the first time he had thought of the rates since leaving Tonson's shop, and he had spent at the tavern all that he had not given to his friend. But his gravity was only of a moment's duration. "Friendship," said he, "has called for the money, and had it; let the collector call again." A second application to Tonson enabled him, however, to satisfy the demands of the parish as well as those of friendship.

It was in this year that the Act for licensing plays was passed, the occasion—perhaps I should say, the pretext—being the performance of Fielding's burlesque, *Pasquin*. Ministers had had their eyes upon the stage for some time, and it must be admitted that the political allusions that were indulged in on the stage were strong, and often spiced with personalities that would not be tolerated at the present day. It is doubtful, however, whether the Act would have passed the House of Commons, but for the folly of Giffard, manager of Goodman's Fields, and sometimes of a booth in Bartholomew Fair. He had a burlesque offered him, called the *Golden Princess*, so full of gross abuse of Parliament, the Privy Council, and even the King, that, impelled by loyalty, and suspecting no ulterior aims or sinister intention, he waited upon Sir Robert Walpole, and laid before him the dreadful manuscript. The minister praised Giffard for his loyalty, while he must have inwardly chuckled at the egregious folly and mental short-sightedness that could be so easily led into such a blunder. He purchased the manuscript, and made such effective use of it in the House of Commons that Parliament was as completely gulled as Giffard had been, and the Dramatic Licensing Bill became law.

In the following year, Hallam appeared at Bartholomew Fair without a partner, setting up his show over against the gate of the hospital, and presenting a medley entertainment, comprising, as set forth in the bills, "the surprising performances of M. Jano, M. Raynard, M. Baudouin, and Mynheer Vander Huff. Also a variety of rope-dancers, tumblers, posture-masters, balance-masters, and comic dancers; being a set of the very best performers that way in Europe. The comic dances to be performed by M. Jano, M. Baudouin, M. Peters, and Mr. Thompson; Madlle. De Frano, Madlle. Le Roy, Mrs. Dancey, and Miss Dancey. To which will be added, the Italian Shadows, performed by the best masters from Italy, which have not been seen these twenty years. The whole to conclude with a grand ballet dance, called *Le Badinage Champêtre*. With a complete band of music of hautboys, violins, trumpets, and kettle-drums. All the decorations entirely new. To begin every day at one o'clock, and continue till eleven at night." Close to this booth was Yeates's, in which *The Lover his own Rival* was performed by wax figures, nearly as large as life, after which Yeates's son performed some juggling feats, and a youth whose name does not appear in the bills gave an acrobatic performance.

In 1738, Hallam's booth occupied the former site of Fielding's, in George Yard, the entertainment consisted of the operatic burlesque, *The Dragon of Wantley*, performed by the Lilliputian company from Drury Lane. During the filling of the booth a posturing performance was given by M. Rapinese. "The passage to the booth," says the advertisements, "is commodiously illuminated by several large moons and lanthorns, for the conveniency of the company, and that persons of quality's coaches may drive up the yard." Penkethman had this year a booth, where Hallam's had stood the preceding year, and presented *The Man's Bewitched* and *The Country Wedding*.

Hallam's booth attended Tottenham Court Fair this year, standing near the turnpike, and presenting a new entertainment called *The Mad Lovers*. At Southwark Fair Lee's theatrical booth stood on the bowling-green, and presented *Merlin, the British Enchanter*, and *The Country Farmer*, concluding with a mimic pageant representing the Lord Mayor's procession in the old times.

In 1739, Bartholomew Fair was extended to four days, and there was a proportionately larger attendance of theatrical booths. Hallam's stood over against the hospital gate, and presented the pantomime of *Harlequin turned Philosopher* and the farce of *The Sailor's Wedding*, with singing and dancing. Hippisley, Chapman, and Legar had a booth in George Yard, where they produced *The Top of the Tree*, in which a famous dog scene was introduced, and the mythological pantomime of *Perseus and Andromeda*. Bullock, who had made his last appearance at Covent Garden in the preceding April, had the largest booth in the fair, and assumed the part of Judge Balance in a new pantomimic entertainment called *The Escapes of Harlequin by Sea and Land*, which was preceded by a variety of humorous songs and dances. Phillips, a comedian from Drury Lane, joined Mrs. Lee this year in a booth at the corner of Hosier Lane, where they presented a medley entertainment, comprising the "grand scene" of *Cupid and Psyche*, a scaramouch dance by Phillips and others (said to have been given, with great applause, on forty successive nights, at the Opera, Paris), a dialogue between Punch and Columbine, a scene of a drunken peasant by Phillips, and a pantomimic entertainment called *Columbine Courtesan*, in which the parts of Harlequin and Columbine were sustained by Phillips and his wife.

In 1740, Hallam, whose show stood opposite the hospital gate, presented *The Rambling Lover*; and Yeates, whose booth was next to Hallam's, the pantomime of *Orpheus and Eurydice*. The growing taste for pantomime, which is sufficiently attested by the play-bills of the period, induced Hippisley and Chapman, whose booth stood in George Yard, to present, instead of a tragedy or comedy, a pantomime called *Harlequin Scapin*, in which the popular embodiment of Molière's humour was adapted with success to pantomimic requirements. Hippisley played Scapin, Chapman was Tim, and Yates, who made his first appearance at Bartholomew Fair, Slyboots. After the pantomime came

43

singing and dancing by Oates, Yates, Mrs. Phillips, and others, "particularly a new whimsical and diverting dance called the Spanish Beauties." The performances concluded with a new musical entertainment called *The Parting Lovers*. Fawkes and Pinchbeck also had a theatrical booth this year in conjunction with a partner named Terwin.

This year the fair was visited again by the Prince of Wales, of which incident an account appeared many years afterwards in the 'New European Magazine.' The shows were all in full blast and the crowd at its thickest, when, says the narrator, "the multitude behind was impelled violently forwards; a broad blaze of red light, issuing from a score of flambeaux, streamed into the air; several voices were loudly shouting, 'room there for Prince George! Make way for the Prince!' and there was that long sweep heard to pass over the ground which indicates the approach of a grand and ceremonious train. Presently the pressure became much greater, the voices louder, the light stronger, and as the train came onward, it might be seen that it consisted, firstly, of a party of the yeomen of the guard, clearing the way; then several more of them bearing flambeaux, and flanking the procession; while in the midst of all appeared a tall, fair, and handsome young man, having something of a plump foreign visage, seemingly about four and thirty, dressed in a ruby-coloured frock-coat, very richly guarded with gold lace, and having his long flowing hair curiously curled over his forehead and at the sides, and finished with a very large bag and courtly queue behind. The air of dignity with which he walked, the blue ribbon and star and garter with which he was decorated, the small three-cornered silk court hat which he wore, whilst all around him were uncovered; the numerous suite, as well of gentlemen as of guards, which marshalled him along, the obsequious attention of a short stout person, who, by his flourishing manner seemed to be a player,—all these particulars indicated that the amiable Frederick, Prince of Wales, was visiting Bartholomew Fair by torch-light, and that Manager Rich was introducing his royal guest to all the entertainments of the place.

"However strange this circumstance may appear to the present generation, yet it is nevertheless strictly true; for about 1740, when the drolls in Smithfield were extended to three weeks and a month, it was not considered as derogatory to persons of the first rank and fashion to partake in the broad humour and theatrical amusements of the place. It should also be remembered, that many an eminent performer of the last century unfolded his abilities in a booth; and that it was once considered as an important and excellent preparation to their treading the boards of a theatre royal."

The narrator then proceeds to describe the duties of the leading actor in a Bartholomew Fair theatre, from which account there is some deduction to be made for the errors and exaggerations of a person writing long after the times which he undertakes to describe, and who was not very careful in his researches, as the statement that the fair then lasted three weeks or a month sufficiently attests. The picture which he gives was evidently drawn from his knowledge of the Richardsonian era, which he endeavoured to make fit into the Bartholomew Fair experiences of the very different showmen of the reign of George II.

"I will," he says, assuming the character of an actor of the period he describes, "as we say, take you behind the scenes. First, then, an actor must sleep in the pit, and wake early to throw fresh sawdust into the boxes; he must shake out the dresses, and wind up the motion-jacks; he must teach the dull ones how to act, rout up the idlers from the straw, and redeem those that happen to get into the watch-house. Then, sir, when the fair begins, he should sometimes walk about the stage grandly, and show his dress; sometimes he should dance with his fellows; sometimes he should sing; sometimes he should blow the trumpet; sometimes he should laugh and joke with the crowd, and give them a kind of a touch-and-go speech, which keeps them merry, and makes them come in. Then, sir, he should sometimes cover his state robe with a great coat, and go into the crowd, and shout opposite his own booth, like a stranger who is struck with its magnificence: by the way, sir, that's a good trick,—I never knew it fail to make an audience; and then he has only to steal away, mount his stage, and strut, and dance, and sing, and trumpet, and roar over again."

Griffin and Harper drop out of the list of showmen at the London fairs in this year. Griffin appeared at Drury Lane for the last time on the 12th of February, and died soon afterwards, with the character of a worthy man and an excellent actor. He made his first appearance at Lincoln's Inn Fields, as Sterling in *The Perplexed Lovers*, in 1714. Harper, the jolly, facetious low comedian, suffered an attack of paralysis towards the close of 1739, and, though he survived till 1742, he never appeared again on the stage.

In the following year, Hippisley and Chapman presented *A Devil of a Duke*; and Hallam relied for success upon *Fair Rosamond*. Lee and Woodward, whose booth stood opposite the hospital gate, produced *Darius, King of Persia*, "with the comical humours of Sir Andrew Aguecheek at the siege of Babylon." Anachronisms of this kind were common at theatrical booths in those days, when comic Englishmen of one type or another were constantly introduced, without regard to the scene or the period of the drama to be represented. Audiences were not sufficiently educated to be critical in such matters, and managers could plead the example of Shakspeare, who was then esteemed a greater authority than he is considered to be at the present day. Yates made his first appearance as a showman this year, in partnership with Turbutt, who set up a booth opposite the King's Head, and produced a pantomime called *Thamas Kouli Khan*, founded on recent news from the East. An epilogue, in the character of a drunken English sailor, was spoken by Yates, of whom Churchill wrote,—

"In characters of low and vulgar mould,
Where nature's coarsest features we behold
Where, destitute of every decent grace,
Unmanner'd jests are blurted in your face;
There Yates with justice strict attention draws,
Acts truly from himself, and gains applause."

There was a second and smaller booth in the name of Hallam, in which tumbling and rope-dancing were performed; but whether belonging to the actor or to another showman of the same name is uncertain. Fawkes and Pinchbeck exhibited the latter's model of the Siege of Carthagena, with which a comic dramatic performance was combined.

The office of Master of the Revels was held at this time by Heidegger, a native of Zurich, who was also manager of the Italian Opera. He was one of the most singular characters of the time, and as remarkable for his personal ugliness as for the eccentricity of his manners. The profanity of his language was less notable in that age than his candour. Supping on one occasion with a party of gentlemen of rank, the comparative ingenuity of different nations became the theme of conversation, when the first place was claimed by Heidegger for his compatriots.

"I am myself a proof of what I assert," said he. "I was born a Swiss, and came to England without a farthing, where I have found means to gain five thousand a year and to spend it. Now, I defy the most able Englishman to go to Switzerland and either to gain that income, or to spend it there."

He was never averse to a joke upon his own ugliness, and once made a wager with Lord Chesterfield that the latter would not be able, within a certain given time, to produce a more ugly man in all London. The time elapsed; and Heidegger won the wager. Yet he could never be persuaded to have his portrait painted, even though requested by the King, and urged by all his friends to comply with the royal wish. The facetious Duke of

Montagu, the concoctor of the memorable bottle-conjuror hoax at the Haymarket, had recourse to stratagem to obtain Heidegger's likeness, which afterwards gave rise to a laughable adventure. He gave a dinner at the Devil Tavern, near Temple Bar, to several of his friends and acquaintances, selecting those whom he knew to be the least accessible to the effects of wine, and the most likely to indulge in vinous conviviality. Heidegger was one of the guests, and, in a few hours after dinner, became so very much inebriated that he was carried out of the room in a state of insensibility, and laid upon a bed.

An artist in wax, a daughter of the famous Mrs. Salmon, was ready to play her part in the plot, and quickly made a mould of Heidegger's face in plaster. From this a mask was made; and all that remained to be done was to learn from his valet what clothes he would wear on a certain night, and procure a similar suit and a man of the same stature. All this the Duke accomplished before a masked ball took place, at which the King had promised to be present, and the band of the Opera House was to play in a gallery. The night came; and as the King entered, accompanied by the Countess of Yarmouth, Heidegger directed the band to play the national anthem. He had scarcely turned his back, however, when the counterfeit Heidegger told them to play "Charlie over the water."

Consternation fell upon all the assembly at the sound of the treasonable strains; everybody looked at everybody else, wondering what the playing of a Jacobite air in the presence of the King might presage. Heidegger ran to the orchestra, and swore, stamped, and raved, accusing the musicians of being drunk, or of being bribed by some secret enemy to bring about his ruin. The treasonable melody ceased, and the loyal strains of the national anthem saluted the royal ears. Heidegger had no sooner left the room, however, than his double stepped forward, and standing before the music-gallery, swore at the musicians as Heidegger had done, imitating his voice, and again directed them to play "Charlie over the water." The musicians, knowing his eccentricity, and likewise his addiction to inebriety, shrugged their shoulders, and obeyed. Some officers of the Guards resented the affront to the King by attempting to ascend to the gallery for the purpose of kicking the musicians out; but the Duke of Cumberland, who, as well as the King and his fair companion, was in the plot, interposed and calmed them.

The company were thrown into confusion, however, and cries of "shame! shame!" arose on every side. Heidegger, bursting with rage, again rushed in, and began to rave and swear at the musicians. The music ceased; and the Duke of Montagu persuaded Heidegger to go to the King, and make an apology for the band, representing that His Majesty was very angry. The counterfeit Heidegger immediately took the same course, and, as soon as Heidegger had made the best apology his agitation would permit, the former stepped to his side and said, "Indeed, sire, it was not my fault, but that devil's in my likeness." Heidegger faced about, pale and speechless, staring with widely dilated eyes at his double. The Duke of Montagu then told the latter to take off his mask, and the frolic ended; but Heidegger swore that he would never attend any public entertainment again, unless that witch, the wax-work woman, broke the mould and melted the mask before him.

In 1742, the first place in Bartholomew Fair was again held, but for the last time, by Hippisley and Chapman, who revived the ever-popular Scapin in what they called "the most humorous and diverting droll, called *Scaramouch Scapin* or the *Old Miser caught in a Sack*," the managers playing the same characters as in 1740. Hallam had made his last appearance at the fair in the preceding year, and his booth was now held by Turbutt and Yates, who set it up opposite the hospital gate, and produced *The Loves of King Edward IV. and Jane Shore*. Yates personated Sir Anthony Lackbrains, Turbutt was Captain Blunderbuss, and Mrs. Yates, Flora. A new aspirant to public favour appeared in Goodwin, whose booth stood opposite the White Hart, near Cow Lane, and presented a three act comedy, called *The Intriguing Footman*, followed by a pantomimic entertainment "between a soldier, a sailor, a tinker, a tailor, and Buxom Joan of Deptford." Fawkes and Pinchbeck announced that "Punch's celebrated company of comical tragedians from the Haymarket," would perform *The Tragedy of Tragedies*, "being the most comical and whimsical tragedy that was ever tragedized by any tragical company of comedians, called *The Humours of Covent Garden*, by Henry Fielding, Esq."

In 1743, the erection of theatrical booths in Smithfield was prohibited by a resolution of the Court of Aldermen, and the interdict was repeated in the following year. The prohibition did not extend to Southwark Fair, however, though held by the Corporation; for Yates was there in the former year, with a strong company from the theatres royal playing *Love for Love*, with Woodward as Tattle, Macklin as Ben, Arthur as Foresight, Mrs. Yates as Mrs. Frail, and Miss Bradshaw as Miss Prue. The after-piece was *The Lying Valet*, in which Yates appeared as Sharp, and his wife as Kitty Pry.

It was in 1744 that the famous Turkish wire-walker appeared at Bartholomew Fair, where he performed without a balancing-pole, at the height of thirty-five feet. He juggled while on the wire with what were supposed to be oranges; but this feat lost much of its marvellousness on his dropping one of them, which revealed by the sound that it was a painted ball of lead. He had formidable rivals in the celebrated Violantes, man and wife, the latter of whom far exceeded in skill and daring the famous Dutch woman of the latter years of the seventeenth century. These Italian *artistes*, like the Turk, performed at a considerable height, which, while it does not require greater skill, gives the performance a much more sensational character.

Violante is the slack-rope performer introduced by Hogarth in his picture of Southwark Fair. The following feat is recorded of the *artiste* by Malcolm, in his 'Londinium Redivivus,' in connection with the building of the church of St. Martin-in-the-Fields:— "Soon after the completion of the steeple, an adventurous Italian, named Violante, descended from the arches, head foremost, on a rope stretched across St. Martin's Lane to the Royal Mews; the princesses being present, and many eminent persons." Hogarth has introduced, in the background of his picture, another performer of this feat, namely, Cadman, who lost his life in 1740 in an attempt to descend from a church steeple in Shrewsbury. The epitaph on his gravestone sets forth the circumstances of the catastrophe as follows:—

"Let this small monument record the name
Of Cadman, and to future times proclaim
Here, by an attempt to fly from this high spire,
Across the Sabrine stream, he did acquire
His fatal end. 'Twas not for want of skill,
Or courage to perform the task, he fell:
No, no—a faulty cord, being drawn too tight,
Hurried his soul on high to take her flight,
Which bid the body here beneath good night."

The fairs of London were in the zenith of their fame during the period embraced in this chapter. During the second quarter of the eighteenth century, they were resorted to by all classes of the people, even by royalty; and the theatrical booths by which they were attended boasted the best talent in the profession. They were not only regarded as the nurseries of histrionic ability, as the provincial theatres afterwards came to be regarded, but witnessed the efforts to please of the best actors of the London theatres, when in the noon of their success and popularity. Cibber, Quin, Macklin, Woodward, Shuter, did not disdain to appear before a Bartholomew Fair audience, nor Fielding to furnish them with the early gushings of his humour. The inimitable Hogarth made the light of his peculiar genius shine upon them, and the memories of the old showmen are preserved in more than one of his pictures.

CHAPTER VI.

A new Race of Showmen—Yeates, the Conjuror—The Turkish Rope-Walker—Pan and the Oronutu Savage—The Corsican Fairy—Perry's Menagerie—The Riobiscay and the Double Cow—A Mermaid at the Fairs—Garrick at Bartholomew Fair—Yates's Theatrical Booth—Dwarfs and Giants—The Female Samson—Riots at Bartholomew Fair—Ballard's Animal Comedians—Evans, the Wire-Walker—Southwark Fair—Waxwork Show—Shuter, the Comedian—Bisset, the Animal Trainer—Powell, the Fire-Eater—Roger Smith, the Bell-Player—Suppression of Southwark Fair.

The limitation of Bartholomew Fair to three days, and the interdiction of theatrical booths in two successive years, was a serious blow, regarding the matter from the professional point of view, to the interests of the fair. Though actors worked hard during the twelve or eighteen days of the fair, they earned higher salaries during that time than they would have received at the theatres, and looked forward to Bartholomew-tide as the labourer to harvest. Though the theatres remained open during the fair when theatrical booths and puppet-shows were interdicted by the Court of Aldermen, actors missed their extra earnings, and managers found their receipts considerably diminished. In these we have only a passing interest; but the glory of the fairs began to wane when the great actors ceased to appear on the boards of the canvas theatres, for the nobility and gentry withdrew their patronage when the luminaries of Drury Lane and Covent Garden were no longer to be seen, and fairs began to be voted low by persons of rank and fashion.

The removal of the interdict on theatrical booths had little or no effect in arresting the progress of the decadence which had commenced; for the three days to which Bartholomew Fair remained limited did not afford to actors engaged at the London theatres, opportunities for earning money sufficient to induce them to set up a portable theatre, which, except for Southwark Fair, they could not use again until the following year. The case was very different when the fair lasted two or three weeks, and the theatres were closed during the time; but when its duration was contracted to three days, the attendance of a theatrical company could be made remunerative only for inferior *artistes* who strolled all through the year from one fair to another.

Towards the middle of the last century, therefore, a new race of showmen came prominently before the visitors to the London fairs, and two or three only of the names familiar to fair audiences afterwards re-appeared in the bills of the temporary theatres. Even these had, with the exception of Mrs. Lee, come into notice only since the fair, by being limited to three days, had lost its attractiveness for actors of the theatres royal. The site made famous by Fielding was occupied in 1746 by a new manager, Hussey, who presented a drama of Shakspeare's (without announcing the title), sandwich-like, between the two parts of a vocal and instrumental concert, concluding the entertainment with a pantomime called *The Schemes of Harlequin*, in which Rayner was Harlequin, and his daughter, who did a tight-rope performance, probably Columbine. Rayner was an acrobat at Sadler's Wells, where his daughter danced on the tight rope. The pantomime concluded with a chorus in praise of the Duke of Cumberland, whose victory at Culloden in the preceding year had finally crushed the hopes of the disaffected Jacobites.

The younger Yeates joined Mrs. Lee in a theatrical booth facing the hospital gate, where they presented *Love in a Labyrinth*, a musical entertainment called *Harlequin Invader*, and "stiff and slack rope-dancing by the famous Dutch woman." This can scarcely be the woman who did such wonders on the rope about the time of the Revolution, though Madame Saqui performed on the rope at a very advanced age; she may have been the same, for she does not appear again, but, considering that she is spoken of as a woman at the time of her first appearance in England, it is more probable that the rope-dancer of Mrs. Lee's booth was another Dutch woman, perhaps a daughter of the elder and more famous performer.

Adjoining Mrs. Lee's booth was one of which Warner and Fawkes were the proprietors, and in which a drama called *The Happy Hero* was performed, followed by a musical entertainment called *Harlequin Incendiary*, in which the parts of Harlequin and Columbine were sustained by a couple named Cushing, who afterwards appeared at Covent Garden. Warner personated Clodpole, a humorous rustic. Not to be outdone in loyalty by Hussey, he concluded the performance by singing a song in praise of the victor of Culloden.

Entertainers are, as a class, loyal, under whatever dynasty or form of government they live, providing that it does not interfere with the exercise of their profession; and in this instance their sympathies accorded with the popular political creed.

In the following year, Hussey's booth again stood in George Yard, and presented *Tamerlane the Great*, with singing and "several curious equilibres on the slack rope by Mahomet Achmed Vizaro Mussulmo, a Turk just arrived from Constantinople, who not only balances without a pole, but also plays a variety of excellent airs on the violin when on the slack rope, which none can perform in England but himself." Though said to have just arrived from Constantinople, this Turk was probably the same that had performed at Bartholomew Fair three years previously.

Warner disconnected himself from Fawkes this year, and joined Yeates and Mrs. Lee, whose booth stood in the same position as before, presenting the *Siege of Troy*, and an entertainment of singing and dancing. Adjoining it stood a new show, owned by Godwin and Reynolds, with "a curious collection of wax-work figures, being the richest and most beautiful in England;" and a panoramic view of the world, "particularly an accurate and beautiful prospect of Bergen-op-Zoom, together with its fortifications and adjacent forts, and an exact representation of the French besieging it, and the Dutch defending it from their batteries, etc." The movements of this exhibition were effected by clock-work. Opposite the Greyhound was another new venture, Chettle's, in which a pantomimic entertainment called *Frolicsome Lasses* was presented, with singing and dancing between the acts, and a display of fireworks at the end.

The only theatrical booth at Southwark Fair this year seems to have been Mrs. Lee's, in which the entertainments were the same as at Bartholomew Fair. In Mermaid Lane was exhibited "the strange and wonderful monstrous production of Nature, a sea-elephant head, having forty-six teeth, some of them ten inches long, fluted, and turning up like a ram's horn."

The shows increased in number and variety, though the theatrical booths could no longer boast of the great names of former years. George Yard was occupied in 1748 by a new theatre, owned by Bridges, Cross, Barton, and Vaughan, from the theatres royal, who availed of the interest created by recent events to present a new historical drama called *The Northern Heroes*, followed by dancing and a farce called *The Volunteers*, founded on the 'Adventures of Roderick Random.' Smollett was now running Fielding hard in the race of fame, and the new managers were keen in turning his popularity to account for their own interests. This booth was the most important one in the fair, and the charge for admission ranged from sixpence to half-a-crown.

Hussey's booth, at which the prices ranged from sixpence to two shillings, stood opposite the gate of the hospital. The entertainments consisted of the comedy of *The Constant Quaker*, singing and dancing, including "a new dance called Punch's Maggot, or Foote's Vagaries," and a pantomime called *Harlequin's Frolics*.

In Lee and Yeates's booth, opposite the Greyhound, *The Unnatural Parents* was revived, "shewing the manner of her (the heroine) being forced to wander from home by the cruelty of her parents, and beg her bread; and being weary, fell into a slumber, in a grove, where a goddess appears to her, and directs her to a nobleman's house; how she was there taken in as a servant, and at length, for her beauty and modest behaviour, married to a gentleman of great fortune, with her return to her parents, and their happy reconciliation. Also the comical humours and adventures of Trusty, her father's man, and the three witches." Then follow the *dramatis personæ*, which show a strong company. "With the original dance performed by three wild cats of the wood. With dancing between the acts by Mr. Adams and Mrs. Ogden. A good band of music is provided, consisting of kettle-drums, trumpets, French horns, hautboys, violins, etc. To begin each day at twelve o'clock. The scenes and clothes are entirely new, and the droll the same that was performed by Mrs. Lee fifteen years ago, with great applause."

Near Cow Lane stood another new theatrical booth, that of Cousins and Reynolds, at which the charges for admission ranged from threepence to a shilling. Here the romantic drama of *The Blind Beggar of Bethnal Green* was presented, with dancing between the acts, an exhibition of life-size wax figures, representing the Court of Maria Theresa, and the performance of the Italian sword-dancers, "who have had the honour of performing before the Prince of Wales, with great applause."

Among the minor shows was one at "the first house on the pavement, from the end of Hosier Lane," where the sights to be seen were a camel, a hyæna, a panther, "the wonderful and surprising satyr, call'd by Latin authors, Pan," and a "young Oronutu savage." On the pavement, at the end of Cow Lane, was a smaller show, the charge for admission to which was threepence, consisting of a large hog, said to weigh a hundred and twenty stones, and announced as "the greatest prodigy in Nature;" and an "amazing little dwarf, being the smallest man in the world."

Bartholomew Fair was visited this year for the first time by the female dwarf who obtained such wide-spread celebrity as the Corsican Fairy. It will be seen from the following copy of the bill issued by her exhibitors that she was not shown in a booth, but in a room hired for the purpose:—

"To the Nobility and Gentry, and to all who are Admirers of the Extraordinary Productions of Nature.

"There is to be seen in a commodious Apartment, at the Corner of Cow Lane, facing the Sheep-Pens, West Smithfield, During the short time of Bartholomew Fair,

MARIA TERESIA,

the Amazing Corsican Fairy, who has had the Honour of being shown three Times before their Majesties.

"☞ She was exhibited in Cockspur Street, Haymarket, at two shillings and sixpence each Person; but that Persons of every Degree may have a Sight of so extraordinary a Curiosity, she will be shown to the Gentry at sixpence each, and to Working People, Servants, and Children at Threepence, during this Fair.

"This most astonishing Part of the Human Species was born in the Island of Corsica, on the Mountain of Stata Ota, in the year 1743. She is only thirty-four Inches high, weighs but twenty-six Pounds, and a Child of two Years of Age has larger Hands and Feet. Her surprising Littleness makes a strong Impression at first Sight on the Spectator's Mind. Nothing disagreeable, either in Person or Conversation, is to be found in her; although most of Nature's Productions, in Miniature, are generally so in both. Her Form affords a pleasing Surprise, her Limbs are exceedingly well proportioned, her admirable Symmetry engages the attention; and, upon the whole, is acknowledged a perfect Beauty. She is possessed of a great deal of Vivacity of Spirit; can speak Italian and French, and gives the inquisitive Mind an agreeable Entertainment. In short, she is the most extraordinary Curiosity ever known, or ever heard of in History; and the Curious, in all countries where she has been shown, pronounce her the finest Display of Human Nature, in Miniature, they ever saw.

"⁂ She is to be seen by any Number of Persons, from Ten in the Morning till Nine at Night."

Hussey's theatrical booth attended Southwark Fair, where it stood on the bowling-green, the entertainments being the same as in Smithfield. Lee and Yeates can scarcely have been absent from a scene with which the former had been so long and intimately associated. Yeates took a benefit this year at the New Wells, near the London Spa, Clerkenwell, where a concert was followed by a performance of the *Beggar's Opera*, with the *bénéficiaire* as Macheath and his wife as Polly, and the farce of *Miss in her Teens*, in which the part of Captain Flash was sustained by the former, and that of Miss Biddy by his wife. The place was probably unlicensed for theatrical performances, as the dramatic portion of the entertainment was announced to be free to holders of tickets for the concert.

Tottenham Court Fair was continued this year for fourteen days, but does not appear to have been attended by any of the shows which contributed so much to the attractiveness of the fairs of Smithfield and Southwark Green. The only advertisement of the entertainments which I have been able to find mentions a "great theatrical booth," but it was devoted on the day to which the announcement relates to wrestling and single-stick playing. As a relic of a bygone time, it is curious enough to merit preservation:—

"For the entertainment of all lovers and encouragers of the sword in its different uses, and for the benefit of Daniel French, at the great theatrical booth at Tottenham Court, on Monday the 14th instant, will be revived a country wake. Three men of Gloucestershire to play at single-stick against three from any part, for a laced hat, value fifteen shillings, or half a guinea in gold; he that breaks most heads fairly in three bouts, and saves his own, to have the prize; half-a-crown for every man breaking a head fairly, besides stage-money. That gentlemen may not be disappointed, every gamester designing to engage is desired to enter his name and place of abode with Mr. Fuller, at the King's Head, next the booth, before the day of sport, or he will not be admitted to play, and to meet by eight in the morning to breakfast and settle the play for the afternoon. Money will be given for the encouragement of wrestling, sword and dagger, and other diversions usual on the stage, besides stage-money. That no time may be lost, while two are taking breath, two fresh men shall engage. The doors to be opened at twelve o'clock, and the sport to begin precisely at three in the afternoon. Note, there will be variety of singing and dancing for prizes, as will be expressed in the bills and papers of the day. Hob, clerk of the revel."

Newspapers of this year contain advertisements of several shows which probably visited the London Fairs, where they were sufficiently announced by their pictures. There are no fewer than three menageries, all on a small scale. The best seems to have been Perry's, advertised as follows:—"This is to give notice to all Gentlemen, Ladies, and others, that Mr. Perry's Grand Collection of Living Wild Beasts is come to the White Horse Inn, Fleet Street, consisting of a large he-lion, a he-tiger, a leopard, a panther, two hyenas, a civet cat, a jackall, or lion's provider, and several other rarities too tedious to mention. To be seen at any time of the day, without any loss of time. Note.—This is the only tiger in England, that baited being only a common leopard." The note alludes to a recent baiting of a leopard by dogs, the animal so abused being described in the announcements of the combat as a tiger.

The second menagerie under notice was advertised as follows:—

"To be seen, at the Flying Horse, near the London workhouse, Bishopsgate Street, from eight in the morning till nine at night, the largest collection of living wild creatures ever seen in Europe. 1. A beautiful large he-tiger, brought from Bengal by Captain Webster, in the Ann. He is very tame, and vastly admired. 2. A beautiful young leopard, from Turkey. 3. A civet cat, from Guinea. 4. A young man-tiger, from Angola. 5. A wonderful hyæna, from the coast of Guinea. 6. A right man-tiger, brought from Angola by Captain D'Abbadie, in the Portfield Indiaman. This is a very curious creature, and the only one that has been seen in England for several years. It comes the nearest to human nature of any animal in the world. With several others too tedious to mention." Perry seems to have been in error in announcing that he had the only tiger in England; though the one exhibited at the Flying Horse may have been a more recent importation. The "man-tigers" of the latter collection were probably gorillas, though those animals seem to have been lost sight of subsequently until attention was recalled to them by M. Du Chaillu.

The third collection was advertised as follows:—

"To be seen, at the White Swan, near the Bull and Gate, Holborn, a collection of the most curious living wild creatures just arrived from different parts of the world. 1. A large and beautiful young camel from Grand Cairo, in Egypt, near eight feet high, though not two years old, and drinks water but once in sixteen days. 2. A surprising hyæna, from the coast of Guinea. 3. A beautiful he-panther, from Buenos Ayres, in the Spanish West Indies. 4. A young Riobiscay, from Russia: and several other creatures, too tedious to mention. Likewise a travelling post-chaise from Switzerland, which, without horses, keeps its stage for upwards of fifty miles a day, without danger to the rider. Attendance from eight in the morning till eight at night." What the riobiscay was is now beyond conjecture; but the panther from Buenos Ayres was, of course, a jaguar, the panther being limited to the eastern hemisphere. This collection was exhibited in Holborn early in the year, and removed at Easter to the Rose and Crown, near the gates of Greenwich Park.

There was a bovine monstrosity shown this year as a "double cow," probably at the fairs, as the following paragraph, extracted from a newspaper of the time, refers to a second locality:—

"As we are well assured that that most wonderful living curiosity, the double cow, has given uncommon satisfaction to the several learned bodies by whom it has hitherto been seen, we hope the following account and description of it will not be disagreeable to our readers. This wonderful prodigy was bred at Cookfield in Sussex, being one entire beautiful cow, from the middle of whose back issues the following parts of the other cow, viz., a leg with the blade-bone quite perfect, and about two feet long; the gullet, bowels, teats, and udder, from which udder, as well as from the udder of the perfect cow, it gives milk in great plenty, though more than a yard asunder; and what is very extraordinary, and has astonished the most curious observers, is the discontinuation of the back-bone about sixteen inches from the shoulder. This wonderful beast is so healthy as to travel twenty miles a day, is extremely gentle, and by all the gentlemen and ladies who have already seen it is thought as agreeable as astonishing. It is now shewn in a commodious room, facing Craigg's Court, Charing Cross, at one shilling each person."

There was also exhibited at the Heath Cock, Charing Cross, "a surprising young Mermaid, taken on the coast of Aquapulca, which, though the generality of mankind think there is no such thing, has been seen by the curious, who express their utmost satisfaction at so uncommon a creature, being half like a woman, and half like a fish, and is allowed to be the greatest curiosity ever exposed to the public view."

In 1749, there was again a large muster of shows on the ancient arena of West Smithfield. Yates re-appeared as a theatrical manager, and in some measure restored the former repute of the fair, Oates and Miss Hippisley being members of his company. His booth stood in George Yard, where he played Gormandize Simple, while Oates personated Jupiter and Miss Hippisley the wanton chambermaid, Dorothy Squeezepurse, in "a New, Pleasant, and Diverting Droll, call'd the Descent of the Heathen Gods, with the Loves of Jupiter and Alcmena; or, Cuckoldom no Scandal. Interspersed with several Diverting Scenes, both Satyrical and Comical, particularly the Surprising Metamorphosis of *Jupiter* and *Mercury*; the very remarkable Tryal before *Judge Puzzlecause*, with many Learned Arguments on both sides, to prove that One can't be Two. Likewise the Adventures and whimsical Perplexities of *Gormandize Simple* the Hungarian Footman; with the wonderful Conversation he had with, and the dreadful Drubbing he received from, *His Own Apparition*; together with the Intrigues of *Dorothy Squeezepurse* the Wanton Chambermaid."

Opposite the George stood the theatrical booth of the elder Yeates, who had been absent from the fair for a few years, and whom Mr. Henry Morley confounds with his son, now in partnership with Warner and Mrs. Lee. He produced *The Blind Beggar of Bethnal Green*, with singing and dancing between the acts, and the pantomime of *The Amours of Harlequin*. Cross and Bridges, whose booth stood opposite the gate of the hospital, produced a new drama, called *The Fair Lunatic*, "founded on a story in real life, as related in the memoirs of the celebrated Mrs. Constantia Phillips," with dancing by Master Matthews and Mrs. Annesley. Next to this booth stood that of Lee, Yeates, and Warner, in which was revived the "true and ancient history of *Whittington*, Lord Mayor of London," as performed in Lee's booth fourteen years before, with singing and dancing between the acts. Cushing whom we have seen playing Harlequin three years before in Warner and Fawkes's booth, but who was now performing at Covent Garden, set up a booth opposite the King's Head, and produced *King John*, the part of Lady Constance being sustained by Miss Yates, a Drury Lane actress, while Cushing's wife personated Prince Arthur, and the manager the mirth-provoking Sir Lubberly Lackbrains.

At a house in Hosier Lane (No. 20), a performing Arabian pony was exhibited. There were also shows in the fair, which did not advertise, and the memory of which has, in consequence, not been preserved. Of one, owned by a person named Phillips, the only record is a very brief newspaper report of a fatal accident, occasioned by the breaking down of the gallery, by which four persons were killed, and several others severely injured.

Garrick, who had married the dancer Violette two months previously, took his bride to Bartholomew Fair, where they visited the theatrical booth of Yates, which was the best in the fair. He was one of the few great actors of the period who had not performed in the fair; and was probably impelled by curiosity, rather than by the expectation of seeing good acting, though it was not many years since he had made his first appearance on any stage at Goodman's Fields, playing Harlequin at a moment's notice when Yates was seized with a sudden indisposition as he was about to go on the stage. The crowd pressing upon his wife and himself very unpleasantly as he approached the portable theatre, he called out to Palmer, the Drury Lane bill-sticker, who was acting as money-taker at the booth, to protect them. "I can't help you here, sir," said Palmer, shaking his head. "There aren't many people in Smithfield as knows Mr. Garrick."

It was probably not at Yates's booth, but at one of much inferior grade, that the money-taker rejected Garrick's offer to pay for admission, with the remark, "We never take money of one another." The story would be pointless if the incident occurred at any booth in which dramatic performances were given by comedians from the principal London theatres.

We now approach a period when a new series of strenuous efforts for the suppression of the London fairs was commenced by persons who would willingly have suppressed amusements of every kind, and were aided in their endeavours by persons who had merely a selfish interest in the matter. In the summer of 1750, a numerously signed petition of graziers, cattle salesmen, and inhabitants of Smithfield was presented to the Court of Aldermen, praying for the suppression of Bartholomew Fair, on the ground that it annoyed them in their occupations, and afforded opportunities for debauchery and riot. The annual Lord Mayor's procession might have been objected to on the same grounds, and the civic authorities well knew that the riots which had sometimes occurred in the fair had been occasioned by their own acts, in the execution of their edicts for the exclusion of puppet-shows and theatrical booths. Their action to this end was generally taken so tardily that booths were put up before the proprietors received notice of the intention of the Court of Aldermen to exclude them; and then the tardiness of the owners in taking them down, and the sudden zeal of the constables, produced quarrels and fights, in which the bystanders invariably took the part of the showmen.

The revenues which the Corporation derived from rents and tolls during the fair constituted an element of the question which could not be overlooked, and which kept it in a state of oscillation from year to year. The civic authorities would have been willing enough to suppress the fair, if the question of finance had not been involved. If the fair was abolished, some other source of revenue would have to be found. So they compounded with their belief that the fair was a fount of disorder and immorality by again limiting its duration to three days, and excluding theatrical booths and puppet-shows, while abstaining from interference with the gambling-tables and the gin-stalls.

Giants and dwarfs, and learned pigs and performing ponies had now the fair to themselves, though their showmen probably took less money than they did when the theatrical booths and puppet-shows attracted larger numbers of people. Henry Blacker, a native of Cuckfield, in Sussex, twenty-seven years of age, and seven feet four inches in height, exhibited himself at the Swan, in Smithfield, during the three days to which the fair was restricted in 1751. The principal show seems to have been one containing two dwarfs, a remarkable negro, a female one-horned rhinoceros, and a crocodile, said to have been the first ever seen alive in this country. The more famous of the two dwarfs was John Coan, a native of Norfolk, who at this time was twenty-three years of age, and only three feet two inches in height, and of thirty-four pounds weight. His fellow pigmy was a Welsh lad, fourteen years of age, two feet six inches in height, and weighed only twelve pounds. The negro could throw back his clasped hands over his head and bring them under his feet, backward and forward; and was probably "the famous negro who swings his arms about in every direction," mentioned in the 'Adventurer.'

The exclusion of the theatrical booths and puppet-shows from the fair produced, in the following year, a serious disturbance in Smithfield, in the suppression of which Birch, the deputy-marshal of the City, received injuries which proved fatal. This resistance to their edict did not, however, deter the civic authorities from applying the same rule to Southwark Fair, which was this year limited to three days, and diminished of its attractions by the exclusion of theatrical booths and puppet-shows. The principal shows were Yeates's, which stood in George Yard, and consisted of an exhibition of wax figures, the conjuring tricks of young Yeates, and the feats on the slack wire of a performer named Steward; and the female Samson's, an Italian woman, who exhibited feats of strength in a booth opposite the Greyhound, similar to those of the French woman seen by Carter at May Fair, with the addition of supporting six men while resting on two chairs only by the head and heels.

Towards the close of this year a man named Ballard brought from Italy a company of performing dogs and monkeys, and exhibited them as a supplementary attraction to the musical entertainments then given at a place in the Haymarket, called Mrs. Midnight's Oratory. The Animal Comedians, as they were called, became famous enough to furnish the theme of an 'Adventurer.' The author states that the repeated encomiums on their performances induced him to be present one evening at the entertainment, when he "was astonished at the sagacity of the monkies; and was no less amazed at the activity of the other quadrupeds—I should have rather said, from a view of their extraordinary elevations, bipeds.

"It is a peculiar happiness to me as an Adventurer," he continues, "that I sally forth in an age which emulates those heroick times of old, when nothing was pleasing but what was unnatural. Thousands have gaped at a wire-dancer daring to do what no one else would attempt; and thousands still gape at greater extravagances in pantomime entertainments. Every street teems with incredibilities; and if the great mob have their little theatre in the Haymarket, the small vulgar can boast their cheaper diversion in two enormous bears, that jauntily trip it to the light tune of a Caledonian jig.

"That the intellectual faculties of brutes may be exerted beyond the narrow limits which we have hitherto assigned to their capacities, I saw a sufficient proof in Mrs. Midnight's dogs and monkies. Man differs less from beasts in general, than these seem to approach man in rationality. But while I applaud their exalted genius, I am in pain for the rest of their kindred, both of the canine and cercopithecan species." The writer then proceeds to comment humorously upon the mania which the exhibition had created for teaching dogs and monkeys to perform the tricks for which the Animal Comedians were famous. "Every boarding-house romp and wanton school-boy," he says, "is employed in perverting the end of the canine creation."

The contributor of this paper seems to have had a familiar acquaintance with the shows attending the London fairs, for it was he, whoever he was, who wrote the third number of the 'Adventurer,' in which, giving the details of a scheme for a pantomime, he says that he has "not only ransacked the fairs of Bartholomew and Southwark, but picked up every uncommon animal, every prodigy of nature, and every surprising performer, that has lately appeared within the bills of mortality." He proceeds to enumerate them, and to assign parts in his intended entertainment for "the Modern Colossus," "all the wonderful tall men and women that have been lately exhibited in this town," "the Female Sampson," "the famous negro who swings his arms about in every direction," "the noted ox, with six legs and two bellies," "the beautiful panther mare," "the noted fire-eater, smoking out of red-hot tobacco pipes, champing lighted brimstone, and swallowing his infernal mess of broth," "the most amazing new English *Chien Savant*," "the little woman that weighs no more than twenty-three pounds," "the wonderful little Norfolk man," "the fellow with Stentorian lungs, who can break glasses and shatter window-panes with the loudness of his vociferation," and "the wonderful man who talks in his belly, and can fling his voice into any part of a room." Incidentally he mentions also "the so much applauded stupendous ostrich," "the sorcerer's great gelding," "the wire dancer," and dancing bears.

The showmen's bills and advertisements of the period enable us to identify most of the wonders enumerated by this writer. The female Samson and the wire-walker had been seen that year in the fairs, the famous negro and the Norfolk dwarf the year before, and the Corsican fairy and the double cow in 1748. The fire-eater was probably Powell, though I have seen no advertisement of that human salamander earlier than 1760.

The Bartholomew Fair riot was repeated in 1753, when Buck, the successor of the unfortunate Birch, was very roughly handled by the rioters, and severely bruised. This tumult was followed by an accident to a wire-walker, named Evans, who, by the breaking of his wire, was precipitated to the ground, breaking one of his thighs and receiving other injuries. This was the year of the demonstration against the claim of the Corporation to levy tolls upon the goods of citizens, as well as upon those of strangers, during the time of Bartholomew Fair. Richard Holland, a leather-seller in Newgate Street, had, in the preceding year, refused the toll demanded on a roll of leather with which he had attempted to enter the fair, and, on the leather being seized by the collector, had called a constable, and charged the impounder with theft. The squabble resulted in an action against the Corporation, which was not tried, however, till 1754, when the judge pronounced in favour of the citizens.

While the action was pending, Holland's cart was driven through the fair with a load of hay, and was not stopped by the collector of the tolls, who had, probably, been instructed to hold his hand until the matter was determined. The horses' heads were decorated with ribbons, and on the leader's forehead was a card, upon which the following doggrel lines were written in a bold round hand:—

"My master keeps me well, 'tis true,
And justly pays whatever is due;
Now plainly, not to mince the matter,
No toll he pays but with a halter."

On each side of the load of hay hung a halter, and a paper bearing the following announcement:—

"The time is approaching, if not already come,
That all British subjects may freely pass on;
And not on pretence of Bartholomew Fair
Make you pay for your passage, with all you bring near.
When once it is try'd, ever after depend on,
'Twill incur the same fate as on Finchley Common.
Give Cæsar his due, when by law 'tis demanded,
And those that deserve with this halter be hanged."

The disturbances occasioned by the interference of the authorities with the entertainers of the fair-goers were not renewed in 1754, though the elements of disorder seem to have been present in tolerable strength; for on a swing breaking down in Smithfield, without any person being seriously hurt, a number of persons broke up the apparatus, and throwing the wreck into a heap, set it on fire. Every swing in the fair was then attacked and wrecked in succession, and the frames and broken cars thrown upon the blazing pile, which soon sent a column of fire high into the air, to the immense danger of the many combustible erections on every side. To keep up the fire, all the tables and benches of the sausage-vendors were next seized, and cast upon it; and the feeble police of that period was inadequate to the prevention of this wholesale destruction, which seems to have gone on without a check.

The exclusion of theatrical entertainments from Southwark Fair was not maintained in 1755, when Warner set up a booth on the bowling-green, in conjunction with the widow of Yeates (who had died about this time), and revived the favourite London fair drama of *The Unnatural Parents*. In the following year, Warner's name appears alone, as the proprietor of a "great tiled booth," in which he produced *The Lover's Metamorphosis*, with dancing between the acts, and a pantomimic entertainment called *The Stratagems of Harlequin*.

In 1757, Yates and Shuter, the former engaged at the time at Drury Lane, and the latter at Covent Garden, tried the experiment of a variety entertainment, at the large concert-room of the Greyhound Inn, in Smithfield, "during the short time of Bartholomew Fair," as all bills and advertisements had announced since the duration of the fair had been limited to three days. By this device, they evaded the edict of the Lord Mayor and the Court of Aldermen, which applied only to temporary erections in Smithfield. They did not repeat the experiment in Southwark, where the only booth advertised was Warner's, with "a company of comedians from the theatres," in *The Intriguing Lover* and *Harlequin's Vagaries*.

Yates and Shuter re-appeared at the Greyhound next year, when they presented *Woman turned Bully*, with singing and dancing between the acts, and a representation of the storming of Louisbourg. Theatrical representations were this year permitted or connived at in the fair, for Dunstall and Vaughan set up a booth in George Yard, associating with them in the enterprise the more experienced Warner, and announcing "a select company from the theatres royal." *The Widow Bewitched* was performed, with an entertainment of singing and dancing. Next door to the George Inn was an exhibition of wax-work, the chief feature of which was a collection of figures representing the royal family of Prussia.

Southwark Fair was this year extended to four days, so fitful and varying was the policy of the Court of Aldermen with regard to the fairs, which, while they professed to regard them as incentives to idleness and vice, they encouraged in some years as much as they restricted in others. The names of Dunstall and Vaughan do not appear in the bills issued by Warner for this fair, but the comedy performed was the same as at Bartholomew Fair, followed by a representation of the capture of Louisbourg, concluding with a procession of colours and standards, and a song in praise of the heroes of the victory.

Yates and Shuter again attended Bartholomew Fair in the following year. Mr. Henry Morley claims for the latter the invention of the showman's device of announcing to the players, by a cant word, that there was another audience collected in front, and that the performances might be drawn to a close as soon as possible. Shuter's mystic words are said to have been "John Audley," shouted from the front. The practice appears, however, to have been in operation in the earliest days of Sadler's Wells, where, according to a description of the place and the entertainments given by Macklin, in a conversation recorded in the fortieth volume of the 'European Magazine,' the announcement was made in the query, "Is Hiram Fistoman here?"

It was about this time that the "cat's opera" was announced by the famous animal-trainer, Bisset, whose pupils, furred and feathered, were regarded as one of the most wonderful exhibitions ever witnessed. Bisset was originally a shoemaker at Perth, where he was born in 1721, but, on coming to London, and entering the connubial state, he commenced business as a broker, and accumulated a little capital. Having read an account of a performing horse, which was exhibited at the fair of St. Germain in 1739, he was induced to try his own skill in the teaching of animals upon a dog, and afterwards upon a horse, which he bought for the purpose. Succeeding with these, he procured a couple of monkeys, one of which he taught to play a barrel-organ, while the other danced and vaulted on the tight-rope.

Cats are generally regarded as too susceptible of nervous excitement to perform in public, though their larger relatives, lions, tigers, and leopards, have been taught to perform a variety of tricks before spectators, and cats are readily taught to perform the same tricks in private. Bisset aimed at something higher than the exhibition of the leaping feats of the species, and succeeded in teaching three cats to play the dulcimer and squall to the notes. By the advice of Pinchbeck, with whom he had become acquainted, he hired a large room in the Haymarket, and announced a public performance of the "cat's opera," supplemented by the tricks of the horse, the dog, and the monkeys. Besides the organ-grinding and rope-dancing performance, the monkeys took wine together, and rode on the horse, pirouetting and somersaulting with the skill of a practised acrobat. One of them also danced a minuet with the dog.

The "cat's opera" was attended by crowded houses, and Bisset cleared a thousand pounds by the exhibition in a few days. He afterwards taught a hare to walk on its hind legs, and beat a drum; a feathered company of canaries, linnets, and sparrows to spell names, tell the time by the clock, etc.; half-a-dozen turkeys to execute a country dance; and a turtle (according to Wilson, but probably a tortoise) to write names on the floor, having its feet blackened for the purpose. After a successful season in London, he sold some of the animals, and made a provincial tour with the rest, rapidly accumulating a considerable fortune. Passing over to Ireland in 1775, he exhibited his animals in Dublin and Belfast, afterwards establishing himself in a public-house in the latter city. There he remained until 1783, when he reappeared in Dublin with a pig, which he had taught to perform all the tricks since exhibited by the learned grunter's successors at all the fairs in the kingdom. He was on his way to London with the pig when he became ill at Chester, where he shortly afterwards died.

The question of suppressing both Bartholomew and Southwark Fairs was considered by the Court of Common Council in 1760, and the City Lands Committee was desired to report upon the tenures of the fairs, with a view to that end. Counsel's opinion was taken, and the committee reported the result of the inquiry, upon which the Court resolved that Southwark Fair should be abolished henceforth, but that the interests of Lord Kensington in the revenues of Bartholomew Fair prevented the same course from being pursued in Smithfield. The latter fair was voted a nuisance, however, and the Court expressed a determination to abate it with the utmost strictness. Shuter produced a masque, called *The Triumph of Hymen*, in honour of the approaching royal nuptials; it was the production of a forgotten poet named Wignell, in a collected edition of whose poems it was printed in 1762. Among the minor entertainers of this year at Bartholomew Fair were Powell, the fire-eater, and Roger Smith, who gave a musical performance upon eight bells, two of which were fixed upon his head-gear, and one upon each foot, while two were held in each hand.

CHAPTER VII.

Yates and Shuter—Cat Harris—Mechanical Singing Birds—Lecture on Heads—Pidcock's Menagerie—Breslaw, the Conjuror—Reappearance of the Corsican Fairy—Gaetano, the Bird Imitator—Rossignol's Performing Birds—Ambroise, the Showman—Brunn, the Juggler, on the Wire—Riot at Bartholomew Fair—Dancing Serpents—Flockton, the Puppet-Showman—Royal Visit to Bartholomew Fair—Lane, the Conjuror—Hall's Museum—O'Brien, the Irish Giant—Baker's Theatre—Joel Tarvey and Lewis Owen, the popular Clowns.

The relations between Yates and Shuter in the last two or three years of their appearance as showmen at Bartholomew Fair are somewhat doubtful; but all the evidence that I have been able to obtain points to the conclusion that they did not co-operate subsequently to 1758. In 1761 they seemed to have been in rivalry, for the former's name appears singly as the director of the "company of comedians from both the theatres" that performed in the concert-room at the Greyhound, while an advertisement of one of the minor shows of the fair describes it as located in George Yard, "leading to Mr. Shuter's booth." I have not, however, been able to find an advertisement of Shuter's booth.

Yates's company performed *The Fair Bride*, which the bills curiously describe as "containing many surprising Occurrences at Sea, which could not possibly happen at Land. The Performance will be highly enlivened with several entertaining Scenes between England, France, Ireland, and Scotland, in the diverting Personages of Ben Bowling, an English Sailor; Mons. Soup-Maigre, a French Captain; O'Flannaghan, an Irish Officer; M'Pherson, a Scotch Officer. Through which the Manners of each Nation will be characteristically and humorously depicted. In which will be introduced as singular and curious a Procession as was ever exhibited in this Nation. The objects that comprise the Pageantry are both Exotic and British. The Principal Figure is the Glory and Delight of OLD ENGLAND, and Envy of our ENEMIES. With Variety of Entertainments of Singing and Dancing. The whole to conclude with a Loyal Song on the approaching Marriage of our great and glorious Sovereign King GEORGE and the Princess CHARLOTTE of Mecklenberg."

There were two shows in George Yard, in one of which "the famous learned canary bird" was exhibited, the other consisting of a moving picture of a city, with an artificial cascade, and "a magnificent temple, with two mechanical birds which have all the exact motions of living animals; they perform a variety of tunes, either singular or in concert. During the performance, the just swelling of the throat, the quick motions of the bills, and the joyous fluttering of the wings, strike every spectator with pleasing astonishment."

Shuter seems to have been the last actor who played at Bartholomew Fair while engaged at a permanent theatre. Some amusing stories are told of his powers of mimicry. When Foote introduced in a comedy a duet supposed to be performed by two cats, in imitation of Bisset's feline opera, he engaged for the purpose one Harris, who was famous for his power of producing the vocal sounds peculiar to the species. Harris being absent one day from rehearsal, Shuter went in search of him, and not knowing the number of the house in which Cat Harris, as he was called, resided, he began to perform a feline solo as soon as he entered the court in which lived the man of whom he was in search. Harris opened his window at the sound, and responded with a beautiful *meeyow*.

"You are the man!" said Shuter. "Come along! We can't begin the cats' opera without you."

There is a story told of Shuter, however, which is strongly suggestive of his ability to have supplied Cat Harris's place. He was travelling in the Brighton stage-coach on a very warm day, with four ladies, when the vehicle stopped to receive a sixth passenger, who could have played Falstaff without padding. The faces of the ladies elongated at this unwelcome addition to the number, but Shuter only smiled. When the stout gentleman was seated, and the coach was again in motion, Shuter gravely inquired of one of the ladies her motive for visiting Brighton. She replied, that her physician had advised sea-bathing as a remedy for mental depression. He turned to the others, and repeated his inquiries; the next was nervous, the third bilious—all had some ailment which the sea was expected to cure.

"Ah!" sighed the comedian, "all your complaints put together are nothing to mine. Oh, nothing!—mine is dreadful but to think of."

"Indeed, sir!" said the stout passenger, with a look of astonishment. "What is your complaint? you look exceedingly well."

"Ah, sir!" responded Shuter, shaking his head, "looks are deceitful; you must know, sir, that, three days ago, I had the misfortune to be bitten by a mad dog, for which I am informed sea-bathing is the only cure. For that purpose I am going to Brighton; for though, as you observe, I am looking well, yet the fit comes on in a moment, when I bark like a dog, and endeavour to bite every one near me."

"Lord have mercy on us!" ejaculated the stout passenger, with a look of alarm. "But, sir, you are not in earnest—you—"

"Bow-wow-wow!"

"Coachman! coachman! Let me out!—let me out, I say!"

"Now, your honour, what's the matter?"

"A mad dog is the matter!—hydrophobia is the matter! open the door!"

"Bow-wow-wow!"

"Open the door! Never mind the steps. Thank God, I am safe out! Let those who like ride inside; I'll mount the roof."

So he rode to Brighton outside the coach, much to the satisfaction of Shuter and his fair companions who were very merry at his expense, the former repeating at intervals his sonorous *bow-wow-wow*!

Theatrical booths and puppet-shows were again prohibited in 1762, and, as the jugglers, the acrobats, and the rope-dancers who attended the fairs did not advertise their performances, only casual notices are to be found in the newspapers of the period of the amusements which that generation flocked into Smithfield in the first week of September to witness, and which lead them somewhat earlier to the greens of Camberwell and Stepney. Some of the entertainers of the period are mentioned in an anonymous poem on Bartholomew Fair, which appeared in 1763. The names are probably fictitious.

"On slender cord Volante treads;
The earth seems paved with human heads:
And as she springs aloft in air,
Trembling they crouch below for fear.
A well-made form Querpero shows,
Well-skilled that form to discompose;
The arms forget their wonted state;
Standing on earth, they bear his weight;
The head falls downward 'twixt the thighs,
The legs mount upward to the skies;
And thus this topsy-turvy creature
Stalks, and derides the human nature.
Agyrta, famed for cup and ball,
Plays sleight of hand, and pleases all:
The certainty of sense in vain
Philosophers in schools maintain;
This man your sharpest wit defies,
He cheats your watchful ears and eyes.
Ah, 'prentice, well your pockets fence,
And yet he steals your master's pence."

In 1765, "the celebrated lecture on heads" was advertised to be given, during the time of Bartholomew Fair, "in a large and commodious room near the end of Hosier Lane." The name of the lecturer was not announced, but the form of the advertisement implies that the lecture was Steevens's. The lecturer may, however, have been only an imitator of that famous humorist; for the newspapers of the preceding week inform us that a similar announcement was made at Alnwick, where the audience, finding that the lecturer was not Steevens, regarded him as an impostor, and demanded the return of their money, with a threat of tossing him in a blanket. The lecturer attempted to vindicate himself, but the production of a blanket completed his discomfiture, and he surrendered, returning to the disappointed audience the money which they had paid for admission.

In 1769, the chief attraction of the London fairs was Pidcock's menagerie, which was the largest and best which had ever been exhibited in a temporary erection, the animals being hired from Cross's collection at Exeter Change. Pidcock exhibited his animals at Bartholomew Fair for several successive years, and was succeeded by Polito, whose zoological collection attracted thousands of spectators every year.

Breslaw, the conjuror, appeared in 1772, in a large room in Cockspur Street, where his tricks of legerdemain were combined with a vocal and instrumental concert by three or four Italians, imitations by a young lady announced as Miss Rose of "many interesting parts of the capital actresses in tragedy and comedy," and imitations by an Italian named Gaetano of the notes of the blackbird, thrush, canary, linnet, bull-finch, sky-lark, and nightingale. In 1774, the entertainment was given on alternate days in the large ball-room of the King's Arms, opposite the Royal Exchange. In 1775, it was given in Cockspur Street only, and in the following year at Marylebone Gardens. He then appears to have been absent from London for a couple of years, as he always was during a portion of each year, when he made a tour through the provinces.

Caulfield says that Breslaw was superior to Fawkes, "both in tricks and impudence," and relates an anecdote, which certainly goes far to bear out his assertion. Breslaw, while exhibiting at Canterbury, requested permission to display his cunning a little longer, promising the Mayor that if he was indulged with the required permission, he would give the receipts of one night for the benefit of the poor. The Mayor acceded to the proposition, and Breslaw had a crowded house; hearing nothing about the money collected on the specified evening, the Mayor called upon Breslaw, and, in as delicate a manner as possible, expressed his surprise.

"Mr. Mayor," said the conjuror, "I have distributed the money myself."

"Pray, sir, to whom?" inquired the Mayor, still more surprised.

"To my own company, than whom none can be poorer," replied Breslaw.

"This is a trick!" exclaimed the Mayor indignantly.

"Sir," returned the conjuror, "we live by tricks."

In 1773, the Corsican fairy reappeared, having probably made the tour of Europe since her first exhibition in London in 1748, which has been overlooked by some writers, though there is no doubt that the girl exhibited at the latter date was the same person. Two years later, the Turkish rope-dancer, who had displayed his feats in 1744, reappeared at Bartholomew Fair. In the same year, Rossignol exhibited his performing birds at Sadler's Wells, and afterwards at the Smock Alley theatre, in Dublin. He returned to Sadler's Wells in 1776, where his clever feathered company attracted as many spectators as before. Twelve or fourteen canaries and linnets were taken from their cages, and placed on a table, in ranks, with paper caps on their heads, and tiny toy muskets under their left wings. Thus armed and accoutred, they marched about the table, until one of them, leaving the ranks, was adjudged a deserter, and sentenced to be shot. A mimic execution then took place, one of the birds holding a lighted match in its claw, and firing a toy cannon of brass, loaded with powder. The deserter fell, feigning death, but rose again at the command of Rossignol.

Breslaw had formidable competitors this year in Ambroise and Brunn, who gave a variety entertainment in a large room in Panton Street, of which we have the following account in their advertisements:—

"On the part of Mr. Ambroise, the manager of the *Ombres Chinoises*, will be performed all those scenes which, upon repeated trial, have had a general approbation, with new pieces every day; the whole to be augmented with a fourth division. By the particular desire of the company, the *danses de caractère* in the intervals are performed to the astonishment of all, and to conclude with the comic of a magician, who performs metamorphoses, etc. He had the honour to represent this spectacle before his Most Christian Majesty Louis XVI. and the Royal Family; likewise before His Serene Highness the Prince d'Orange and the whole Court, with an approbation very flattering for the performer.

"The Saxon Brunn, besides various tricks of his dexterity, will give this day a surprising circular motion with three forks and a sword; to-morrow, with a plate put horizontally upon the point of a knife, a sword fixed perpendicularly, on the top of which another plate, all turning with a remarkable swiftness; and on Saturday the singular performance with a bason, called the Clag of Manfredonia; all which are of his own invention, being the *non plus ultra* for equilibriums on the wire. The applause they have already received makes them hope to give an equal satisfaction to the company for the future. To begin at seven precisely. Admittance, five shillings."

In 1778, a foreigner exhibited in Bartholomew Fair the extraordinary spectacle of serpents dancing on silken ropes to the sound of music, which performance has never, I believe, been repeated since. The serpents exhibited by Arab and Hindoo performers, of whose skill an example was afforded several years ago in the Zoological Gardens in the Regent's Park, dance on the ground. It was in this year that the fair was visited by the Duke and Duchess of Gloucester, who entered at Giltspur Street, and passing the puppet-shows of Flockton and Jobson, the conjuring booths of Lane and Robinson, and several other shows the names only of whose proprietors—Ives, Basil, Clarkson,—have been preserved, rode through Cow Lane into Holborn.

This year appears to have been the first in which puppet-shows were allowed to be set up in Smithfield after being excluded for several years; as in 1776 a more than ordinary degree of irritation was produced by their exclusion, "Lady Holland's mob" proclaiming the fair without any restriction, and a disturbance arising afterwards, in the course of which the windows of nearly every house round Smithfield were broken by the rioters. Flockton and Jobson attended the fair regularly for many years. The former used to perform some conjuring tricks on the outside of his show to attract an audience, but Strutt says that he was a very poor conjuror. Lane's performances were varied by posturing and dancing by his two daughters. The following doggrel appears in one of his bills:—

"It will make you laugh, it will drive away gloom,
To see how the egg it will dance round the room;
And from another egg a bird there will fly,
Which makes the company all for to cry,
'O rare Lane! cockalorum for Lane! well done, Lane!
You are the Man!'"

One of the chief shows of the fair in 1779 was the fine collection of preserved animals of Hall, of the City Road, who was famous for his skill in that art. This museum did not prove so attractive as Pidcock's menagerie, however, the frequenters of the fair preferring to see the animals living; and in the following year even the expedient of parading a stuffed zebra round the fair did not attract spectators enough to induce Hall to attend again. His museum remained open in the City Road, however, for many years.

Breslaw, the conjuror, had a room in 1779 at the King's Head, near the Mansion House, as well as in Cockspur Street (opposite the Haymarket), and a bill of this year shows, better than any of his earlier announcements, the nature of the tricks which he performed. His exposition of "how it is done" was probably not more intelligible than Dr. Lynn's. "Between the different parts," says the bill, "Mr. Breslaw will discover the following deceptions in such a manner, that every person in the company shall be capable of doing them immediately for their amusement. First, to tell any lady or gentleman the card that they fix on, without asking any questions. Second, to make a remarkable piece of money to fly out of any gentleman's hand into a lady's pocket-handkerchief, at two yards distance. Third, to change four or five cards in any lady's or gentleman's hand several times into different cards. Fourth, to make a fresh egg fly out of any person's pocket into a box on the table, and immediately to fly back again into the pocket."

Breslaw had Rossignol in his company at this time, as will be seen from the following programme:—"1. Mr. Breslaw will exhibit a variety of new magical card deceptions, particularly he will communicate the thoughts from one person to another, after which he will perform many new deceptions with letters, numbers, dice, rings, pocket-pieces, &c., &c. 2. Under the direction of Sieur Changee, a new invented small chest, consisting of three divisions, will be displayed in a most extraordinary manner. 3. The famous Rossignol, from Naples, will imitate various birds, to the astonishment of the spectators. 4. Mr. Breslaw will exhibit several new experiments on six different metals, watches, caskets, gold boxes, silver machineries, &c., &c."

Rossignol (said to be an assumed name) afterwards obtained an engagement at Covent Garden Theatre, where he attracted attention by an imitation of the violin with his mouth; but, being detected in the use of a concealed instrument, he lost his reputation, and we hear of him no more. Breslaw filled up the vacancy in his company by engaging Novilli, who played "at one time on the German flute, violin, Spanish castanets, two pipes, trumpet, bassoon, bass, Dutch drum, and violin-cello, never attempted before in this kingdom." I have not been able to discover anything that would throw some light upon the manner in which this extraordinary performance was accomplished. He engaged for his London season this year a large room in Panton Street, probably the one in which Ambroise and Brunn performed in 1775. The entertainment commenced, as before, with a vocal and instrumental concert, between the parts of which lyrical and rhetorical imitations were given by "a young gentleman, not nine years of age;" the concluding portion consisting of the exhibition of Breslaw's "new invented mechanical watches, sympathetic bell, pyramidical glasses, magical card deceptions, &c., &c.," and particularly "a new grand apparatus and experiments never attempted before in this kingdom."

It was in this year that the famous Irish giant, Patrick O'Brien, first exhibited himself at Bartholomew Fair, being then nineteen years of age, and over eight feet high. His name was Cotter, that of O'Brien being assumed when he began to exhibit himself, to accord with the representation that he was a descendant of the ancient royal race of Munster. His parents, who were both of middle height only, apprenticed him to a bricklayer; but, at the age of eighteen, his extraordinary stature attracted the attention of a showman, by whom he was induced to sign an agreement to exhibit himself in England for three years, receiving a yearly salary of fifty pounds. Soon after reaching England, however, on his refusing his assent to a proposed cession of his person to another showman, his exhibitor caused him to be arrested at Bristol for a fictitious debt, and lodged in the city goal.

Obtaining his release, and the annulment of the contract, by the interposition of a benevolent inhabitant of Bristol, he proceeded to London, and exhibited himself on his own account in Bartholomew Fair, realising thirty pounds by the experiment in three days. He exhibited in this fair four or five successive years, but, as he made money, he changed the scene of his "receptions," as they would now be called, to public halls in the metropolis, and the assembly-rooms of provincial hotels. He attained the height of eight feet seven inches, and was proportionately stout, but far from symmetrical; and so deficient in stamina that the effort to maintain an upright attitude while exhibiting himself was painful to him.

Theatrical booths again appeared at Bartholomew Fair in 1782, when Mrs. Baker, manageress of the Rochester Theatre, took her company to Smithfield. Tradition says that Elizabeth Inchbald was at this time a member of Mrs. Baker's company, but I have not been able to discover any ground for the belief. The diary of the actress would have set the matter at rest; but she destroyed it before her death, and Boaden's memoirs of her were based chiefly upon her letters. They show her to have performed that year at Canterbury, and it is within the limits of probability that she may have performed at

Rochester also; though it would still remain doubtful whether she accompanied Mrs. Baker to Bartholomew Fair. According to Boaden, she proceeded to Edinburgh on the termination of her Canterbury engagement.

Lewis Owen, who was engaged by Mrs. Baker as clown for her Bartholomew Fair performances, was a young man of reputable family and good education, who had embraced the career of a public entertainer from choice, as more congenial to his tastes and habits than any other. His eccentric manners and powers of grimace, joined with a considerable fund of natural wit, caused him to be speedily recognised as a worthy successor of Joel Tarvey, who, after amusing more than one generation, as the Merry Andrew of various shows and places of amusements, had died at Hoxton of extreme old age in 1777.

CHAPTER VIII.

Lady Holland's Mob—Kelham Whiteland, the Dwarf—Flockton, the Conjuror and Puppet-Showman—Wonderful Rams—Miss Morgan, the Dwarf—Flockton's Will—Gyngell, the Conjuror—Jobson, the Puppet-Showman—Abraham Saunders—Menageries of Miles and Polito—Miss Biffin—Philip Astley.

While the character of the theatrical entertainments presented at the London fairs declined from the middle of the eighteenth century, when Yates and Shuter ceased to appear in Smithfield "during the short time of Bartholomew Fair," the various other shows underwent a gradual improvement. Menageries became larger and better arranged, while with the progress of zoological science, they were rendered better media for its diffusion. Panoramas and mechanical exhibitions began to appear, and, though it is impossible to estimate the degree in which such agencies were instrumental in educating the people, it is but fair to allow them some share in the intellectual progress of the latter half of the century.

The good or evil arising from the amusements of any class of the people can only be fairly judged by comparing the amusements with those of other classes at the same period; and those who will study the dramas and novels, and especially the newspapers of the last century, will not find more to commend in the manners and pursuits of the upper and middle classes than in those of the lower orders of society, as exemplified in the London fairs. The hand that painted Gin Lane for the contemplation of posterity left an instructive picture of the morals and manners of the upper strata of society in the 'Rake's Progress' and the 'Midnight Conversation.'

The amusements of the people partake of the mutability of all mundane matters, and the newspapers of the period show that the London fairs had begun, at the beginning of the last quarter of the eighteenth century, to be regarded by the educated portion of society much less favourably than they had been in earlier times. When St. James's ceased to patronize them, Bloomsbury voted them low, and Cornhill declared them a nuisance. Journalists, having as yet no readers in the slums, and therefore writing exclusively for St. James's, or Bloomsbury, or Cornhill, as the case might be, adapted their tone to the views current in those sections of London society. If we first place a paragraph of the 'Times' of the present day recording a cock-fight or a pugilistic contest, by the side of a report of a similar encounter in a journal of thirty years ago, we shall have no difficulty in understanding why Bartholomew Fair was described by the 'Morning Chronicle' in 1784 in language so different to that used by Pepys and Evelyn a century before.

After recounting the misdoings of "Lady Holland's mob," the paragraphist tells his readers that:—

"The elegant part of the entertainment was confined to a few booths. At the Lock and Key, near Cloth Fair, a select company performed the musical opera of the *Poor Soldier*, with Columbine's escape from Smithfield. Mr. Flockton, whose name can never be struck off Bartholomew roll, had a variety of entertainments without and within. The King's conjuror, who takes more money from out the pocket than he puts in, made the lank-haired gentry scratch their pates; the walking French puppet-show had hired an apartment, with additional performers; Punch and the Devil, in his little moving theatre, were performing without doors, to invite the company into the grand theatre. Men with wooden mummies in show-boxes were found straggling about the fair; tall women in cellars, dropping upon their knees to be kissed by short customers; dwarfs mounted on stools for the same civil purposes; and men without arms writing with their feet."

The sneering tone, and the disposition to write down the fair, perceptible in this account, are more strongly exhibited in the 'Public Advertiser' of the 5th of September, in the following year:—

"Saturday being Bartholomew Fair day, it was, according to annual custom, ushered in by Lady Holland's Mob, accompanied with a charming band of music, consisting of marrow-bones and cleavers, tin kettles, &c., &c., much to the gratification of the inhabitants about Smithfield; great preparations were then made for the reception of the Lord Mayor, the Sheriffs, and other City officers, who, after regaling themselves with a cool tankard at Mr. Akerman's, made their appearance in the fair about one o'clock, to authorise *mimic* fools to make *real* ones of the gaping spectators. The proclamation being read, and the Lord Mayor retiring, he was saluted by a flourish of trumpets, drums, rattles, salt-boxes, and other delightful musical instruments. The noted Flockton, and the notorious Jobson, with many new managers, exhibited their tragic and comic performers, as did Penley his drolls. There were wild beasts from all parts of the world roaring, puppets squeaking, sausages frying, Kings and Queens raving, pickpockets diving, roundabouts twirling, hackney coaches and poor horses driving, and all Smithfield alive-o! The Learned Horse paid his obedience to the company, as did about a score of monkeys, several *beautiful young* ladies of forty, Punches, Pantaloons, Harlequins, Columbines, three giants, a dwarf, and a giantess. These were not all who came to Smithfield to gratify the public; there were several sleight-of-hand men and fire-eaters; the last, however, were not quite so numerous as those who eat of the deliciously flavoured sausages and oysters with which the fair abounded. The company were *remarkably genteel* and crowded, and the different performances went off with loud and unbounded bursts of applause; they will be repeated this day and to-morrow for the last times this season." Reports similar in tone to the foregoing continued to appear in the newspapers for many years.

That the fairs were visited at and from this time almost exclusively by the lower orders of society is tolerably obvious from the fact that, though the number and variety of the shows were greater, and advertising was more largely resorted to every year as a medium of publicity, the showmen had ceased to use the columns of the London press for this purpose. Bills were given away in the fair, or displayed on the outsides of the shows, but few of these have been preserved, though the few extant are the only memorials of the London fairs during several years.

The only bill of 1787 which I have succeeded in finding announces a dwarf with the remarkable name of Kelham Whiteland; he is said to have been born at Ipswich, but his height, strange to say, is not stated, a blank being left before the word *inches*. Probably he was growing, and his exhibitor deemed it advisable, as a matter of financial economy, to have a large number of bills printed at one time.

Flockton, who was the leading showman of this period, was the sole advertiser of 1789, when he put forth the following announcement:—

"Mr. Flockton's Most Grand and Unparalleled Exhibition. Consisting, first, in the display of the Original and Universally admired Italian Fantoccini, exhibited in the same Skilful and Wonderful Manner, as well as Striking Imitations of Living Performers, as represented and exhibited before the Royal Family, and the most illustrious Characters in this Kingdom. Mr. Flockton will display his inimitable Dexterity of Hand, Different from all pretenders to the said Art. To which will be perform'd an ingenious and Spirited Opera called The Padlock. Principal vocal performers, Signor Giovanni Orsi and Signora Vidina. The whole to conclude with his grand and inimitable Musical Clock, at first view, a curious organ, exhibited three times before their Majesties."

In this clock nine hundred figures were said to be shown at work at various trades.

In the following year, two wonderful rams were exhibited in Bartholomew Fair. One of them had a single horn, growing from the centre of the forehead, like the unicorn of the heralds; the other had six legs. One of the principal shows of this year was advertised as "the Original Theatre (Late the celebrated Yates and Shuter, of facetious Memory), Up the Greyhound Inn Yard, the only real and commodious place for Theatrical Performances. The Performers selected from the most distinguished Theatres in England, Scotland, &c. The Representation consists of an entirely New Piece, called, The Spaniard Well Drub'd, or the British Tar Victorious." This clap-trap drama concluded with "a Grand Procession of the King, French Heroes, Guards, Municipal Troops, &c., to the Champ de Mars, to swear to the Revolution Laws, as established by the Magnificent National Assembly, on the 14th of July, 1790." There was "hornpipe dancing by the renowned Jack Bowling," and an "Olio of wit, whim, and fancy, in Song, Speech, and Grimace."

Two years later, the London Fairs were visited by a couple of dwarfs, almost as famous in their day as Tom Thumb and his Lilliputian bride in our own. These were Thomas Allen, described in the bill of the show as "the most surprising small man ever before the public," and who had previously been exhibited at the Lyceum, where he was visited by the Duke of York and the Duke of Clarence; and, again to quote the bill, which seems to have been based on the announcements of the Corsican Fairy, some of the passages being identical,—

"Miss Morgan, the Celebrated Windsor Fairy, known in *London* and *Windsor* by the Addition of LADY MORGAN, a Title which His Majesty was pleased to confer on her.

"This unparallelled Woman is in the 35th year of her age, and only 18 pounds weight. Her form affords a pleasing surprise, and her admirable symmetry engages attention. She was introduced to their Majesties at the *Queen's Lodge, Windsor*, on Saturday the 4th of August, 1781, by the recommendation of the late Dr. *Hunter*; when they were pleased to pronounce her the finest Display of Human Nature in *miniature* they ever saw.—But we shall say no more of these great Wonders of Nature: let those who honour them with their visits, judge for themselves.

"Let others boast of stature, or of birth,
This glorious Truth shall fill our souls with mirth.
'That we now are, and hope, for years, to sing,
The Smallest subject of the Greatest King!'

"☞ Admittance to Ladies and Gentlemen, 1*s*. Children, Half Price.

"⁂ In this and many other parts of the Kingdom, it is too common to show deformed persons, with various arts and deceptions, under denominations of persons in miniature, to impose on the public.

"This little couple are, beyond contradiction, the most wonderful display of nature ever held out to the admiration of mankind.

"N.B. The above Lady's mother is with her, and will attend at any Lady or Gentleman's house, if required."

Flockton died in 1794, at Peckham, where he had lived for several years in comfort and respectability, having realised what was then regarded as a considerable fortune. He had attended the London Fairs, and many of the chief provincial ones, for many years, retiring to his cottage at Peckham in the winter. His representation of Punch was not only superior in every way to that of the open air puppet shows, but famous for the introduction of a struggle between the mimic representative of the Prince of Darkness and a fine Newfoundland dog, in which the canine combatant seized the enemy by the nose, and finally carried him off the stage.

Flockton had no children, and probably no other relatives, for he bequeathed his show, with all the properties pertaining to it, to Gyngell, a clever performer of tricks of sleight of hand, and a widow named Flint, both of whom had travelled with it for several years; and between these two persons and other members of his company he divided the whole of his accumulated gains, amounting to five thousand pounds. His successors were announced next Bartholomew Fair as "the Widow Flint and Gyngell, at Flockton's original Theatre, up the Greyhound Yard." Gyngell exhibited his conjuring tricks, and performed on the musical glasses; and his wife sang between this part of the entertainment and the exhibition of the *fantoccini* and Flockton's celebrated clock, which seems either to have been over-puffed by its original exhibitor, or to have fallen out of repair, for it was now said to contain five hundred figures, instead of the nine hundred originally claimed for it. Perhaps, however, the larger number was a misprint.

Widow Flint seems to have died soon after Flockton, or to have disposed of her share in the show to Gyngell; for the bill of 1795 is the only one I have found with her name as co-proprietor. Gyngell attended the London fairs, and the principal fairs for many miles round the metropolis, for thirty years after Flockton's death, and is spoken of by persons old enough to remember him as a quiet, gentlemanly man.

Jobson, the puppet-showman, who had been in the field as long as Flockton, was prosecuted in 1797, with several other owners of similar shows, for making his puppets speak, which was held to be an infraction of the laws relating to theatrical licences. This circumstance proves Strutt to have been in error in describing Flockton as the last of the "motion-masters," the latter having been dead three years when his contemporaries were prosecuted. I have not found Jobson's name among the showmen at the London fairs in later years, however; and Gyngell's puppets appear to have dropped out of existence with the musical clock, during the early years of his career as a showman.

The suppression of Bartholomew Fair was strongly urged upon the Court of Common Council in 1798, and the expediency of the measure was referred by the Court to the City Lands Committee, but nothing came of the discussion at that time. It was proposed to limit the duration of the fair to one day, but this suggestion was rejected by the Court of Common Council on the ground that the limitation would cause the fair to be crowded to an extent that would be dangerous to life and limb. It is doubtful, however, whether the showmen would have found the profits of one day sufficient to induce them, had the experiment been tried, to incur the expense of putting up their booths.

The fair went on as before, therefore, and Rowlandson's print sets before us the scene which it presented in 1799 as thoroughly and as vividly as Setchel's engraving has done the Bartholomew Fair of the first quarter of the century. Gyngell's "grand medley" (a name adopted from Jobson) was there; and the menageries of Miles and Polito, the Italian successor of Pidcock, and very famous in his day; and Abraham Saunders, whom we meet with for the first time, with the theatre which he appears to have sometimes substituted for the circus, perhaps when an execution had deprived him of his horses, or a bad season had obliged him to sell them; and Miss Biffin, who, having been born without arms, painted portraits with a brush affixed to her right shoulder, and exhibited herself and her productions at fairs as the best mode of obtaining patronage.

Down to the end of the last century there are no records of a circus having appeared at the London fairs. Astley is said to have taken his stud and company to Bartholomew Fair at one time, but I have not succeeded in finding any bill or advertisement of the great equestrian in connection with fairs. The amphitheatre which has always borne his name (except during the lesseeship of Mr. Boucicault, who chose to call it the Westminster Theatre, a title about as appropriate as the Marylebone would be in Shoreditch), was opened in 1780, and he had previously given open air performances on the same site, only the seats being roofed over. The enterprising character of Astley renders it not improbable that he may have tried his fortune at the fairs when the circus was closed, as it has usually been during the summer; and he may not have commenced his season at the amphitheatre until after Bartholomew Fair, or have given there a performance which he was accustomed to give in the afternoon at a large room in Piccadilly, where the tricks of a performing horse were varied with conjuring and *Ombres Chinoises*, a kind of shadow pantomime.

But though Astley's was the first circus erected in England, equestrian performances in the open air had been given before his time by Price and Sampson. The site of Dobney's Place, at the back of Penton Street, Islington, was, in the middle of the last century, a tea-garden and bowling-green, to which Johnson, who leased the premises in 1767, added the attraction of tumbling and rope-dancing performances, which had become so popular at Sadler's Wells. Price commenced his equestrian performances at this place in 1770, and soon had a rival in Sampson, who performed similar feats in a field behind the Old Hats public-house. It was not until ten years later, according to the historians of Lambeth, that Philip Astley exhibited his feats of horsemanship in a field near the Halfpenny Hatch, forming his first ring with a rope and stakes, after the manner of the mountebanks of a later day, and going round with his hat after each performance to collect the largesses of the spectators, a part of the business which, in the slang of strolling acrobats and other entertainers of the public in bye-streets and market-places, and on village greens, is called "doing a nob."

This remarkable man was born in 1742, at Newcastle-under-Lyme, where his father carried on the business of a cabinet maker. He received little or no education—no uncommon thing at that time,—and, having worked a few years with his father, enlisted in a cavalry regiment. His imposing appearance, being over six feet in height, with the proportions of a Hercules, and the voice of a Stentor, attracted attention to him; and his capture of a standard at the battle of Emsdorff, made him one of the celebrities of his regiment. While serving in the army, he learned many feats of horsemanship from an itinerant equestrian named Johnson, and often exhibited them for the amusement of his comrades. On his discharge from the army, being presented by General Elliot with a horse, he bought another in Smithfield, and with these two animals gave the open air performances in Lambeth, which have been mentioned.

CHAPTER IX

Edmund Kean—Mystery of his Parentage—Saunders's Circus—Scowton's Theatre—Belzoni—The Nondescript—Richardson's Theatre—The Carey Family—Kean, a Circus Performer—Oxberry, the Comedian—James Wallack—Last Appearance of the Irish Giant—Miss Biffin and the Earl of Morton—Bartholomew Fair Incidents—Josephine Girardelli, the Female Salamander—James England, the Flying Pieman—Elliston as a Showman—Simon Paap, the Dutch Dwarf—Ballard's Menagerie—A Learned Pig—Madame Gobert, the Athlete—Cartlich, the Original Mazeppa—Barnes, the Pantaloon—Nelson Lee—Cooke's Circus—The Gyngell Family

With the present century commenced a period of the history of shows and showmen specially interesting to the generation which remembers the London fairs as they were forty or fifty years ago, and to which the names of Gyngell, Scowton, Samwell, Richardson, Clarke, Atkins, and Wombwell have a familiar sound. It introduces us, in its earliest years, to the celebrated Edmund Kean, "the stripling known in a certain wayfaring troop of *Atellanæ* by the name of Carey," as Raymond wrote, and whom we find performing at the London fairs, sometimes tumbling in Saunders's circus, and sometimes playing juvenile characters in the travelling theatres of Scowton and Richardson. The early life of this remarkable man is as strange as any that has ever afforded materials for the biographer, and the mystery surrounding his parentage as inscrutable a problem as the authorship of the letters of Junius.

Phippen, the earliest biographer of Kean, says that he was born in 1788, and was the illegitimate offspring of *Aaron* Kean, a tailor, and Anne Carey, an actress. Proctor, whose account is repeated by Hawkins, states that his parentage was unknown, but that, according to the best conclusion he was able to form, he was the son of *Edmund* Kean, a mechanic employed by a London builder, and Anne Carey, an actress. Raymond says, on the authority of Miss Tidswell, who was many years at Drury Lane Theatre, that he was the son of *Edward* Kean, a carpenter, and Nancy Carey, the actress. While these various writers agree as to the name and profession of the future great tragedian's mother, and the patronymic of his father, they give us the choice of three baptismal names for the latter, and at least two occupations. There seems no doubt, however, that his father, whether he was a carpenter or a tailor, was the brother of Moses Kean, a popular reciter and imitator of the leading actors at the beginning of the present century.

No register of his birth or baptism has ever been discovered, and it is even a matter of doubt whether he was born in Westminster or in Southwark. Miss Tidswell seems to have been the only person who possessed any knowledge of his birth and parentage that was ever revealed, a circumstance which caused her to be suspected of herself standing in the maternal relationship to him. Kean, when a child, called her sometimes mother, and sometimes aunt; but, according to her own account, she was in no way related to him, but had adopted him on his being deserted by his real mother, Anne Carey.

His first appearance in public was made in the character of a monkey, in the show of Abraham Saunders, at Bartholomew Fair, probably in 1801. He was then twelve or thirteen years of age, and already inured to a wandering and vagabond mode of life; being in the habit of absenting himself for days together from the lodging of Miss Tidswell, in order to visit the fairs, and sleeping under the trees in St. James's Park, to avoid being locked up by his guardian, and thus prevented from gazing at the parades of Saunders and Scowton on the morrow.

Proctor says, somewhat vaguely, though probably with as much exactness as the materials for a memoir of Kean's boyhood render possible, that when about fourteen years of age, he was sometimes in Richardson's company, and sometimes in Scowton's or Saunders's; and that, besides tumbling in the circus of the latter, he rode and danced on the tight-rope. In performing an equestrian act at Bartholomew Fair, he once fell from the pad, and hurt his legs, which never quite recovered from the effects of the accident.

In 1803, another notability of the age made his appearance at Bartholomew Fair, namely, Belzoni, afterwards famous as an explorer of the pyramids and royal tombs of Egypt. He was a remarkably handsome and finely proportioned man, and of almost gigantic stature, his height being six feet six inches. His muscular strength being proportionate to his size, he was engaged by Gyngell to exhibit feats of strength, as the young Hercules, *alias* the Patagonian Samson, in which character he lifted four men of average weight off the ground, and held out prodigious weights at arm's length. He afterwards went to Edmonton Fair, where he performed in a field behind the Bell Inn. Of his engagements during the following six or seven years we have no account, but in 1810 he sustained the character of Orson at the Edinburgh theatre, when he was hissed for not being sufficiently demonstrative in his attentions to the maternal bear. Five years later, he was exploring the pyramids and sarcophagi of Egypt, as assistant to the British Consul at Alexandria, and in 1820 his name was famous.

In the same year that Belzoni performed his feats of strength in Gyngell's show, there was exhibited in Bartholomew Fair, together with a two-headed calf, and a double-bodied calf, "a surprising large fish, the Nondescript," which "surprising inhabitant of the watery kingdom was," according to the bill, "drawn on the shore by seven horses and about a hundred men. She measured twenty-five feet in length and about eighteen in circumference, and had in her belly when found, one thousand seven hundred mackerel."

The first mention of Richardson's theatre in the annals of the London Fairs occurs in 1804. Of his early career there is no record; probably it did not differ much from that of his pupil, Kean, or his successor, Nelson Lee, or of the famous "roving English clown," Charlie Keith, and numerous others whose lives have been passed in wandering from place to place, amusing the public as actors, jugglers, conjurors, acrobats, etc. Whatever his antecedents may have been, there is no doubt as to his character, all who knew him concurring in representing him as illiterate and ignorant, but possessing a large fund of shrewdness and common sense; irritable in temper, but agreeable in his manners so long as nothing occurred to excite his irascibility; sensitive to any unprovoked insult, which he never failed to revenge, but always ready and willing to lend a helping hand to those who had been less fortunate than himself.

Many stories are current among showmen and the theatrical profession of Richardson's goodness of heart and his occasional eccentricities of conduct. On one occasion, while his portable theatre was at St. Albans, a fire occurred in the town, and many small houses were destroyed, the poor tenants of which by that means lost all their furniture, and almost everything they possessed. A subscription was immediately opened for their relief, and a public meeting was held to promote the benevolent purpose. Richardson attended, and when the Mayor, who presided, had read a list of donations, varying in amount from five shillings to twice as many pounds, he advanced to the table, and presented a Bank of England note for a hundred pounds.

"To whom is the fund indebted for this munificent donation?" inquired the astonished Mayor.

"Put it down to Muster Richardson, the showman," replied the donor, who then walked quietly from the room.

He often paid the ground-rent of the poorer proprietors of travelling shows, booths, and stalls, whose receipts, owing to bad weather, had not enabled them to pay the claims of the owner of the field, and who, but for Richardson's kindness, would have been obliged to remain on the ground, losing the chance of making money elsewhere, until they could raise the required sum. He never seemed to expect repayment in such cases, and never referred to them afterwards. Saunders, who seems to have passed through an unusually long life in a chronic condition of impecuniosity, once borrowed ten pounds of him, and honourably and punctually repaid the money at the appointed time. Richardson seemed surprised, but he took the money, and made no remark. No very long time elapsed before Saunders wanted another loan, when, to his surprise, Richardson met his application with a decided refusal.

"I paid you honourably the money you lent me before," observed Saunders with an aggrieved air.

"That's it, Muster Saunders," rejoined Richardson. "You did pay me that money, and I was never more surprised in my life; and I mean to take care you don't surprise me again, either in that way, *or any other way*."

In recruiting his company, he preferred actors who had learned a trade, such being, in his opinion, steadier and more to be depended upon than those who, like Kean, had been strollers from childhood. His pay-table was the head of the big drum, and his way of discharging an actor or musician with whom he was dissatisfied was to ask him, when giving him his week's salary, to leave his name and address with the stage-manager, who was also wardrobe-keeper and scene-shifter. This post was held for many years by a man named Lewis, who was also the general servant of Richardson's "living carriage," and at his winter quarters, Woodland Cottage, Horsemonger Lane, long since pulled down, the site being occupied by a respectable row of houses, called Woodland Terrace.

He always strengthened his company, and produced his best dresses, for the London fairs, where his theatre, decked with banners and a good display of steel and brass armour, presented a striking appearance. His wardrobe and scene-waggon were always well stocked, and the dresses were not, as some persons imagined, the off castings of the theatres, but were made for him, and, having to be worn by daylight, were of really excellent quality. Cloaks were provided for the company to wear on parade when the weather happened to be wet.

It was a frequent boast of Richardson, that many of the most eminent members of the theatrical profession had graduated in his company, and it is known that Edmund Kean, James Wallack, Oxberry, and Saville Faucit were of the number. Kean always acknowledged that he made his first appearance in a principal part as Young Norval in Richardson's theatre; but it is obvious from what is known of his boyhood that he must have been in the company several years before he could have essayed that character. So far as can be made out from his supposed age, he seems to have joined Richardson's company in 1804, to the early part of which year we must assign the story told by Davis, who was afterwards associated in partnership with the younger Astley in the lesseeship of the Amphitheatre.

"I was passing down Great Surrey Street one morning," Davis is reported to have said, "when just as I came to the place where the Riding House now stands, at the corner of the Magdalen as they call it, I saw Master Saunders packing up his traps. His booth, you see, had been standing there for some three or four days, or thereabouts; and on the parade-waggon I saw a slim young chap with marks of paint—and bad paint it was, for all the world like raddle on the back of a sheep—on his face, tying up some of the canvas. And when I had shook hands with Master Saunders, he turns him right round to this young chap, who had just threw a somerset behind his back, and says, 'I say, you Mr. King Dick, if you don't mind what you're arter, and pack up that wan pretty tight and nimble, we shan't be off afore to-morrow; and so, you mind your eye, my lad.' That Mr. King Dick, as Master Saunders called him, was young Carey, that's now your great Mr. Kean."

Kean's engagement with Richardson brings us to a portion of his personal history which is involved in the profoundest mystery. His biographers state that his mother, Anne Carey, was at the time a member of Richardson's company, that Kean was unaware of the fact when he engaged, and that he left the *troupe* not very long afterwards, in consequence of his mother claiming and receiving his salary, the last circumstance being said to rest on the authority of Kean himself. Not much credence is due to the story on that account; for the great actor exercised his imagination on the subject of his origin and antecedents as freely as the Josiah Bounderby of the inimitable Dickens. But the results of a patient search among the gatherings relating to Bartholomew Fair in the library of the British Museum clearly prove that Kean's mother was, when a member of Richardson's company, the wife of an actor named Carey.

The only Careys whose names are to be found in any of the bills of Richardson's theatre which have been preserved were a married couple, who for many years, including the whole period of Kean's engagement, sustained the principal parts in those wonderful melodramas for which the establishment was so famous. If these people were Kean's parents, what becomes of the story which has been told by his biographers, on the authority of Miss Tidswell? That they assumed to be his parents is undoubted, and it is equally beyond doubt that the relationship was unquestioned by Richardson, and the claims founded upon it acquiesced in by Kean.

"Windsor Fair," said Richardson, in relating the story of Kean's professional visit to Windsor Castle, "commenced on a Friday, and after all our impediments we arrived safe, and lost no time in erecting our booth. We opened with *Tom Thumb* and the *Magic Oak*. To my great astonishment, I received a note from the Castle, commanding Master Carey to recite several passages from different plays before his Majesty King George the Third at the Palace. I was highly gratified at the receipt of the above note; but I was equally perplexed to comply with the commands of the King. The letter came to me on Saturday night; and as Master Carey's wardrobe was very scanty, it was necessary to add to it before he could appear in the presence of royalty. My purse was nearly empty, and to increase my dilemma, all shops belonging to Jews were shut, and the only chance we had left was their being open on Sunday morning.

"Among the Jews, however, we at last purchased a smart little jacket, trousers, and body linen; we tied the collar of his shirt through the button-holes with a piece of black ribbon; and when dressed in his new apparel, Master Carey appeared a smart little fellow, and fit to exhibit his talents before any monarch in the world. The King was highly delighted with him, and so were all the nobility who were present. Two hours were occupied in recitations; and his abilities were so conspicuous to every person present that he was pronounced an astonishing boy, and a lad of great promise. The present he received for his performance was rather small, being only two guineas, though, upon the whole, it turned out fortunate for the family. The principal conversation in Windsor for a few days was about the talents displayed by Master Carey before the King. His mother, therefore, took advantage of the circumstance, and engaged the market-hall for three nights for Edmund's recitations. This was an excellent speculation, and the hall overflowed with company every night.

"Mrs. Carey joined me on the following Monday at Ewell Fair; and all the family, owing to their great success, came so nicely dressed that I scarcely knew them. Mrs. Carey and her children did not quit my standard during the summer. After a short period, I again got my company together, and with hired horses went to Waltham Abbey. I took a small theatre in that town, the rent of which was fifteen shillings per week. It was all the money too much. My company I considered very strong, consisting of Mr. Vaughan, Mr.

Thwaites, Master Edmund, his mother, and the whole of his family, Mr. Saville Faucit, Mr. Grosette, Mr. and Mrs. Jefferies, Mr. Reed, Mrs. Wells, and several other performers, who are now engaged at the different theatres in the kingdom. Notwithstanding we acted the most popular pieces, the best night produced only nine shillings and sixpence. Starvation stared us in the face, and our situation was so truly pitiable that the magistrate of the town, out of compassion for our misfortunes, bespoke a night."

It is singular that Richardson does not mention Carey, his chief actor, in this communication; but the words "the whole of his family" must be supposed to include Carey and, I believe, a daughter. In every bill of the period the names of Mr. H. Carey and Mrs. H. Carey appear as the representatives of the heroes and heroines of the Richardsonian drama; and the absence of any direct mention of the former is much less remarkable than the fact that he has been altogether ignored by every biographer of Kean, while the supposed mother of the tragedian is invariably styled *Miss* Carey.

It is exceedingly improbable that the mystery involved in these discrepancies and contradictions will now ever be cleared up in a satisfactory manner. One thing alone, amidst all the confusion and obscurity, seems certain; namely, that the Careys were in Richardson's company before Kean joined it, and that, whether or not he believed them to be his parents, he dropped their acquaintance when he threw off their authority. Raymond says that when Kean, after his marriage, visited Bartholomew Fair, he was recognised by Carey, who was standing on the parade of Richardson's theatre, and ran down the steps to greet him; the tragedian seemed mortified, treated the strolling actor coldly, and "slunk away, literally like a dog in a fair."

In pondering the probabilities of the case, it is obvious that considerable allowance must be made for the obscurity which envelopes the origin of Kean's existence. Their only authority being Miss Tidswell, it is natural that the biographers should suppose the woman who passed for Kean's mother with Richardson and his company to be the Nancy Carey of her story, and mention her as Miss Carey. But the evidence of the bills, which cannot have been known to them, forces upon us the re-consideration of the story of Kean's parentage which has hitherto passed current. Miss Tidswell's story can be reconciled with the facts only by the hypothesis that Anne Carey, subsequently to Kean's birth, became the wife of H. Carey, the sameness of name being due to cousinship, or perhaps merely a coincidence. Kean's illegitimacy may have been known to Richardson, whose knowledge of the circumstance would explain the reason of his speaking of Mrs. Carey as the mother of Master Carey, while he says nothing to warrant the supposition that he regarded her husband as the lad's father.

But everything about Kean's early life is mysterious and obscure. How and when did he acquire the classical lore which he seems to have possessed? Certainly not while he was roaming the streets of London, frequenting all the fairs, and practising flip-flaps; nor while travelling with Saunders, Scowton, and Richardson, and rejoicing in the cognomen of Mr. King Dick. As little likely does it seem that he could have acquired it at that subsequent period of his life when the leisure which his profession left him was passed in disreputable taverns, in low orgies with the worst companions.

"You see this inequality in the bridge of my nose?" he once observed to Benson Hill, the author of a couple of amusing volumes of theatrical anecdotes and adventures. "It was dealt me by a demmed pewter pot, hurled from the hand of Jack Thurtell. We were borne, drunk and bleeding, to the watch-house, for the night. When I was taken out, washed, plastered, left to cogitate on any lie, of an accident in a stage fight, I told it, and was believed, for the next day I dined with the Bishop of Norwich."

My task does not, however, require me to follow Kean's fortunes from the time when he left Richardson's company, and obtained an engagement at a provincial theatre. The date is uncertain, but his name does not appear in the bills of 1807, and he had probably turned his back on the travelling theatre in the preceding year.

Patrick O'Brien, the Irish giant, exhibited himself for the last time in 1804, when he advertised as follows:—

"Just arrived in town, and to be seen in a commodious room, at No. 11, Haymarket, nearly opposite the Opera House, the celebrated Irish Giant, Mr. O'Brien, of the Kingdom of Ireland, indisputably the tallest man ever shown; is a lineal descendant of the old puissant king, Brien Boreau, and has, in person and appearance, all the similitudes of that great and grand potentate. It is remarkable of this family, that, however various the revolutions in point of fortune and alliance, the lineal descendants thereof have been favoured by Providence with the original size and stature, which have been so peculiar to their family. The gentleman alluded to measures nearly nine feet high. Admittance one shilling."

O'Brien had now realised a considerable fortune, and he resolved to retire from the public gaze. Having purchased an old mansion near Epping, and on the borders of the forest, he took up his abode there, keeping a carriage and pair of horses, and living quietly and unostentatiously the brief remainder of his life. He died in 1806, in his forty-seventh year, when his servants made use of his fame and his wardrobe for their own emolument, dressing a wax figure in his clothes, and exhibiting it at rooms in the Haymarket, the Strand, and other parts of the metropolis.

The rival theatres of Richardson and Scowton attended Bartholomew Fair in 1807, when the former produced a romantic and highly sensational drama, called *The Monk and the Murderer*, in which Carey played the principal character, Baron Montaldi, and his wife that of Emilina, the Baron's daughter. The following announcement appears in the head of the bill:—

"Mr. Richardson has the honour to inform the Public, that for the extraordinary Patronage he has experienced, it has been his great object to contribute to the convenience and gratification of his audience. Mr. R. has a splendid collection of Scenery, unrivalled in any Theatre; and, as they are painted and designed by the first Artists in England, he hopes with such Decorations, and a Change of Performances each day, the Public will continue him that Patronage it has been his greatest pride to deserve."

The scenery of the drama comprised a Gothic hall in the Baron's castle, a rocky pass in Calabria, a forest, a rustic bridge, with a distant view of the castle, a Gothic chamber, and a baronial hall, decorated with banners and trophies. In the fourth scene a chivalric procession was introduced, and in the last a combat with battle-axes. The drama was followed, as usual, by a pantomime entitled *Mirth and Magic*, which concluded with a "grand panoramic view of Gibraltar, painted by the first artists."

Saunders was there, with a circus, and seems to have attended the fair with considerable regularity. He was often in difficulties, however, and on one occasion, after borrowing a trick horse of Astley, his stud was taken in execution for debt, and the borrowed horse was sold with the rest. Some time afterwards, two equestrians of Astley's company were passing a public-house, when they recognised Billy, harnessed to a cart which was standing before the door. Hearing their voices, the horse erected his ears, and, at a signal from one of them, stood up on his hind legs, and performed such extraordinary evolutions that a crowd collected to witness them. On the driver of the cart coming from the public-house, an explanation of Billy's appearance in cart-harness was obtained with the observation that "he was a werry good 'orse, but so full o' tricks that we calls 'im the mountebank." Billy, I scarcely need say, was returned to his stall in Astley's stables very soon after this discovery.

Miss Biffin was still attending the fairs, painting portraits with her right shoulder, and in 1808 attracted the attention of the Earl of Morton, who sat to her for his likeness, and visited her "living carriage" several times for that purpose. In order to test her ability, he took the portrait away with him, after each sitting, and thus became satisfied that it was entirely the work of her own hand, or rather shoulder. Finding that the armless little lady really possessed artistic talent, he showed the portrait to George III., who was pleased to direct that she should receive instruction in drawing at his expense.

The Earl of Morton corresponded with this remarkable artist during a period of twenty years. She was patronised by three successive sovereigns, and from William IV. she received a small pension. She then yielded to the wish of the Earl of Morton that she should cease to travel, and settled at Birmingham, where, several years afterwards, she married, and resumed, as Mrs. Wright, the pursuit of her profession.

Ballard's menagerie held a respectable position between the time of Polito and Miles and that of Wombwell and Atkins. The newspapers of the period do not inform us, however, from whose menagerie it was that the leopard escaped which created so much consternation one summer night in 1810. The caravans were on their way to Bartholomew Fair, when, between ten and eleven o'clock at night, while passing along Piccadilly, the horses attached to one of them were scared by some noise, or other cause of alarm, and became restive. The caravan was overturned and broken, and a leopard and two monkeys made their escape. The leopard ran into the basement of an unfinished house near St. James's Church, and one of the monkeys into an oyster-shop, the proprietor of which, hearing that a leopard was loose, immediately closed the door. What became of the other monkey is not stated.

The keepers ran about, calling for a blanket and cords, to secure the leopard; but every person they accosted shut their doors, or took to their heels, on learning the purpose for which such appliances were required. After some delay, a cage was backed against the opening by which the leopard had entered the building, below which it growled threateningly as it crouched in the darkness. With some risk and difficulty, it was got into the cage, but not until it had bitten the arm of one of the keepers so severely that he was obliged to proceed to St. George's hospital for surgical aid.

Malcolm, describing Bartholomew Fair as it was seventy years ago, says,—"Those who wish to form an idea of this scene of depravity may go at eleven o'clock in the evening. They may then form some conception of the dreadful scenes that have been acted there in former days. The visitor will find all uproar. Shouts, drums, trumpets, organs, the roaring of beasts, assailing the ear; while the blaze of torches and glare of candles confuse sight, and present as well the horror of executions, and the burning of martyrs, and the humours of a fair." Though, "the blaze of torches and glare of candles" cannot be said to constitute a "scene of depravity," and "shouts, drums, trumpets, organs, the roaring of beasts," though tending to produce an "uproar," cannot be accepted as evidence of vice, since the former sounds accompany the civic procession of the 9th of November, and the latter are heard in the Zoological Gardens, the newspapers of the period bear testimony to the existence of a considerable amount of riot and disorder at the late hour mentioned by Malcolm.

In those days, when the lighting was defective and the police inefficient, it is not surprising that the "roughs" had their way when the more respectable portion of the frequenters of the fair had retired, and that scenes occurred such as the more efficient police of the present day have had some difficulty in suppressing on Sunday evenings in the principal thoroughfares of Islington and Pentonville. The newspapers of the period referred to by Malcolm afford no other support to his statement than accounts of the disorder and mischief produced by the rushing through the fair at night of hordes of young men and boys, apparently without anything being attempted for the prevention of the evil. In 1810, two bands of these ruffians met, and their collision caused two stalls to be knocked down, when the upsetting of a lamp on a stove caused the canvas to ignite, and a terrible disaster was only prevented by the exertions of a gentleman who was on the spot in extinguishing the flames. In 1812 many persons were thrown down in one of the wild rushes of the "roughs," and an infant was dashed from its mother's arms, and trampled to death.

Richardson, who was always on the alert for novelties, introduced in 1814, at Portsmouth, the famous Josephine Girardelli, who in the same year exhibited her remarkable feats in a room in New Bond Street. The following hand-bill sufficiently indicates their nature:—

"Wonders will never cease!—The great Phenomena of Nature. Signora Josephine Girardelli (just arrived from the Continent), who has had the honour of appearing before most of the Crowned Heads of Europe, will exhibit the Powers of Resistance against Heat, every day, until further notice, at Mr. Laxton's Rooms, 23, New Bond Street. She will, without the least symptoms of pain, put boiling melted lead into her mouth, and emit the same with the imprint of her teeth thereon; red-hot irons will be passed over various parts of her body; she will walk over a bar of red-hot iron with her naked feet; will wash her hands in aquafortis; put boiling oil in her mouth! The above are but a few of the wonderful feats she is able to go through. Her performances will commence at 12, 2, 4, and 6 o'clock. Admission 3s. Any lady or gentleman being dubious of the above performances taking place, may witness the same, gratis, if not satisfied. Parties may be accommodated by a private performance, by applying to the Conductor."

The portrait of this Fire Queen, as she would be styled at the present day, was engraved by Page, and published by Smeeton, St. Martin's Lane. It represents her in her performing costume, a short spangled jacket, worn over a dress of the fashion of that day; the features are regular and striking, but their beauty is of a rather masculine type. The hair appears dark, and is arranged in short curls.

Elliston engaged in a show speculation at this time, having contracted with a Dutchman, named Sampœman, for the exhibition of a dwarf, named Simon Paap. He hired a room in Piccadilly for the purpose and engaged an interpreter; but the speculation was a failure, and Elliston was glad to obtain Sampœman's consent to the cancelling of the contract. He made a more successful venture when, at the close of a bad theatrical season at Birmingham, he announced the advent of a Bohemian giant, who would toss about, like a ball, a stone weighing nearly a ton. Few modern giants have possessed the strength ascribed to the seven-feet men of old, and such an athlete as the Bohemian would have been worth a visit. The theatre was filled, therefore, for the first time that season; but when the overture had been performed, and the occupants of the gallery were beginning to testify impatience, Elliston appeared before the curtain, looking grave and anxious, as on such occasions he could look to perfection. Evincing the deepest emotion, he informed the expectant audience that the perfidious Bohemian had disappointed him, and had not arrived.

"Here," said he, producing a number of letters from his pockets, "are letters which must satisfy every one that I am not to blame for this disappointment, which I assure you, ladies and gentlemen, is to me one of the bitterest of my existence. As they are numerous and lengthy, and are all written in German, you will, I am sure, excuse me from reading them; but, as further evidence of the good faith in which I have acted in this matter, you shall see the stone."

The curtain was drawn half-way up, and the disappointed Brums were consoled with the sight of an enormous mass of stone, and with the announcement that they would receive, on leaving the theatre, vouchers entitling them to admission to the boxes on the following night, on payment of a shilling. Elliston thus obtained two good houses at no other extra expense than a few shillings for the cartage of the pretended giant's stone ball, the Bohemian being merely a creation of his own fertile imagination.

Sampœman's arrangement with Elliston having proved a failure, the little Dutchman was transferred to Gyngell, who exhibited him in his show in Bartholomew Fair and elsewhere, in 1815. There are three portraits of Simon Paap in existence, showing a striking resemblance to little Mr. Stratton, commonly known as Tom Thumb. One of them, drawn by Woolley, and engraved by Worship, probably for advertising purposes, bears the following inscription:—

Mr. Simon Paap.

"*The celebrated Dutch dwarf, 26 years of age, weighs 27 pounds, and only 28 inches high; had the honour of being presented to the Prince Regent and the whole of the Royal Family at Carleton House, May 5th, 1815, and was introduced by Mr. Dan. Gyngell to the Right Honourable the Lord Mayor, Sept. 1st, 1815; and was exhibited in the course of 4 days in Smithfield to upwards of 20,000 persons; is universally admitted to be the greatest wonder of the age.*"

Another portrait, engraved by Cooper, and published by Robins and Co., is better executed; but the third is a poor sketch, taken three years later, and unsigned.

Richardson presented this year, on the first day of Bartholomew Fair, *The Maid and the Magpie*, and a pantomime, "expressly written for this theatre," entitled *Harlequin in the Deep*, terminating with a panorama, "taken from the spot, by one of our most eminent artists," representing Longwood, in the island of St. Helena, and the adjacent scenery, interesting to the public at that time as the place of exile selected by the Powers lately in arms against France for Napoleon I. Pocock's drama was, of course, greatly abridged, for drama and pantomime, with a comic song between, were got through in half an hour, and often in twenty minutes, when the influx of visitors rendered it expedient to abbreviate the performance. Shuter's signal, corrupted into *John Orderly*, was used by Richardson on such occasions.

A daily change of performances had at this time become necessary, and Richardson presented on the second day "an entire new Chinese romantic melodrama," called *The Children of the Desert*, and a comic pantomime, entitled *Harlequin and the Devil*. On the third day the pantomime was the same, preceded by "an entire new melodrama," called *The Roman Wife*.

This year there first appeared in the fair an eccentric character named James Sharp England, known as "the flying pieman." He was always neatly dressed, with a clean white apron before him, but wore no hat, and had his hair powdered and tied behind in a queue. Like the famous Tiddy-dol of a century earlier, he aimed at a profitable notoriety through a fantastic exterior and a droll manner; and he succeeded, his sales of plum-pudding, which he carried before him on a board, and vended in slices, being very great wherever he appeared. The present representative of the perambulating traders of the eccentric order is a man who has for many years strolled about the western districts of the metropolis, wearing clean white sleeves and a black velvet cap placed jauntily on his head, and carrying before him a tray of what, in oily and mellifluous accents, he proclaims to be, "Brandy balls as big as St. Paul's! Oh, *so* nice! They are all sugar and brandy!"

The following year is memorable among showmen, and especially among menagerists, for the attack of Ballard's lioness on the Exeter mail-coach. On the night of the 20th of October, the caravans containing the animals were standing in a line along the side of the road, near the inn called the Winterslow Hut, seven miles from Salisbury, to the fair of which city the menagerie was on its way. The coach had just stopped at this inn for the guard to deliver his bag of local letters, when one of the leaders was attacked by some large animal. The alarm and confusion produced by this incident were so great that two of the inside passengers left the coach, ran into the house, and locked themselves in a room above stairs; while the horses kicked and plunged so violently that the coachman feared that the coach would be overturned. It was soon perceived by the coachman and guard, by the light of the lamps, that the assailant was a large lioness. A mastiff attacked the beast, which immediately left the horse, and turned upon him; the dog then fled, but was pursued and killed by the lioness about forty yards from the coach.

An alarm being given, Ballard and his keepers pursued the lioness to a granary in a farm-yard, where she ran underneath the building, and was there barricaded in to prevent her escape. She growled for some time so loudly as to be heard half a mile distant. The excited spectators called loudly to the guard to despatch her with his blunderbuss, which he seemed disposed to attempt, but Ballard cried out, "For God's sake, don't kill her! She cost me five hundred pounds, and she will be as quiet as a lamb if not irritated." This arrested the guard's hand, and he did not fire. The lioness was afterwards easily enticed from beneath the granary by the keepers, and taken back to her cage. The horse was found to be severely lacerated about the neck and chest, the lioness having fastened the talons of her fore feet on each side of his throat, while the talons of her hind feet were forced into his chest, in which position she hung until attacked by the dog. Death being inevitable, a fresh horse was procured, and the coach proceeded on its journey, after having been detained three-quarters of an hour.

A coloured print of this encounter adorns, or did thirty years ago adorn, the parlour of the Winterslow Hut, and was executed, according to the inscription, from the narrative of Joseph Pike, the guard, who, next to the lioness, is the most conspicuous object in the group. The lioness has seized the off leader by the throat, and the guard is standing on his seat with a levelled carbine, as if about to fire. In the foreground is the dog, which looks small for a mastiff, as if diminished by the artist for the purpose of making the lioness appear larger by the comparison, as the human figures on the show-cloths of the menageries always are. The terrified faces in the inside of the coach, and at the upper windows of the inn, and the blue coats and yellow vests of the outside passengers, each grasping an umbrella or a carpet-bag, as if determined not to die without a struggle, make up a vivid and sensational picture, which would have found immediate favour with the conductor of the 'Police News,' had such a periodical existed in those days.

The following year was signalised by the first appearance at Bartholomew Fair of the learned pig, Toby, who was exhibited by a showman named Hoare. There seems to have been a succession of learned pigs bearing the same name, on the same principle, probably, as Richardson's theatre continues to be advertised at Easter or Whitsuntide as at the Crystal Palace, or the Agricultural Hall, or the Spaniards, at Hampstead Heath, twenty years after the component parts of the structure were dispersed under the auctioneer's hammer.

The wonder of 1818 was an athletic French woman, who was advertised as follows:—

"The strongest woman in Europe, the celebrated French Female Hercules, Madame Gobert, who will lift with her teeth a table five feet long and three feet wide, with several persons seated upon it; also carry thirty-six weights, fifty-six pounds each, equal to 2016 lbs. and will disengage herself from them without any assistance; will carry a barrel containing 340 bottles; also an anvil 400 pounds weight, on which they will forge with four hammers at the same time she supports it on her stomach; she will also lift with her hair the same anvil, swing it from the ground, and suspend it in that position to the astonishment of every beholder; will take up a chair by the hind stave with her teeth, and throw it over her head ten feet from her body. Her travelling caravan (weighing two tons) on its road from Harwich to Leominster, owing to the neglect of the driver and badness of the road, sunk in the mud, nearly to the box of the wheels; the two horses being unable to extricate it, she descended, and, with apparent ease, disengaged the caravan from its situation, without any assistance whatever."

Caulfield says that he visited the show "for the purpose of accurately observing her manner of performance, which was by lying extended at length on her back on three chairs; pillows were then placed over her legs, thighs, and stomach, over those two thick blankets, and then a moderately thick deal board; the thirty-six weights were then placed on the board, beginning at the bottom of the legs, and extending upwards above the knees and thighs, but none approaching towards the stomach. She held the board on each side with her hands, and when the last weight was put on, she pushed the board upwards on one side, and tumbled the weights to the ground. On the whole, there appeared more of trick than of personal strength in this feat. Her next performance was raising the anvil (which might weigh nearly 200 lbs.) from the ground with her hair, which is thick, black, and as strong as that in the tail of a horse; this is platted on each side, and fixed to two cords, which are attached to the anvil; then rising from a bending to an erect posture, she raises and swings the anvil several times backwards and forwards through her legs. Her next feat was raising a table with her teeth, a slight, rickety thing, made of deal, with a bar across the legs, which, upon her grasping it, is sustained against her thighs, and enables her more easily to swing it round several times, maintaining her hold only by her teeth. The chair she makes nothing of, but canters it over her head like a plaything. That she is a wonderfully strong woman is evident, but that she can perform what is promised in her bills is a notorious untruth. She has an infant which now sucks at her breast, about eleven months old, that lifts, with very little exertion, a quarter of a hundred weight."

Greenwich and Stepney Fairs became popular places of resort with the working classes of the metropolis during the second decade of the present century. Old showmen assert that the former was then declining, a state of things which they ascribe to the growing popularity of the latter; and it is certain that the number of persons who resort to a fair is no criterion of the number, size, and quality of the shows by which it is attended, or of the gains of the showmen. Croydon Fair was never visited by so many thousands of persons as in the years of its decadence, which commenced with the opening of the railway; but the average expenditure of each person, so far from increasing in the same proportion, must have considerably diminished.

The Easter Fair at Greenwich was the opening event of the season, and during its best days Richardson's theatre always occupied the best position. John Cartlitch, the original representative of Mazeppa, and James Barnes, afterwards famous as the pantaloon of the Covent Garden pantomimes, were members of Richardson's company at this time; and it was joined at Greenwich by Nelson Lee, well known to the present generation as an enterprising theatrical manager and a prolific producer of pantomimes, but at that time fresh from school, with no other experience of theatrical business than he had gained during a brief engagement as a supernumerary at the old Royalty to serve as the foundation of the fame to which he aspired.

James and Nelson Lee were the sons of Colonel Lee, who commanded a line regiment of infantry during the period of the Peninsular war. At their father's death, the elder boy was articled to a wine merchant in the City of London, but evinced so much dislike to trade, and such strong theatrical proclivities, that the articles were cancelled, and he was placed under the tuition of Bradley, the famous swordsman of the Coburg. He declined a second time, however, to fulfil his engagement, and, leaving Bradley at the expiration of the first year, joined Bannister's circus company, in what capacity my researches have failed to show.

The Whitsuntide Fair at Greenwich was followed at this time by a small fair at Deptford, on the occasion of the annual official visit of the Master of the Trinity House, which was always made on the morrow of the festival of the Trinity. Ealing, Fairlop,

Mitcham, and Camberwell followed; then came Bartholomew; the round of the fairs within ten miles of the metropolis being completed by Enfield and Croydon.

Richardson generally proceeded from Ealing to Portsmouth, where the three weeks' town fair was immediately followed by another of a week's duration on Portsdown Hill. One of the many stories which are current among showmen and actors of his eccentricities of character has its scene at a public-house on the Portsmouth road, at which he had, in the preceding year, been refused water and provender for his horses, the innkeeper growling that he had been "done" once by a showman, and did not want to have anything more to do with show folks. Richardson bore the insult in his mind, and on approaching the house again sent his company forward, desiring each to order a glass of brandy-and-water, but not to touch it until he joined them. Twenty glasses of brandy-and-water, all wanted at once, was an unprecedented demand upon that roadside hostelry; and the landlord, as he summoned all his staff to assist him, wondered what could be the cause of such an influx of visitors. While the beverage was being concocted the waggons came up, with Richardson walking at the head.

"Here we are, governor!" exclaimed one of the actors, who had, in the meantime, strolled out upon a little green before the inn.

"Hullo!" said Richardson, affecting surprise. "I thought you had gone on to the Black Bull. What are you all doing here?"

"Waiting for you to pay for the brandy-and-water, governor," replied the comedian.

"Not if I know it!" returned Richardson, with a scowl at the expectant innkeeper. "That's the crusty fellow that wouldn't give the poor beasts a pail of water and a mouthful of hay last year, and not a shilling of my money shall ever go into his pocket. So come on, my lads, and I'll stand glasses all round at the Black Bull."

And with these words he strode on, followed by his company, leaving the disappointed innkeeper aghast behind his twenty glasses of brandy-and-water.

At Portsmouth some dissension arose between Richardson and William Cooke, whose equestrians, as the consequence or the cause, paraded in front of the theatre, and prevented free access to it.

"We must move them chaps from before our steps, Lewis," said Richardson to his stage-manager; and having a basket-horse among his properties, he had some squibs and crackers affixed to it, and sent one of the company to caper in it in the rear of Cooke's horses.

Very few of the horses used for circus parades being trained for the business of the ring, the fireworks no sooner began to fizz and bang than the equine obstructives became so restive that Cooke found it expedient to recall them to his own parade waggon.

Richardson always returned to the metropolis for Bartholomew Fair, where the shows were, in 1820, arranged for the first time in the manner described by Hone five years later. They had previously formed a block on the site of the sheep-pens; but this year swings and roundabouts were excluded, so as to preserve the area open, and the shows were built round the sides of the quadrangle. As the fair existed at this time, there were small uncovered stalls from the Skinner Street corner of Giltspur Street, along the whole length of the churchyard; and on the opposite side of Giltspur Street there were like stalls from the Newgate Street corner, along the front of the Compter prison. At these stalls were sold fruit, oysters, toys, gingerbread, baskets, and other articles of trifling value. They were held by the small fry of the stall-keeping fraternity, who lacked means to pay for space and furnish out a tempting display. The fronts of these standings were towards the passengers in the carriage-way.

Then, with occasional distances of three or four feet for footways from the road to the pavement, began lines of covered stalls, with their open fronts opposite the fronts of the houses and close to the curbstone, and their enclosed backs to the road. On the St. Sepulchre's side they extended to Cock Lane, and thence to the Smithfield corner of Giltspur Street, then, turning the corner into Smithfield, they extended to Hosier Lane, and from thence all along the west side of Smithfield to Cow Lane, where, on that side, they terminated in a line with the opposite corner leading to St. John Street, where the line was resumed, and continued to Smithfield Bars, and there, on the west side, ended. Crossing over to the east side, and returning south, these covered stalls commenced opposite to their termination on the west, and ran towards Smithfield, turning into which they extended westerly towards the pig-market, and thence to Long Lane, from which point they ran along the east side of Smithfield to the great gate of Cloth Fair. From Duke Street they continued along the south side to the great front gate of St. Bartholomew's Hospital, and from thence to the carriage entrance of the hospital, from whence they extended along Giltspur Street to the Compter, where they joined the uncovered stalls.

These covered stalls, thus surrounding Smithfield, belonged to dealers in gingerbread, toys, hardwares, pocketbooks, trinkets, and articles of all prices, from a halfpenny to ten shillings. The largest stalls were those of the toy-sellers, some of which had a frontage of twenty-five feet, and many of eighteen feet. The frontage of the majority of the stalls was eight to twelve feet; they were six or seven feet high in front, and five at the back, and all formed of canvas stretched upon a light frame-work of wood; the canvas roofs sloped to the backs, which were enclosed by canvas to the ground. The fronts were open to the thronging passengers, for whom a clear way was preserved on the pavements between the stalls and the houses, all of which, necessarily, had their shutters up and their doors closed.

The shows had their fronts towards the area of Smithfield, and their backs to the backs of the stalls, without any passage between them in any part. The area of Smithfield was thus entirely open, and persons standing in the carriage-way could see all the shows at one view. They surrounded Smithfield entirely, except on the north side. Against the pens in the centre there were no shows, the space between being kept free for spectators and persons making their way to the exhibitions. Yet, although no vehicle of any kind was permitted to pass, this immense carriage-way was always so thronged as to be almost impassable. Officers were stationed at the Giltspur Street, Hosier Lane, and Duke Street entrances to prevent carriages and horsemen from entering, the only ways by which these were allowed ingress to Smithfield being through Cow Lane, Chick Lane, Smithfield Bars, and Long Lane; and they were to go on and pass, without stopping, through one or other of these entrances, and without turning into the body of the fair. The city officers, to whom was committed the execution of these regulations, enforced them with rigour, never swerving from their instructions, but giving no just ground of offence to those whom the regulations displeased.

The shows were very numerous this year. There were four menageries, the proprietors of which are not named in the newspapers of the day, which inform us further that there was "the usual variety of conjurors, wire-dancers, giants, dwarfs, fat children, learned pigs, albinoes, &c." Ballard, Wombwell, and Atkins were probably among the menagerists, though I have found no bill or other memorial of either of the two great menageries of the second quarter of the eighteenth century of an earlier date than 1825.

Gyngell, like Richardson, never missed Bartholomew Fair in those days; and he was now supported by a clever grown-up family, consisting of Joseph, who was a good juggler and balancer; Horatio, who, besides being a dancer, was a self-taught artist of considerable ability; George, who was a pyrotechnist; and Louisa, a very beautiful young woman and graceful tight-rope dancer, who afterwards fell, and broke one of her arms, in ascending from the stage of Covent Garden Theatre to the gallery. Nelson Lee joined Gyngell's company on the termination of his engagement with Richardson; and, having learned the juggling business from a Frenchman in the *troupe*, shortly afterwards exhibited his skill at the Adelphi, and other London theatres.

CHAPTER X.

Saker and the Lees—Richardson's Theatre—Wombwell, the Menagerist—The Lion Fights at Warwick—Maughan, the Showman—Miss Hipson, the Fat Girl—Lydia Walpole, the Dwarf—The Persian Giant and the Fair Circassian—Ball's Theatre—Atkins's Menagerie—A Mare with Seven Feet—Hone's Visit to Richardson's Theatre—Samwell's Theatre—Clarke's Circus—Brown's Theatre of Arts—Ballard's Menagerie—Toby, the Learned Pig—William Whitehead, the Fat Boy—Elizabeth Stock, the Giantess—Chappell and Pike's Theatre—The Spotted Boy—Wombwell's "Bonassus"—Gouffe, the Man-Monkey—De Berar's Phantasmagoria—Scowton's Theatre—Death of Richardson.

Nelson Lee had just completed a round of engagements at the London theatres when, in 1822, his brother, having terminated his engagement with Bannister's circus, came to the metropolis, and fitted up an unoccupied factory in the Old Kent Road as a theatre. Nelson joined him in the enterprise, which for a time was tolerably successful; but they had omitted the requisite preliminary of obtaining a licence, and one night a strong force of constables invaded the theatre, and arrested every one present, audience as well as actors, with one exception. Saker, who afterwards won some distinction as a comedian, ascended into a loft on the first alarm, and drew up the ladder by which he had escaped. When all was quiet, he descended, and left the building through a window. The watch-houses of Southwark, Newington, Camberwell, and Greenwich were filled with the offenders, most of whom, however, were discharged on the following day, while the Lees, who pleaded ignorance of the law, escaped with a small fine.

The same year witnessed the final performances of "Lady Holland's Mob." About five thousand of the rabble of the City assembled in the neighbourhood of Skinner Street, about midnight of the eve of St. Bartholomew, and roared and rioted till between three and four o'clock next morning, without interference from the watch or the constables. From this time, however, this annual Saturnalia was not observed, or was observed so mildly that the newspapers contain no record of the circumstance.

In 1823, Richardson presented his patrons with a drama called *The Virgin Bride*, and an extravaganza entitled *Tom, Logic, and Jerry*, founded upon Moncrieff's drama, and concluding with a panorama of the metropolis. On the third day, a romantic drama called *The Wanderer* was substituted.

Wombwell's menagerie comes prominently into notice about this time. Its proprietor is said to have begun life as a cobbler in Monmouth Street, Seven Dials, then a famous mart of the second-hand clothes trade, and now called Dudley Street. The steps by which he subsequently advanced to the position of an importer of wild animals and proprietor of one of the largest and finest collections that ever travelled are unknown; but that he preceded Jamrach and Rice in the former vocation is proved by the existence of a small yellow card, bearing the device of a tiger, and the inscription—

Wombwell,
Wild Beast Merchant,

Commercial Road,
London.

All sorts of Foreign Animals, Birds, &c., bought, sold, or exchanged, at the Repository, or the Travelling Menagerie.

Wombwell never missed Bartholomew Fair, as long as it continued to be held, but a story is told of him which shows that he was once very near doing so. His menagerie was at Newcastle-on-Tyne within a fortnight of the time when it should be in Smithfield, and it did not seem possible to reach London in time; but, being in the metropolis on some business connected with his Commercial Road establishment, he found that Atkins was advertising that his menagerie would be "the only wild beast show in the fair." The rivalry which appears to have existed at that time between the two great menagerists prompted Wombwell to post down to Newcastle, and immediately commence a forced march to London. By making extraordinary exertions, he succeeded in reaching the metropolis on the morning of the first day of the fair. But his elephant had exerted itself so much on the journey that it died within a few hours after its arrival on the ground.

Atkins heard by some means of his rival's loss, and immediately placarded the neighbourhood with the announcement that his menagerie contained "the only living elephant in the fair." Wombwell resolved that his rival should not make capital of his loss in this manner, and had a long strip of canvas painted with the words—"The only dead elephant in the fair." This bold bid for public patronage proved a complete success. A dead elephant was a greater rarity than a live one, and his show was crowded every day of the fair, while Atkins's was comparatively deserted. The keen rivalry which this story illustrates did not endure for ever, for, during the period of my earliest recollections, from forty to fifty years ago, the two great menageries never visited Croydon Fair together, their proprietors agreeing to take that popular resort in their tours in alternate years.

I never failed, in my boyhood, to visit Wombwell's, or Atkins's show, whichever visited Croydon Fair, and could never sufficiently admire the gorgeously-uniformed bandsmen, whose brazen instruments brayed and blared from noon till night on the exterior platform, and the immense pictures, suspended from lofty poles, of elephants and giraffes, lions and tigers, zebras, boa constrictors, and whatever else was most wonderful in the brute creation, or most susceptible of brilliant colouring. The difference in the scale to which the zoological rarities within were depicted on the canvas, as compared with the figures of men that were represented, was a very characteristic feature of these pictorial displays. The boa constrictor was given the girth of an ox, and the white bear should have been as large as an elephant, judged by the size of the sailors who were attacking him among his native ice-bergs.

I have a perfect recollection of Wombwell's two famous lions, Nero and Wallace, and their keeper, "Manchester Jack," as he was called, who used to enter Nero's cage, and sit upon the animal, open his mouth, etc. It is said that, when Van Amburgh arrived in England with his trained lions, tigers, and leopards, arrangements were made for a trial of skill and daring between him and Manchester Jack, which was to have taken place at Southampton, but fell through, owing to the American showing the white feather. The story seems improbable, for Van Amburgh's daring in his performances has never been excelled.

Lion-tamers, like gymnasts, are generally killed half-a-dozen times by rumour, though they die in their beds in about the same proportion as other men; and I remember hearing an absurd story which conferred upon Manchester Jack the unenviable distinction of having his head bitten off by a lion. He was said to have been exhibiting the fool-hardy trick, with which Van Amburgh's name was so much associated, of putting his head in the lion's mouth, and to have been awakened to a sense of his temerity and its consequences by hearing the animal growl, and feeling its jaw close upon his neck.

"Does he whisk his tail, Bill?" he was reported to have said to another keeper while in this horrible situation.

"Yes," replied Bill.

"Then I am a dead man!" groaned Manchester Jack.

A moment afterwards, the lion snapped its formidable jaws, and bit off the keeper's head. Such was the story; but it is contradicted by the fact that Manchester Jack left the menagerie with a whole skin, and for many years afterwards kept an inn at Taunton, where he died in 1865.

Nero's tameness and docility made him a public favourite, but the "lion," *par excellence*, of Wombwell's show, after the lion-baitings at Warwick, was Wallace. At the time when the terrible death of the lion-tamer, Macarthy, had invested the subject with extraordinary interest, a narrative appeared in the columns of a metropolitan morning journal, purporting to relate the experiences of "an ex-lion king," in which the story of these combats was revived, but in a manner not easily reconciled with the statement of the man who communicated his reminiscences to the "special commissioner" of the journal in question, that he knew the animals and their keeper.

"Did you ever," the ex-lion king was reported to have said, "hear of old Wallace's fight with the dogs? George Wombwell was at very low water, and not knowing how to get his head up again, he thought of a fight between an old lion he had—sometimes called Wallace, sometimes Nero—and a dozen of mastiff dogs. Wallace was as tame as a sheep; I knew him well—I wish all lions were like him. The prices of admission ranged from a guinea up to five guineas, and every seat was taken, and had the menagerie been three times as large it would have been full. It was a queer go, and no mistake! Sometimes the old lion would scratch a lump out of a dog, and sometimes the dogs would make as if they were going to worry the old lion; but neither side showed any serious fight, and at length the patience of the audience got exhausted, and they went away in disgust. George's excuse was, 'We can't make 'em fight, can we, if they won't?' There was no getting over this, and George cleared over two thousand pounds by the night's work."

According to the newspaper reports of the time, two of these lion-baitings took place; and some vague report or dim recollection of the events as they actually occurred seems to have been in the mind of the "ex-lion king" when he gave the preceding account of them. The combats were said to have originated in a bet between two sporting gentlemen, and the dogs were not a dozen mastiffs, but six bull-dogs, and attacked the lion in "heats" of three. The first fight, the incidents of which were similar in character to those described in the foregoing story, was between Nero and the dogs, and took place in July, 1825; at which time the menagerie was located in the Old Factory Yard, in the outskirts of Warwick, on the road to Northampton. This not being considered satisfactory and conclusive, a second encounter was arranged, in which Wallace, a younger animal, was substituted for the old lion, with very different results. Every dog that faced the lion was killed or disabled, the last being carried about in Wallace's mouth as a rat is by a terrier or a cat.

Shows had been excluded from Greenwich Fair this year, and Bartholomew's was looked forward to by the showmen as the more likely on that account to yield an abundant harvest. Hone says that Greenwich Fair was this year suppressed by the magistrates, and the absence of shows may be regarded as evidence of some bungling and wrong-headed interference; but a score of booths for drinking and dancing were there, only two of which, Algar's and the Albion, made any charge for admission to the "assembly room," the charge for tickets at these being a shilling and sixpence respectively. Algar's was three hundred and twenty-three feet long by sixty wide, seventy feet of the length constituting the refreshment department, and the rest of the space being devoted to dancing, to the music of two harps, three violins, bass viol, two clarionets, and flute.

According to the account preserved in Hone's 'Everyday Book,' the number of shows assembled in Smithfield this year was twenty-two, of which, one was a theatre for dramatic performances, five theatres for the various entertainments usually given in circuses, four menageries, one an exhibition of glass-blowing, one a peep-show, one a mare with seven feet, and the remaining nine, exhibitions of giants, dwarfs, albinoes, fat children, etc. Of course, the theatre was Richardson's, and the following bill was posted on the exterior, and given to every one who asked for it on entering:—

⁂ *Change of Performance each Day.*
RICHARDSON'S THEATRE.
This day will be performed, an entire new Melo-Drama, called the
"Wandering Outlaw;
or, the Hour of Retribution.

"Gustavus, Elector of Saxony, *Mr. Wright*. Orsina, Baron of Holstein, *Mr. Cooper*. Ulric and Albert, Vassals to Orsina, *Messrs. Grove* and *Moore*. St. Clair, the Wandering Outlaw, *Mr. Smith*. Rinalda, the Accusing Spirit, *Mr. Darling*. Monks, Vassals, Hunters, &c. Rosabella, Wife to the Outlaw, *Mrs. Smith*. Nuns and Ladies.

"The Piece concludes with the Death of Orsina, and the Appearance of the
ACCUSING SPIRIT!

"*The Entertainments to conclude with a New Comic Harlequinade, with New Scenery, Tricks, Dresses, and Decorations, called*

"Harlequin Faustus
or, the
Devil will have his own.

"Luciferno, *Mr. Thomas*. Dæmon Amozor, afterwards Pantaloon, *Mr. Wilkinson*. Dæmon Ziokos, afterwards Clown, *Mr. Hayward*. Violencello Player, *Mr. Hartem*. Baker, *Mr. Thompson*. Landlord, *Mr. Wilkins*. Fisherman, *Mr. Rae*. Doctor Faustus, afterwards Harlequin, *Mr. Salter*. Adelada, afterwards Columbine, *Miss Wilmot*. Attendant Dæmons, Sprites, Fairies, Ballad Singers, Flower Girls, &c., &c.

The Pantomime will finish with
A SPLENDID PANORAMA,
Painted by the First Artists.
Boxes, 2*s.* Pit, 1*s.* Gallery, 6 *d.*"

The theatre had an elevation exceeding thirty-feet, and occupied a hundred feet in width. The back of the exterior platform, or parade-waggon, was formed of green baize, before which deeply fringed crimson curtains were festooned, except at two places where the money-takers sat in wide and roomy projections, fitted up like Gothic shrines, with columns and pinnacles. Fifteen hundred variegated lamps were disposed over various parts of this platform, some of them depending from the top in the shape of chandeliers and lustres, and others in wreaths and festoons. A band of ten performers, in scarlet dresses, similar to those worn by the Queen's yeomen, played continually, passing alternately from the parade-waggon and the orchestra, and from the interior to the open air again.

The auditorium was about a hundred feet long, and thirty feet wide, and was hung with green baize and crimson festoons. The seats were rows of planks, rising gradually from the ground at the end, and facing the stage, without any distinction of boxes, pit, or gallery. The stage was elevated, and there was a painted proscenium, with a green curtain, and the royal arms above, and an orchestra lined with crimson cloth. Between the orchestra and the bottom row of seats was a large space, which, after the seats were filled, and greatly to the discomfiture of the lower seat-holders, was nearly occupied by spectators. There were at least a thousand persons present on the occasion of Hone's visit.

"The curtain drew up," he says, "and presented the Wandering Outlaw, with a forest scene and a cottage; the next scene was a castle; the third was another scene in the forest. The second act commenced with a scene of an old church and a market-place. The second scene was a prison, and a ghost appeared to the tune of the evening hymn. The third scene was the castle that formed the second scene in the first act, and the performance was here enlivened by a murder. The fourth scene was rocks, with a cascade, and there was a procession to an unexecuted execution; for a ghost appeared, and saved the Wandering Outlaw from a fierce-looking headsman, and the piece ended. Then a plump little woman sang, 'He loves, and he rides away,' and the curtain drew up to Harlequin Faustus, wherein, after Columbine and a Clown, the most flaming character was the devil, with a red face and hands, in a red Spanish mantle and vest, red 'continuations,' stockings and shoes ditto to follow, a red Spanish hat and plume above, and a red 'brass bugle horn.' As soon as the fate of Faustus was concluded, the sound of a gong announced the happy event, and these performances were, in a quarter of an hour, repeated to another equally intelligent and brilliant audience."

John Clarke, an elderly, gentlemanly-looking showman, whom I saw a few years afterwards "mountebanking" on a piece of waste land at Norwood, and whose memory, in spite of his infirmity of temper, is cherished by the existing generation of equestrians and acrobats, was here with his circus, a large show, with its back against the side of Samwell's, and its front in a line with Hosier Lane, and therefore looking towards Smithfield Bars. The admission to this show was sixpence. The spacious platform outside was lighted with gas, a distinction from the other shows in the fair which extended to the interior, where a single hoop, about two feet six inches in diameter, with little jets of gas about an inch and a half apart, was suspended over the arena.

"The entertainment," says Hone, "commenced by a man dancing on the tight rope. The rope was removed and a light bay horse was mounted by a female in trousers, with a pink gown fully frilled, flounced, and ribboned, with the shoulders in large puffs. While the horse circled the ring at full speed, she danced upon him, and skipped with a hoop like a skipping-rope; she performed other dexterous feats, and concluded by dancing on the saddle with a flag in each hand, while the horse flew round the ring with great velocity. These and the subsequent performances were enlivened by tunes from a clarionet and horn, and jokes from a clown, who, when she had concluded, said to an attendant, 'Now, John, take the horse off, and whatever you do, rub him down well with a cabbage.' Then a man rode and danced on another horse, a very fine animal, and leaped from him three times over garters, placed at a considerable height and width apart, alighting on the horse's back while he was going round. This rider was remarkably dexterous.

"In conclusion, the clown got up, and rode with many antic tricks, till, on the sudden, an apparently drunken fellow rushed from the audience into the ring, and began to pull the clown from the horse. The manager interfered, and the people cried, 'Turn him out;' but the man persisted, and the clown getting off, offered to help him up, and threw him over the horse's back to the ground. At length the intruder was seated, with his face to the tail, though he gradually assumed a proper position, and, riding as a man thoroughly intoxicated would ride, fell off; he then threw off his hat and great coat, and his waistcoat, and then an under waistcoat, and a third, and a fourth, and more than a dozen waistcoats. Upon taking off the last, his trousers fell down, and he appeared in his shirt; whereupon he crouched, and drawing his shirt off in a twinkling, appeared in a handsome fancy dress, leaped into the saddle, rode standing with great grace, received great applause, made his bows, and so the performance concluded."

The remainder of the shows of this class charged a penny only for admission. Of Samwell's, Hone says,—"I paid my penny to the money-taker, a slender 'fine lady,' with three feathers in a 'jewelled turban,' and a dress of blue and white muslin, and silver; and within-side I saw the 'fat, contented, easy' proprietor, who was arrayed in corresponding magnificence. If he loved leanness, it was in 'his better half,' for himself had none of it. Obesity had disqualified him for activity, and therefore in his immensely tight and large satin jacket, he was, as much as possible, the active commander of his active performers. He superintended the dancing of a young female on the tight rope. Then he announced 'A little boy will dance a horn-pipe on the rope,' and he ordered his 'band' inside to play; this was obeyed without difficulty, for it merely consisted of one man, who blew a hornpipe tune on a Pan's-pipe; while it went on, the little boy danced on the tight rope; so far it was a hornpipe dance, and no farther. 'The little boy will stand on his head on the rope,' said the manager; and the little boy stood on his head accordingly. Then another female danced on the slack wire; and after her came a horse, not a dancing horse, but a 'learned' horse, quite as learned as the horse at Ball's theatre."

At the show last mentioned was a man who balanced chairs on his chin, and holding a knife in his mouth, balanced a sword on the edge of the knife; he then put a pewter plate on the hilt of the sword horizontally, and so balanced the sword with the plate on the edge of the knife as before, the plate having previously had imparted to it a rotary motion, which it communicated to the sword, and preserved during the balance. He also balanced the sword and plate in like manner, with a crown-piece placed edge-wise between the point of the sword and the knife; and afterwards with two crown-pieces, and then with a key. These feats were accompanied by the jokes and grimaces of a clown, and succeeded by an acrobatic performance by boys, and a hornpipe by the lady of the company. Then a learned horse was introduced, and, as desired by his master, indicated a lady who wished to be married, a gentleman who preferred a quart of ale to a sermon, a lady who liked lying in bed when she should be up, and other persons of various proclivities amusing to the rest of the spectators.

Chappell and Pike's was a very large show, fitted up after the manner of Richardson's, with a parade, on which a clown and several acrobats in tights and trunks, and young ladies in ballet costume, alternately promenaded and danced, until the interior filled, and the performances commenced. These consisted of tumbling, slack-rope dancing, etc., as at Ball's, but better executed. The names of these showmen do not appear again in the records of the London fairs, from which it may be inferred that the show was a new venture, and failed. There was a performer named Chappell in the company of Richardson's theatre, while under the management of Nelson Lee; but whether related to the showman of 1825 I am unable to say.

The performances of "Brown's Grand Troop, from Paris," commenced with an exhibition of conjuring; among other tricks, the conjurer gave a boy beer to drink out of a funnel, making him blow through it to show that it was empty, and afterwards applying it to each of the boy's ears, from whence, through the funnel, the beer appeared to reflow, and poured on the ground. Afterwards girls danced on the single and double slack wire, and a melancholy-looking clown, among other things, said they were "as clever as the barber and blacksmith who shaved magpies at twopence a dozen." The show concluded with a learned horse.

The menageries of Wombwell and Atkins were two of the largest shows in the fair. The back of the former abutted on the side of Chappell and Pike's theatre, on the north side of Smithfield, with the front looking towards Giltspur Street, at which avenue it was the first show. The front was entirely covered with painted show-cloths representing the animals, with the proprietor's name in immense letters above, and the inscription, "The Conquering Lion," very conspicuously displayed. There were other show-cloths along the whole length of the side, surmounted by this inscription, stretching out in one line of large capital letters, "Nero and Wallace, the same lions that fought at Warwick." One of the front show-cloths represented the second fight; a lion stood up, with a bleeding dog in his mouth, and his left fore paw resting upon another dog. A third dog was in the act of flying at him ferociously, and one, wounded and bleeding, was retreating. There were seven other show-cloths on this front, with the inscription "Nero and Wallace" between them. One of these show-cloths, whereon the monarch of the forest was painted, was inscribed, "Nero, the Great Lion, from Caffraria."

Wombwell's collection comprised at this time four lions and a lioness, two leopardesses, with cubs, a hyena, a bitch wolf and cubs, a polar bear, a pair of zebras, two onagers or wild asses, and a large assortment of monkeys and exotic birds. The bills announced "a remarkably fine tigress in the same den with a noble British lion;" but Hone notes that this conjunction, the announcement of which was probably suggested by the attractiveness of the lion-tiger cubs and their parents in Atkins's menagerie, was not to be seen in reality. The combats at Warwick produced a strong desire on the part of the public to see the lions who had figured in them, and the menagerie was crowded each day from morn till night. "Manchester Jack" entered Nero's cage, and invited the visitors to follow, which many ventured to do, paying sixpence for the privilege, on his assurance that they might do so with perfect safety.

Hone complains of the confusion and disorder which prevailed, and which are inseparable from a crowd, and may be not uncharitably suspected of being exaggerated in some degree by the evident prejudice which had been created in his mind by the lion-baitings at Warwick. It is certain, however, that gardens like those of the Zoological Society afford conditions for the health and comfort of the animals, and for their exhibition to the public, much more favourable than can be obtained in the best regulated travelling caravan, or in buildings such as the Tower menagerie and Exeter Change. It is impossible to do justice to animals which are cooped within the narrow limits of a travelling show, or in any place which does not admit of thorough ventilation. Apart from the impracticability of allowing sufficient space and a due supply of air, a considerable amount of discomfort to the animals is inseparable from continuous jolting about the country in caravans, and from the braying of brass bands and the glare of gas at evening exhibitions.

It took even the Zoological Society some time to learn the conditions most favourable to the maintenance of the mammal tribes of tropical countries in a state of health, while subject to the restraint necessary for their safe keeping. Too much importance was at first attached to warming the cages in which the monkeys and carnivora of India and Africa were kept, and too little to ventilating them. I remember the time when the carnivora-house in the Society's gardens was a long, narrow building, with double folding-doors at each end, and a range of cages on each side. The cages were less than half the size of the light and lofty apartments now appropriated to the same species, and were artificially heated to such a degree that the atmosphere resembled that of the small glass-house in Kew Gardens in which the paper-reed and other examples of the aquatic vegetation of tropical countries are grown, and was rendered more stifling by the strong ammoniacal odour which constantly prevaded it.

It was found, however, that the mortality among the animals, notwithstanding all the care that was taken to keep them warm, was very great; and the idea gradually dawned upon the minds of the Council of the Society that ventilation might be more conducive to the health and longevity of the animals than any amount of heat. As lions and tigers, leopards and hyenas, baboons and monkeys, live, in a state of nature, in the open air of their native forests, the imperfect ventilation of the old carnivora-house and monkey-house seemed, when once the idea was broached, to be a very likely cause of the excessive mortality, which, as lions and tigers cost from a hundred and fifty to two hundred and fifty pounds, was a constant source of heavy demands upon the Society's funds. It was determined, therefore, to try the experiment of constructing larger cages, and admitting the pure external air to them; and the results were so satisfactory that everybody wondered that the improved hygienic conditions had not been thought of before.

Atkins had a very fine collection of the feline genus, and was famous for the production of hybrids between the lion and the tigress. The cubs so produced united some of the external characteristics of both parents, their colour being tawny, marked while they were young with darker stripes, such as may be observed in black kittens, the progeny of a tabby cat. These markings disappeared, however, as the lion-tigers approached maturity, at which time the males had the mane entirely deficient, or very little developed. I remember seeing a male puma and a leopardess in the same cage in this menagerie, but I am unable to state whether the union was fruitful.

The display of show-cloths on the outside of this menagerie extended about forty feet in length, and the proprietor's name flamed along the front in coloured lamps. A brass band of eight performers, wearing scarlet tunics and leopard-skin caps, played on the outside; and Atkins shouted from time to time, "Don't be deceived! The great performing elephant is *here*; also the only lion and tigress in one den to be seen in the fair, or I'll forfeit a thousand guineas! Walk up!—walk up!"

The following singularly descriptive bill was posted on the outside and wherever else it could be displayed:—

"More Wonders in
Atkins's Royal Menagerie.
Under the Patronage of His Majesty.

G.　　　　R.

"Wonderful Phenomenon in Nature! The singular and hitherto deemed impossible occurrence of a Lion and Tigress cohabiting and producing young, has actually taken place in this menagerie, at Windsor. The tigress, on Wednesday, the 27th of October last, produced *three fine cubs*; one of them strongly resembles the tigress; the other two are of a lighter colour, but striped. Mr. Atkins had the honour (through the kind intervention of the Marquis of Conyngham) of exhibiting the *lion-tigers* to His Majesty, on the first of November, 1824, at the Royal Lodge, Windsor Great Park; when His Majesty was pleased to observe, they were the greatest curiosity of the beast creation he had ever witnessed.

"The royal striped *Bengal Tigress* has again whelped three fine cubs, (April 22,) two males and one female; the males are white, but striped; the female resembles the tigress, and, singular to observe, she fondles them with all the care of an attentive mother. The sire of the young cubs is the noble male lion. This remarkable instance of subdued temper and association of animals to permit the keeper to enter their den, and introduce their young to the spectators, is the greatest phenomenon in natural philosophy.

"That truly singular and wonderful animal, the Aurochos. Words can only convey but a very confused idea of this animal's shape, for there are few so remarkably formed. Its head is furnished with two large horns, growing from the forehead, in a form peculiar to no other animal; from the nostrils to the forehead is a stiff tuft of hair, and underneath the jaw to the neck is a similar brush of hair, and between the forelegs is hair growing about a foot and a half long. The mane is like that of a horse, white, tinged with black, with a beautiful long flowing white tail; the eye remarkably keen, and as large as the eye of the elephant: colour of the animal, dark chesnut; the appearance of the head, in some degree similar to the buffalo, and in some part formed like the goat, the hoof being divided; such is the general outline of this quadruped, which seems to partake of several species. This beautiful animal was brought over by Captain White, from the south of Africa, and landed in England, September 20th, 1823; and is the same animal so frequently mistaken by travellers for the unicorn: further to describe its peculiarities would occupy too much space in a handbill. The only one in England.

"That colossal animal, the wonderful performing
Elephant,

Upwards of ten feet high!! Five tons weight!! His consumption of hay, corn, straw, carrots, water, &c., exceeds 800 lbs. daily. The elephant, the human race excepted, is the most respectable of animals. In size, he surpasses all other terrestrial creatures, and by far exceeds any other travelling animal in England. He has ivory tusks, four feet long, one standing out on each side of his trunk. His trunk serves him instead of hands and arms, with which he can lift up and seize the smallest as well as the largest objects. He alone drags machines which six horses cannot move. To his prodigious strength, he adds courage, prudence, and an exact obedience. He remembers favours as well as injuries; in short, the sagacity and knowledge of this extraordinary animal are beyond anything human imagination can possibly suggest. He will lie down and get up at the word of command, notwithstanding the many fabulous tales of their having no joints in their legs. He will take a sixpence from the floor, and place it in a box he has in the caravan; bolt and unbolt a door; take his keeper's hat off, and replace it; and by the command of his keeper, will perform so many wonderful tricks that he will not only astonish and entertain the audience, but justly prove himself the half-reasoning beast. He is the only elephant now travelling.

"A full grown Lion and Lioness with four cubs, produced December 12, 1824, at Cheltenham.

"*Male Bengal Tiger.* Next to the lion, the tiger is the most tremendous of the carnivorous class; and whilst he possesses all the bad qualities of the former, seems to be a stranger to the good ones; to pride, to strength, to courage, the lion adds greatness, and sometimes, perhaps, clemency; while the tiger, without provocation, is fierce—without necessity, is cruel. Instead of instinct, he hath nothing but a uniform rage, a blind fury; so blind, indeed, so undistinguishing, that he frequently devours his own progeny; and if the tigress offers to defend them he tears in pieces the dam herself.

"The *Onagra*, a native of the Levant, the eastern parts of Asia, and the northern parts of Africa. This race differs from the Zebra, by the size of the body, (which is larger,) slenderness of the legs, and lustre of the hair. The only one now alive in England.

"*Two Zebras*, one full grown, the other in its infant state, in which it seems as if the works of art had been combined with those of nature in this wonderful production. In symmetry of shape, and beauty of colour, it is the most elegant of all quadrupeds ever presented; uniting the graceful figure of a horse, with the fleetness of a stag; beautifully striped with regular lines, black and white.

"A Nepaul *Bison*, only twenty-four inches high.

"*Panther*, or spotted tiger of Buenos Ayres, the only one travelling.

"A pair of *rattle-tail Porcupines.*

"Striped untamable *Hyæna*, a tiger-wolf.

"An elegant *Leopard*, the handsomest marked animal ever seen.

"Spotted *Laughing Hyæna*, the same kind of animal described never to be tamed; but, singular to observe, it is perfectly tame, and its attachment to a dog in the same den is very remarkable.

"The spotted *Cavy*.

"Pair of *Jackalls*.

"Pair of interesting *Sledge Dogs*, brought over by Captain Parry from one of the northern expeditions; they are used by the Esquimaux to draw the sledges on the ice, which they accomplish with great velocity.

"A pair of *Rackoons*, from North America.

"The *Oggouta*, from Java.

"A pair of Jennetts, or wild cats.

"The *Coatimondi*, or ant-eater.

"A pair of those extraordinary and rare birds, Pelicans of the wilderness; the only two alive in the three kingdoms.—These birds have been represented on all crests and coats of arms, to cut their breasts open with the points of their bills, and feed their young with their own blood, and are justly allowed by all authors to be the greatest curiosity of the feathered tribe.

"*Ardea Dubia*, or adjutant of Bengal, gigantic emew, or Linnæus's southern ostrich. The peculiar characteristics that distinguish this bird from the rest of the feathered tribe,—it comes from Brazil, in the new continent; it stands from eight to nine feet high when full grown; it is too large to fly, but is capable of outrunning the fleetest horses of Arabia; what is still more singular, every quill produces two feathers. The only one travelling.

"A pair of rapacious *Condor Minors*, from the interior of South America, the largest birds of flight in the world when full grown; it is the same kind of bird the Indians have asserted to carry off a deer or young calf in their talons, and two of them are sufficient to destroy a buffalo, and the wings are as much as eighteen feet across.

"The great *Horned Owl* of Bohemia. Several species of gold and silver pheasants, of the most splendid plumage, from China and Peru. Yellow-crested cockatoo. Scarlet and buff macaws.—Admittance to see the whole menagerie, 1s.—Children 6d.—Open from ten in the forenoon till feeding-time, half-past nine, 2s."

Hone says that this menagerie was thoroughly clean, and that the condition of the animals told that they were well taken care of. The elephant, with his head protruded between the stout bars of his house, whisked his proboscis diligently in search of eatables from the spectators, who supplied him with fruit and biscuits, or handed him halfpence which he uniformly conveyed by his trunk to a retailer of gingerbread, and got his money's worth in return. Then he unbolted the door to let in his keeper, and bolted it after him; took up a sixpence with his trunk, lifted the lid of a little box fixed against the wall, and deposited it within it, and some time afterwards relifted the lid, and taking out the sixpence with a single motion, returned it to the keeper; he knelt down when told, fired off a blunderbuss, took off the keeper's hat, and afterwards replaced it on his head as well as the man's hand could have done it; in short, he was perfectly docile, and well maintained the reputation of his species for a high degree of intelligence.

"The keeper," says Hone, "showed every animal in an intelligent manner, and answered the questions of the company readily and with civility. His conduct was rewarded by a good parcel of halfpence when his hat went round with a hope that 'the ladies and gentlemen would not forget the keeper before he showed the lion and tigress.' The latter was a beautiful young animal, with playful cubs about the size of bull-dogs, but without the least fierceness. When the man entered the den, they frolicked and climbed about him like kittens; he took them up in his arms, bolted them in a back apartment, and after playing with the tigress a little, threw back a partition which separated her den from the lion's, and then took the lion by the beard. This was a noble animal; he was couching, and being inclined to take his rest, only answered the keeper's command to rise by extending his whole length, and playfully putting up one of his magnificent paws, as a cat does when in a good humour. The man then took a short whip, and after a smart lash or two upon his back, the lion rose with a yawn, and fixed his eye on his keeper with a look that seemed to say, 'Well, I suppose I must humour you.'

"The man then sat down at the back of the den, with his back at the partition, and after some ordering and coaxing, the tigress sat on his right hand, and the lion on his left, and, all three being thus seated, he threw his arms round their necks, played with their noses, and laid their heads in his lap. He rose, and the animals with him; the lion stood in a fine majestic position, but the tigress reared, and putting one foot over his shoulder, and patting him with the other, as if she had been frolicking with one of her cubs, he was obliged to check her playfulness. Then by coaxing, and pushing him about, he caused the lion to sit down, and while in that position opened the animal's ponderous jaws with his hands, and thrust his face down into the lion's throat, wherein he shouted, and there held his head nearly a minute. After this he held up a common hoop for the tigress to leap through, and she did it frequently. The lion seemed more difficult to move to this sport. He did not appear to be excited by command or entreaty; at last, however, he went through the hoop, and having been once roused, he repeated the action several times; the hoop was scarcely two feet in diameter. The exhibition of these two animals concluded by the lion lying down on his side, when the keeper stretched himself to his whole length upon him, and then calling to the tigress she jumped upon the man, extended herself with her paws upon his shoulders, placed her face sideways upon his, and the whole three lay quiescent till the keeper suddenly slipped himself off the lion's side, with the tigress on him, and the trio gambolled and rolled about on the floor of the den, like playful children on the floor of a nursery.

"Of the beasts there is not room to say more than that their number was surprising, considering that they formed a better selected collection, and showed in higher condition from cleanliness and good feeding, than any assemblage I ever saw. Their variety and beauty, with the usual accessory of monkeys, made a splendid picture. The birds were equally admirable, especially the pelicans and the emew. This show would have furnished a dozen sixpenny shows, at least, to a Bartlemy Fair twenty years ago."

The other menageries were penny shows. One was Ballard's, of which the great attraction was still, though nine years had elapsed since the event, the lioness which attacked the Exeter mail-coach. The collection contained besides a fine lion, a tiger, a large polar bear, and several smaller quadrupeds, monkeys, and birds. Hone has not preserved the name of the owner of the fourth collection, which he says was "a really good exhibition of a fine lion, with leopards, and various other beasts of the forest. They were mostly docile and in good condition. One of the leopards was carried by his keeper a pick-a-back." This was probably Morgan's, which we find at this fair three years later.

The daily cost of the food of the animals in a menagerie is no trifle. The amount of animal food required for the carnivora in a first class menagerie is about four hundredweight daily, consisting chiefly of the shins, hearts, and heads of bullocks. A full-grown lion or tiger will consume twelve pounds of meat per day, and this is said to have been the allowance in Wombwell's menagerie; but it is more, I believe, than is allowed in the gardens of the Zoological Society. Bears are allowed meat only in the winter, their food at other seasons consisting of bread, sopped biscuit, or boiled rice, sweetened with sugar. Then there are the elephants, camels, antelopes, etc., to be provided for; and the quantity of hay, cabbages, bread, and boiled rice which an elephant will consume, in addition to the buns and biscuits given to it by the visitors, is, as Dominie Sampson would say, prodigious. There is a story told of an elephant belonging to a travelling menagerie which escaped from the stable in which it had been placed for the night, and, wandering through the village, found a baker's shop open. It pushed its head in, and, helping itself with its trunk, devoured sixteen four-pound loaves, and was beginning to empty the glass jars of the sweets they contained when the arrival of its keeper interrupted its stolen repast.

I now come to the minor exhibitions, of which the first from Hosier Lane, where it stood at the corner, was a peep-show, in which rudely painted pictures were successively lowered by the showmen, and viewed through circular apertures, fitted with glasses of magnifying power. A green curtain separated the spectators from the outer throng while they gazed upon such strangely contrasted scenes as the murder of Weare and the Queen of Sheba's visit to Solomon, the execution of Probert and the conversion of St. Paul, the Greenland whale fishery and the building of Babel, Wellington at Waterloo and Daniel in the lions' den!

Next to this stood a show, on the exterior of which a man beat a drum with one hand, and played a hurdy-gurdy with the other, pausing occasionally to invite the gazers to walk up, and see the living wonders thus announced on the show-cloths:—"*Miss Hipson, the Middlesex Wonder, the Largest Child in the Kingdom, when young the Handsomest Child in the World.—The Persian Giant.—The Fair Circassian with Silver Hair.—The Female Dwarf, Two Feet Eleven Inches high.—Two Wild Indians from the Malay Islands in the East.*" When a company had collected, the wonders were shown from the floor of a caravan on wheels, one side being taken out, and replaced by a curtain, which was drawn or thrown back as occasion required. After the audience had dispersed, Hone was permitted by the proprietor of the show, Nicholas Maughan, of Ipswich, to go "behind the curtain," where the artist who accompanied him completed his sketches for the illustrations in the 'Every-day Book,' while Hone entered into conversation with the persons exhibited.

"Miss Hipson, only twelve years of age, is," he says, "remarkably gigantic, or rather corpulent, for her age, pretty, well-behaved, and well-informed; she weighed sixteen stone a few months before, and has since increased in size; she has ten brothers and sisters, nowise remarkable in appearance: her father, who is dead, was a bargeman at Brentford. The name of the 'little lady' is Lydia Walpole; she was born at Addiscombe, near Yarmouth, and is sociable, agreeable, and intelligent. The fair Circassian is of pleasing countenance and manners. The Persian giant is a good-natured, tall, stately negro. The two Malays could not speak English, except three words, 'drop o' rum,' which they repeated with great glee. One of them, with long hair reaching below the waist, exhibited the posture of drawing a bow. Mr. Maughan described them as being passionate, and showed me a severe wound on his finger which the little one had given him by biting, while he endeavoured to part him and his countryman, during a quarrel a few days ago. A 'female giant' was one of the attractions of this exhibition, but she could not be shown for illness: Miss Hipson described her to be a very good young woman.

"There was an appearance of ease and good condition, with content of mind, in the persons composing this show, which induced me to put several questions to them, and I gathered that I was not mistaken in my conjecture. They described themselves as being very comfortable, and that they were taken great care of, and well treated by the proprietor, Mr. Maughan, and his partner in the show. The 'little lady' had a thorough good character from Miss Hipson as an affectionate creature; and it seems the females obtained exercise by rising early, and being carried out into the country in a post-chaise, where they walked, and thus maintained their health. This was to me the most pleasing show in the fair."

Between this show and Richardson's theatre was a small temporary stable, in which was exhibited a mare with seven feet: the admission to this sight was threepence. The following is a copy of the printed bill:—

"To Sportsmen and Naturalists.—Now exhibiting, one of the greatest living natural curiosities in the world; namely, a thorough-bred chesnut Mare, with seven legs! four years of age, perfectly sound, free from blemish, and shod on six of her feet. She is very fleet in her paces, being descended from that famous horse Julius Cæsar, out of a thorough-bred race mare descended from Eclipse, and is remarkably docile and temperate. She is the property of Mr. J. Checketts, of Belgrave hall, Leicestershire; and will be exhibited for a few days as above."

Each of this mare's hind legs, besides its natural foot, had another growing out from the fetlock joint; one of these additions was nearly the size of the natural foot; the third and least grew from the same joint of the fore leg. Andrews, the exhibitor, told Hone that they grew slowly, and that the new hoofs were, at first, very soft, and exuded during the process of growth.

The line of shows on the east side of Smithfield, commencing at Long Lane, began with an exhibition of an Indian woman, a Chinese lady, and a dwarf; and next to this stood a small exhibition of wax-figures, to which a dwarf and a Maori woman were added. On a company being assembled, the showman made a speech: "Ladies and gentlemen, before I show you the wonderful prodigies of nature, let me introduce you to the wonderful works of art;" and then he drew a curtain, behind which the wax-figures stood. "This," said he, "ladies and gentlemen, is the famous old Mother Shipton; and here is the unfortunate Jane Shore, the beautiful mistress of Edward the Fourth; next to her is his Majesty George the Fourth of most glorious memory; and this is Queen Elizabeth in all her glory; then here you have the Princess Amelia, the daughter of his late Majesty, who is dead; this is Mary, Queen of Scots, who had her head cut off; and this is O'Brien, the famous Irish giant; this man here is Thornton, who was tried for the murder of Mary Ashford; and this is the exact resemblance of Othello, the Moor of Venice, who was a jealous husband, and depend upon it every man who is jealous of his wife will be as black as that negro. Now, ladies and gentlemen, the two next are a wonderful couple, John and Margaret Scott, natives of Dunkeld, in Scotland; they lived about ninety years ago; John Scott was a hundred and five years old when he died, and Margaret lived to be a hundred and twelve; and, what is more remarkable, there is not a soul living can say he ever heard them quarrel."

Here he closed the curtain, and while undrawing another, continued his address as follows: "Having shown you the dead, I have now to exhibit to you two of the most extraordinary wonders of the living; this is the widow of a New Zealand chief, and this is the little old woman of Bagdad; she is thirty inches high, twenty-two years of age, and a native of Boston, in Lincolnshire."

The next show announced, for one penny, "*The Black Wild Indian Woman—The White Indian Youth—and the Welsh Dwarf—All Alive!*" There was this further announcement on the outside: "*The Young American will Perform after the Manner of the French Jugglers at Vauxhall Gardens, with Balls, Rings, Daggers, &c.*" The Welsh dwarf was William Phillips, of Denbigh, fifteen years of age. The "White Indian youth" was an Esquimaux; and the exhibitor assured the visitors upon his veracity that the "black wild Indian woman" was a Court lady of the island of Madagascar. The young American was the exhibitor himself, an intelligent and clever fellow in a loose striped frock, tied round the middle. He commenced his performances by throwing up three balls, which he kept constantly in the air, as he afterwards did four, and then five, with great dexterity, using his hands, shoulders, and elbows apparently with equal ease. He afterwards threw up three rings, each about four inches in diameter, and then four, which he kept in motion with similar success. To end his performance, he produced three knives, which, by throwing up and down, he contrived to preserve in the air altogether. The young American's dress and knives were very similar to those of the Anglo-Saxon glee-man, as Strutt has figured them from a MS. in the Cotton collection.

The inscriptions and paintings on the outside of the next show announced "*The White Negro, who was rescued from her Black Parents by the bravery of a British Officer—the only White Negro Girl Alive—The Great Giantess and Dwarf—Six Curiosities Alive!—Only a Penny to see them All Alive!*" One side of the interior was covered by a pictorial representation of a tread-mill, with convicts at work upon it, superintended by warders. On the other side were several monkeys in cages, an old bear in a jacket, and sundry other animals. When a sufficient number of persons had assembled, a curtain was withdrawn, and the visitors beheld the giantess and the white negro, whom the showman pronounced "the greatest curiosity ever seen—the first that has been exhibited since the reign of George II.—look at her head and hair, ladies and gentlemen, and feel it; there's no deception—it's like ropes of wool!" The girl, who had the flat nose, thick lips, and peculiarly-shaped skull of the negro, stooped to have her hair examined. It was of a dull flaxen hue, and hung, according to Hone's description, "in ropes, of a clothy texture, the thickness of a quill, and from four to six inches in length." Her skin was the colour of an European's. Then there stepped forth a little fellow about three feet high, in a military dress, with top boots, who "strutted his tiny legs, and held his head aloft with not less importance than the proudest general officer could assume upon his promotion to the rank of field marshal."

The next show was announced as an "exhibition of real wonders," and the following bill was put forth by its proprietor:—

"Real Wonders!
See and believe.
Have you seen
The beautiful Dolphin,
The Performing Pig, and the Mermaid?

If not, pray do! as the exhibition contains more variety than any other in England. Those ladies and gentlemen who may be pleased to honour it with a visit will be truly gratified.

Toby,
*The Swinish Philosopher, and Ladies' Fortune
Teller.*

That beautiful animal appears to be endowed with the natural sense of the human race. He is in colour the most beautiful of his race; in symmetry the most perfect; in temper the most docile; and far exceeds anything yet seen for his intelligent performances. He is beyond all conception: he has a perfect knowledge of the alphabet, understands arithmetic, and will spell and cast accounts, tell the points of the globe, the dice-box, the hour by any person's watch, &c.

The Real Head of
Mahoura,
The Cannibal Chief!

At the same time the public will have an opportunity of seeing what was exhibited so long in London, under the title of

The Mermaid:
The wonder of the deep! not a fac-simile or copy, but the same curiosity

Admission Moderate.

Open from Eleven in the Morning till Nine in the Evening."

Foremost among the attractions of this show were the performing pig and the show-woman, who drew forth the learning of the "swinish philosopher" admirably. He went through the alphabet, and spelt monosyllabic words with his nose; and did a sum of two figures in addition. Then, at her desire, he indicated those of the company who were in love, or addicted to excess in drink; and grunted his conviction that a stout gentleman, who might have sat to John Leech for the portrait of John Bull "loved good eating, and a pipe, and a jug of ale better than the sight of the Living Skeleton." The "beautiful dolphin" was a fish-skin stuffed. The mermaid was the last manufactured imposture of that name, exhibited for half-a-crown in Piccadilly, about a year before. The "real head of Mahoura, the cannibal chief," was a skull, with a dried skin over it, and a black wig; "but it looked sufficiently terrific," says Hone, "when the show-woman put the candle in at the neck, and the flame illuminated the yellow integument over the holes where eyes, nose, and a tongue had been."

Adjoining this was another penny show, with pictures large as life on the show-cloths outside of the living wonders within, and the following inscription:—"*All Alive! No False Paintings! The Wild Indian, the Giant Boy, and the Dwarf Family! Never here before. To be seen alive!*" Thomas Day, the reputed father of the dwarf family, was also proprietor of the show; he was thirty-five years of age, and only thirty-five inches high. There was a boy six years old, only twenty-seven inches high. The "wild Indian" was a mild-looking mulatto. The "giant boy," William Wilkinson Whitehead, was fourteen years of age, stood five feet two inches high, measured five feet round the body, twenty-seven inches across the shoulders, twenty inches round the arm, twenty-four inches round the calf, and thirty-one inches round the thigh, and weighed twenty-two stones. His father and mother were "travelling merchants" of Manchester; he was born at Glasgow, during one of their journeys, and was a fine healthy youth, fair complexioned, intelligent looking, active in his movements, and sensible in speech. He was lightly dressed in plaid to show his limbs, with a bonnet of the same.

Holden's glass-working and blowing was the last show on the east side of Smithfield, and was limited to a single caravan. The first on the south side, with its side towards Cloth Fair, and the back towards the corner of Duke Street, presented pictures of a giant, a giantess, and an Indian chief, with the inscription, "*They're all alive! Be assured they're all alive! The Yorkshire Giantess—Waterloo Giant—Indian Chief. Only a penny!*" An overgrown girl was the Yorkshire giantess. A tall man with his hair frizzed and powdered, aided by a military coat and a plaid roquelaire, made the Waterloo giant.

Next to this stood another show of the same kind and quality, the attractions of which were a giantess and two dwarfs. The giantess was a Somerset girl, who arose from the chair whereon she was seated to the height of six feet nine inches and three-quarters, with "Ladies and gentlemen, your most obedient." She was good-looking and affable, and obliged the company by taking off her tight-fitting slipper, and handing it round for their examination. It was of such dimensions that the largest man present could have put his booted foot into it. She said that her name was Elizabeth Stock, and that she was only sixteen years of age. This completed the number of shows pitched in Smithfield in 1825.

There was a visible falling off in the following year, when the number of shows diminished to eight. The west side of Giltspur Street, along its whole length, was occupied by book-stalls; and grave-looking men in black suits, with white cravats, looking like waiters out of employment, walked solemnly through the fair, giving to all who would take them tracts headed with the startling question—"*Are you prepared to die?*" Richardson's theatre was there, and Clarke's circus; but Samwell, and Ball, and

Chappell and Pike did not attend, and Wombwell's was the only menagerie. "Brown's grand company, from Paris," presented a juggling and tight-rope performance, with the learned horse, and a clown who extracted musical sounds from a salt-box, with the aid of a rolling-pin; Holden, the glass-blower, in a glass wig, made tea-cups for threepence each, and tobacco-pipes for a penny; the learned pig displayed his acquirements in orthography and arithmetic; there was a twopenny exhibition of rattlesnakes and young crocodiles, hatched by steam from imported eggs; and a show in which a dwarf and a "silver-haired lady" were exhibited for a penny.

Among the unique of the living curiosities exhibited by the showmen of this period was the famous spotted boy, described in the bills issued by his original exhibitor as "one of those wonderful productions of Nature, which excite the curiosity, and gratify the beholder with the surprising works of the Creator; he is the progeny of Negroes, being beautifully covered over by a diversity of spots of transparent brown and white; his hair is interwoven, black and white alternately, in a most astonishing manner; his countenance is interesting, with limbs finely proportioned; his ideas are quick and penetrating, yet his infantine simplicity is truly captivating. He must be seen to convince; it is not in the power of language to convey an adequate idea of this Fanciful Child of Nature, formed in her most playful mood, and allowed by every lady and gentleman that has seen it, the greatest curiosity ever beheld. May be seen from Ten in the Morning till Ten in the Evening. Admittance for Ladies and Gentlemen 1s. Servants and Children half price. Ladies and Gentlemen wishing to see this Wonderful Child at their own houses, may be accommodated by giving a few hours' notice. Copper plate Likenesses of the Boy may be had at the Place of Exhibition."

Richardson introduced this boy several seasons, between the drama and the pantomime; and became so much attached to him that he directed, by his will, that he should be buried in the grave in which, a few years before, he had deposited the remains of the lively, docile, and affectionate African lad, in the church-yard of Great Marlow.

I have found no account of the number of shows which attended Bartholomew Fair in 1827, but in the following year they must have been nearly as numerous as in 1825, an enumeration of the principal ones reaching to sixteen. All the menageries attended, and, besides Richardson's and Ball's theatres, Keyes and Laine's, Frazer's, Pike's, and a couple of clever Chinese jugglers. The receipts of these and the other principal shows were returned, in round numbers, as follows:—Wombwell's menagerie, £1,700; Richardson's theatre, £1,200; Atkins's menagerie, £1,000; Morgan's menagerie, £150; exhibition of "the pig-faced lady," £150; ditto, fat boy and girl, £140; ditto, head of William Corder, who was hanged at Chelmsford for the murder of Maria Martin, a crime which had created a great sensation, owing to its discovery through a dream of the victim's mother, £100; Ballard's menagerie, £90; Ball's theatre, £80; diorama of the battle of Navarino, £60; the Chinese jugglers, £50; Pike's theatre, £40; a fire-eater, £30; Frazer's theatre, £26; Keyes and Laine's theatre, £20; exhibition of a Scotch giant, £20. Some curious lights are thrown by these figures on the comparative attractiveness of different entertainments and exhibitions.

Considerable excitement was created among the visitors to the fair in the following year by the announcement that Wombwell had on exhibition "that most wonderful animal, the bonassus, being the first of the kind which had ever been brought to Europe." As no one had ever seen or heard of the animal before, or had the faintest conception of what it was, the curious flocked in crowds to see the beast, which proved to be a very fine bull bison, or American buffalo. Under the name given to it by Wombwell, it was introduced into the epilogue of the Westminster play as one of the wonders of the year. It was afterwards sold by Wombwell to the Zoological Society, and placed in their collection in the Regent's Park; but it had been enfeebled by confinement and disease, and it died soon afterwards. The Hudson's Bay Company subsequently supplied its place by presenting the Society with a young cow.

Atkins offered the counter attractions of an elephant ten feet high, and another litter of lion-tigers, the latter addition to his collection being announced as follows:—

"Wonderful Phenomenon in Nature—The singular and hitherto deemed impossible occurrence of a Lion and Tigress cohabiting and producing young has again taken place in the Menagerie, on the 28th of October, 1828, at Windsor, when the Royal Tigress brought forth three fine cubs!!! And they are now to be seen in the same den with their sire and dam. The first litter of these extraordinary animals were presented to Our Most Gracious Sovereign, when he was pleased to express considerable gratification, and to denominate them Lion-Tigers, than which a more appropriate name could not have been given. The great interest the Lion and Tigress have excited is unprecedented; they are a source of irresistible attraction, especially as it is the only instance of the kind ever known of animals so directly opposite in their dispositions forming an attachment of such a singular nature; their beautiful and interesting progeny are most admirable productions of Nature. The Group is truly pleasing and astonishing, and must be witnessed to form an adequate idea of them. The remarkable instance of subdued temper and association of animals to permit the Keeper to enter their Den, and to introduce their performance to the Spectators, is the greatest Phenomenon in Natural History."

Most of the shows enumerated in the list of 1828 attended Bartholomew Fair in 1830, and there were a few additional ones, making the total number about the same. They comprised the menageries of Wombwell, Atkins, and Ballard, the first containing "the great Siam elephant, and the two smallest elephants ever seen in Europe," and the last offering an unique attraction in a seal, floundering in a large tub of water; Richardson's theatre, Ball's tumbling and rope-dancing, Keyes and Laine's conjuring, Frazer's conjuring, a learned pony, the pig-faced lady, a shaved bear (to expose the imposture preceding), the "living skeleton," the fire-eater, the Scotch giant, the diorama of Navarino, the fat boy and girl, and a couple of peep-shows, one exhibiting, as its chief attraction, the lying in state of George IV., the other the murder of Maria Martin.

One of the novel characters whom Richardson picked up in his wanderings was the once famous Gouffe, "the man-monkey," as he was called. His real name was Vale, and when the old showman became acquainted with him he was following the humble occupation of a pot-boy in a low public-house. Richardson, happening to enter the tap-room in which Master Vale waited, found the young gentleman amusing the guests by walking about on pewter pint measures, with his hobnailed boots turned towards the smoke-begrimed ceiling. The performance was a novel one, and Richardson, calling the lad aside on its conclusion, made him an offer too gratifying to be refused. After travelling with Richardson for some time, Vale appeared at several of the minor theatres of the metropolis, always in the part of an ape, and under the assumed name of Gouffe. His pantomimic powers were considerable, and his agility was scarcely inferior to that of the four-handed brutes whom he represented.

The receipts of the shows were not always so large as in 1828. In 1831, which seems to have been a bad year for them, Richardson lost fifty pounds by Bartholomew Fair, though he had half the receipts of Ewing's wax-work exhibition in addition to those of the theatre, under an agreement with the proprietor, by which he paid for the ground and the erection of the show. Wombwell only cleared his expenses, though he had at that time acquired Morgan's menagerie, which stood at the corner of the Greyhound Yard, and by that means secured the pennies as well as the sixpences.

In 1832, the charge for admission to Clarke's circus was reduced from sixpence to threepence. There was a novelty in Bartholomew Fair that year in the show of an Italian conjuror, named Capelli, namely, a company of cats, that beat a drum, turned a spit, ground knives, played the organ, hammered upon an anvil, ground coffee, and rang a bell. One of them understood French as well as Italian, obeying orders in both languages. Capelli's bills announce also a wonderful dog, to "play any gentleman at dominoes that will play with him."

In 1833, the number of shows at this fair rose to thirty-two, Richardson's theatre, Clarke's circus, five for tumbling, rope-dancing, etc., three menageries, four wax-work exhibitions, three phantasmagorias, Holden's glass-blowing, two learned pigs, six exhibitions of giants, dwarfs, etc., and six peep-shows, in which the coronation of William IV., the battle of Navarino, the murder of Maria Martin, and other events of contemporary interest were shown. Only two shows charged so much as sixpence for admission, namely, Richardson's and Wombwell's. The threepenny shows were Ewing's and Clarke's, the latter giving "an excellent display for the money," according to a contemporary account, which continues as follows:—

"The performance began by tight-rope dancing by Miss Clarke, with and without the balance pole, through hoops, with 'flip-flaps,' standing on chairs, &c. Slack-rope vaulting by a little boy named Benjamin Saffery, eight years of age; he exhibited several curious feats. There was also some very extraordinary posturing by two young men, one dressed as a Chinese, the other in the old costume of Pierrot; among many other exploits, they walked round the ring with each a leg put up to their neck, and another on each other's shoulders. They also performed an extraordinary feat of lying on their backs, and throwing their legs up under their arms, and going round the ring by springing forward upon the ground, without the aid of their hands; one of them, while on the ground, supported two men on his thighs. A black man also exhibited some feats of strength; among others, he threw himself backward and, resting on his hands, formed an arch, and then bore two heavy men on his stomach with ease. The horsemanship commenced with the old performance of the rider going round the ring tied up in a sack. During the going round a transformation took place, and he who went into the sack a man came out to all appearance a woman on throwing the sack off. The whole concluded with a countryman who, suddenly starting from the ring, desires to be permitted to ride, which is at first refused, but at length allowed; he mounts, and after a short time, beginning to grow warm, pulls off his coat, then his waistcoat, then another and another to the number of thirteen, at last with much apparent modesty and reluctance his shirt; having done this, he appears a splendid rider, and after a few evolutions, terminates the performance. This rider's name was Price. The show was well attended."

The other shows of this class were Ball's, which, besides tumbling and rope-dancing, gave a pantomime, but without scenery; Keyes and Laine's, which now presented posturing, balancing, and rope-dancing; Samwell's, in which, besides tumbling and dancing, a real Indian executed the war-dance of his tribe; the Chinese jugglers; and a posturing and tumbling show, the proprietor of which was too modest to announce his name. The Chinese jugglers had performed during the summer at Saville House, the building on the north side of Leicester Square, which, after being the locality of several exhibitions, was converted into a music-hall, called the Imperial, and afterwards Eldorado. One of these pig-tailed entertainers pretended to swallow fifty needles, which were afterwards produced from his mouth, each with a thread in its eye. Another balanced a bowl on a stick nine feet long; while a third played the Chinese violin with a single string.

Wombwell's menagerie extended from the hospital gate nearly to Duke Street, and was the largest show in the fair. Drury and Drake's was a small but interesting collection, consisting of a very tame leopard, a couple of hyenas, a good show of monkeys, and several very fine boa constrictors. The third menagerie was Wombwell's smaller concern, formerly Morgan's.

The best of the wax-work exhibitions was Ewing's, which was well arranged in ten caravans. The others were Ferguson's, with the additional attraction of "the beautiful albiness," a really beautiful woman, named Shaw, who was then in her twenty-second year; Hoyo's; and a small and poor collection at a house in Giltspur Street, where the wax figures were supplemented by the exhibition of twin infants united at the breast, "extremely well preserved."

Phantasmagorial exhibitions were at this time a novelty to the masses. The best of those shown this year in Smithfield was the *Optikali Illusio* of a Frenchman, named De Berar, who startled the spectators with the appearance of a human skeleton, the vision of Death on a pale horse, etc. There was another in Long Lane; and a third at a house in Giltspur Street, where the public were invited to witness "the raising of the devil!" A fire-eater named Haines stood at the door of the last show, emitting a shower of sparks from a lump of burning tow in his mouth. Sir David Brewster, who witnessed a phantasmagorial exhibition at Edinburgh, describes it as follows:—

"The small theatre of exhibition was lighted only by one hanging lamp, the flame of which was drawn up into an opaque chimney or shade when the performance began. In this 'darkness visible' the curtain rose, and displayed a cave, with skeletons and other terrific figures in relief upon its walls. The flickering light was then drawn up beneath its shroud, and the spectators, in total darkness, found themselves in the midst of thunder and lightning. A thin transparent screen had, unknown to the spectators, been let down after the disappearance of the light, and upon it the flashes of lightning, and all the subsequent appearances, were represented. This screen, being halfway between the spectators and the cave which was first shown, and being itself invisible, prevented the observers from having any idea of the real distance of the figures, and gave them the entire character of aerial pictures.

"The thunder and lightning were followed by the figures of ghosts, skeletons, and known individuals, whose eyes and mouths were made to move by the action of combined sliders. After the first figure had been exhibited for a short time, it began to grow less and less, as if removed to a great distance, and at last vanished in a small cloud of light. Out of this same cloud the germ of another figure began to appear, and gradually grew larger and larger, and approached the spectators, till it attained its perfect development. In this manner the head of Dr. Franklin was transformed into a skull; figures which retired with the freshness of life came back in the form of skeletons, and the retiring skeletons returned in the drapery of flesh and blood. The exhibition of these transmutations was followed by spectres, skeletons, and terrific figures, which, instead of receding and vanishing as before, suddenly advanced upon the spectators, becoming larger as they approached them, and finally vanished by appearing to sink into the ground. The effect of this part of the exhibition was naturally the most impressive. The spectators were not only surprised, but agitated, and many of them were of opinion that they could have touched the figures."

Dupain's French theatre combined the exhibition of a dwarf, Jonathan Dawson, three feet high, and fifty years of age, with posturing by a performer named Finch, and two mechanical views, one representing Algiers, with the sea in motion, and vessels entering and leaving the harbour; the other a storm at sea, with a vessel in distress, burning blue lights, firing guns, and finally becoming a wreck.

Broomsgrove's show, which made its first appearance, contained three human curiosities, namely, Clancy, an Irishman, whose height was seven feet two inches; Farnham, who was only three feet two inches in height, but so strong that he carried two big men on his shoulders with ease; and Thomas Pierce, "the gigantic Shropshire youth," aged seventeen years, five feet ten inches in height, and thirty-five stones in weight.

Simmett's show contained four "living wonders" of this kind, namely, Priscilla and Amelia Weston, twin Canadian giantesses, twenty years of age; Lydia Walpole, the dwarf exhibited in Maughan's show in 1825; and an albino woman, aged nineteen. Harris added to a peep-show a twelve years old dwarf, named Eliza Webber; a sheep with singularly formed hind hoofs; and a very fine boa constrictor. Another show combined the performances of a monkey, which, in the garb of an old woman, smoked a pipe, wheeled a barrow, etc., with the exhibition of several mechanical figures, representing artisans working at their various trades, and a juvenile albino, named Mary Anne Chapman. Another exhibited, as an "extraordinary hermit," a man named Daniel Mackenzie, whose only distinction rested upon his statement that he had voluntarily secluded himself from the world for five years, which he had passed in a coal-mine near Dalkeith.

Toby, the learned pig, if he was the original porcine wonder of that name, must have been, at least, seventeen years of age, but showed no symptoms of declining vigour or diminished intelligence. He was now exhibited by James Burchall, in conjunction with the proprietor's monstrously fat child, and was announced as,—

"The Unrivalled Chinese Swinish Philosopher, Toby the Real Learned Pig. He will spell, read, and cast accounts, tell the points of the sun's rising and setting, discover the four grand divisions of the Earth, kneel at command, perform blindfold with 20 handkerchiefs over his eyes, tell the hour to a minute by the watch, tell a card, and the age of any party. He is in colour the most beautiful of his race, in symmetry the most perfect, in temper the most docile. And when asked a question, he will give an Immediate Answer."

Toby had a rival this year in the "amazing pig of knowledge," exhibited by James Fawkes, at the George Inn. This pig could tell the number of pence in a shilling, and of shillings in a pound, count the spectators, tell their thoughts (so at least it was pretended), distinguish colours, and do many other wonderful things. The following doggrel verses, extracted from Fawkes's bill, are offered as a curiosity; they seem *apropos* of nothing, and show that the exhibitor was ignorant or oblivious of the fact that George IV. had been dead three years:—

"A learned Pig in George's reign
To Æsop's Brutes an equal Boast;
Then let Mankind again combine
To render Friendship still a Toast.

"Let Albion's Fair superior soar,
To Gallic Fraud, or Gallic Art;
Britons will e'er bow down before
The Virtues seated in the Heart."

In 1836, a new show appeared in the field, namely, Brown's Theatre of Arts, in which were shown mechanical representations of the battle of Trafalgar, the passage of the Alps by the French army, and the Marble Palace at St. Petersburg, the ships in the first and the figures in the others being in actual motion.

Scowton, who had been absent from Bartholomew Fair for several years, made a final appearance there in 1837, when his bills contained the following announcement:—

"Mr. Scowton, deeply impressed with heartfelt gratitude for the liberal Patronage and Support which he has for a series of Years experienced from his Friends and a Generous Public, and which will enable him to spend his future Days in comfortable Retirement: begs leave to announce that the whole of his Extensive Concern, is to be disposed of by Private Contract; and, therefore, at the same time, as he takes leave, requests them to believe that the Memory of their favours and indulgence will never be eradicated from his Memory."

Richardson's theatre stood beside Scowton's, and it is remarked by a newspaper of the time that "the former displayed the trappings of modern grandeur, and the latter evinced his taste for the ancient by exposing to view a couple of centaurs and a sphynx." Scowton presented a "new grand dramatic romance," called *The Treacherous Friend*, in which he played the character of Alphonsus himself.

This was the last appearance of both these veteran showmen. Scowton retired, and Richardson died shortly afterwards at his cottage in Horsemonger Lane, and was buried, as his will directed, at Great Marlow, in the same grave with the spotted boy. He bequeathed the greater part of his property to Charles Reed, who had travelled with him for many years; his old friend, Johnson, afterwards co-lessee with Nelson Lee of the City of London Theatre, received a legacy of five hundred pounds, and Davy, who had superintended the building and removal of the theatre from the beginning of its existence, two hundred pounds.

Looking backward forty years, I can recall the quaint figure of the old showman as he stood on the steps of his portable theatre, clad in a loose drab coat and a long scarlet vest, which looked as if it had been made in the reign of George II. As I think of Croydon Fair as it used to be in Richardson's days, with the show standing between Clarke's circus and Wombwell's menagerie, I can almost fancy that I hear the booming of the old man's gong. Many a time afterwards have I seen Nelson Lee beating that memorable instrument of discord, and heard him shouting, "Walk up! walk up! Just going to begin!" But *he* wore a suit of black, and did not impress me half so much as his predecessor. The change seemed, indeed, a symptom of the declining glory of the fair, which has, within the last few years, become a thing of the past.

CHAPTER XI.

Successors of Scowton and Richardson—Nelson Lee—Crowther, the Actor—Paul Herring—Newman and Allen's Theatre—Fair in Hyde Park—Hilton's Menagerie—Bartholomew Fair again threatened—Wombwell's Menagerie—Charles Freer—Fox Cooper and the Bosjesmans—Destruction of Johnson and Lee's Theatre—Reed's Theatre—Hales, the Norfolk Giant—Affray at Greenwich—Death of Wombwell—Lion Queens—Catastrophe in a Menagerie—World's Fair at Bayswater—Abbott's Theatre—Charlie Keith, the Clown—Robson, the Comedian—Manders's Menagerie—Macomo, the Lion-Tamer—Macarthy and the Lions—Fairgrieve's Menagerie—Lorenzo and the Tigress—Sale of a Menagerie—Extinction of the London Fairs—Decline of Fairs near the Metropolis—Conclusion.

The change in the proprietorship of the travelling theatres conducted during so many years by Scowton and Richardson may be regarded as a stage in the history of the people's amusements. The decline which showmen had noted during the preceding years had not been perceptible to the public, who had crowded the London fairs more densely than ever, and found as many showmen catering for their entertainment as in earlier years. But while the crowds that gazed at Wombwell's show-cloths, and the parades of Richardson's theatre and Clarke's circus, became more dense every year, the showmen found their receipts diminish and their expenses increase. The people had more wants than formerly, and their means of supplying them had not, at the time of the decadence of the London fairs, experienced a corresponding increase. The vast and ever-growing population of the metropolis furnished larger crowds, but the middle-class element had diminished, and continued to diminish; and the showmen found reduced charges to be a necessity, without resulting in the augmented gains which follow a reduction of prices in trade.

Scowton's theatre was sold by private contract to Julius Haydon, who, after expending a considerable sum upon it, making it rival Richardson's in size, found the results so little to his advantage that he disposed of the whole concern a year afterwards to the successors of Richardson.

These were the showman's old friends, John Johnson, to whom he left a legacy of five hundred pounds, and Nelson Lee, who, after the unfortunate speculation with his brother in the Old Kent Road, had travelled for a time with Holloway's show, then gone to Scotland with Grey's *fantoccini*, and, after a turn at Edinburgh with Dodsworth and Stevens's automatons, had returned to London, and was at the time of Richardson's death managing Sadler's Wells theatre for Osbaldiston. When he saw Richardson's property advertised for sale, he conferred with Johnson on the subject of its purchase by them, which they effected by private contract, Lee resigning his post at Sadler's Wells to undertake the management.

The new proprietors furnished the theatre with a new front, and provided new dresses for the ballet in *Esmeralda*, which was then attracting large audiences to the Adelphi. They did not propose to open with this drama, but they thought the ballet would be a success on the parade outside, which managers of travelling theatres find it necessary to make as attractive as possible, the public forming their anticipations of the entertainment to be witnessed inside by what they see outside, as they do of tenting circus performances by the extent and splendour of the parade round the town and neighbourhood which precedes them. I once saw a very pretty harvest-dance of reapers and gleaners on the parade of Richardson's theatre, and on another occasion a fantastic dance of Indians, who held cocoa-nuts in their hands, and struck them together, assuming every variety of attitude, each dancer sometimes striking his own nuts together, and sometimes his own against those of his *vis-à-vis*.

They were in time for the Whitsuntide Fair at Greenwich, where the theatre stood at the extreme end of the fair, near the bridge at Deptford Creek. The Esmeralda dance was a great success, and Oscar Byrne, who had arranged the ballet for the Adelphi, visited the theatre, and complimented Lee on the manner in which it was produced. The drama was *The Tyrant Doge*, and the pantomime, arranged by Lee for the occasion, had local colour given to it, and the local title of *One Tree Hill*. The season opened very favourably, though both the management and the public experienced considerable annoyance from a party of dissolute young men, of whom the Marquis of Waterford was one, and who threw nuts at the actors, and talked and laughed loudly throughout the performance.

Delamore had succeeded Lewis as stage-manager, scene-shifter, and wardrobe-keeper, a few years before Richardson's death, and he was retained in that position by the new proprietors. John Douglass and Paul Herring were in the company at this time; also Crowther, who was subsequently engaged at Astley's, and married Miss Vincent, who was for so many years a popular favourite at the Victoria as the heroine of a series of successful domestic dramas.

Among the minor shows attending the fairs of the southern counties at this period was the portable theatre of Newman and Allen, which, towards the end of the summer, was pitched upon a piece of waste ground at Norwood, and remained there two or three weeks. The fortunes of the company seemed at low ebb, and the small "houses" which they had nightly, with a charge for admission of twopence to front seats, and a penny to the back, did not place the treasury in a very flourishing condition. Small as the company was, they aimed at a higher performance than was usually given in a portable theatre, for on the two occasions that I patronised the canvas temple of Thespis the plays were *Virginius* and *John Bull*, considerably cut down, as was to have been expected, the smallness of the company rendering it necessary to excise some of the characters.

Only one performance was given each night, and a farce preceded the play, the interval between the pieces being filled up with a comic song, sung by the low comedy man, and an acrobatic performance by a young lady whose name I learned was Sarah Saunders. Whether she was related to old Abraham Saunders, I do not know; but the tendency of show-folks to make their vocations hereditary renders it very probable. She was the first female acrobat I ever saw, and an actress besides; and the peculiarity of her acrobatic performance was, that she did not don trunks and tights for it, like Madame Stertzenbach and others of her sex at the present day, but did her "flips," etc., in her ordinary attire, like the little drabs from the back slums of Westminster who may sometimes be seen turning heels over head in St. James's Park.

When the brief season of the canvas theatre was brought to a close, and the fittings, scenery, properties, etc., had left the village behind a bony horse, it seemed that the proprietors had dissolved the partnership which had existed between them; for a living carriage remained on the ground, the occupants of which were old Newman, who had played the heavy parts, and his nephew, Charles Little, the low comedy man. Whether the old gentleman had realised a competency which satisfied his wants, or had some small pension or annuity, or investment of some kind, never became known; but there the wheeled abode of the two men stood for several years, Newman cultivating a patch of the waste, and producing therefrom all the vegetables they required for their own table, while his nephew perambulated the neighbourhood with a basket, offering for sale tapes and cottons, needles and pins, and other small wares of a similar description. This new vocation seemed more lucrative than that of low comedian and comic singer in a travelling theatre; for Charlie, as he was familiarly called, dressed better every year, and, on the death of his uncle, took to himself a wife, and, abandoning the living carriage, settled in a neighbouring cottage.

From this episode of show-life I must return to Johnson and Lee, who, after visiting Deptford and Camberwell Fairs, took their renovated theatre to Smithfield, where it stood with its back to the George Inn. At Croydon Fair it occupied its usual position between Clarke's circus and Wombwell's menagerie; and there a singular and amusing adventure occurred to the clown, who, however, did not find it so amusing himself. The first day being very wet, and the fair in consequence very thinly attended, he thought to divert the tedium of the situation by strolling through the town, and for this purpose put on the uniform over-coat of a policeman, a character then, as now, always diverting in the pantomime. Some short time previously, several robberies had been committed in the town by a thief similarly dressed; and a constable on duty in High Street, seeing a seeming policeman whom he did not know, and who gazed about him as if he was a stranger, took the astonished clown into custody on the charge of personating a constable and loitering about for an unlawful purpose. On being taken to the station-house, the clown made an explanatory statement, and the inspector sent a constable to the theatre to ascertain its truth, testimony to which was given by Lee. The clown was thereupon released from custody, and hurried back to the fair, vowing that he would never promenade in the garb of a policeman again.

In the following year, Johnson and Lee presented a memorial to the Home Office, asking permission to hold a fair in Hyde Park, to celebrate the coronation of the Queen. The Government acceded to the request, and Superintendent Mallalieu was associated with the memorialists in the organisation and management of the undertaking. A tent was pitched in the centre of the ground selected for the purpose, and the three managers attended daily to arrange the plan, classify the shows, stalls, etc., and receive applications for space, which were so numerous that it became necessary to post constables before the tent to maintain order. As each applicant stated the nature of his business, the application was entered in a book kept for the purpose, and a day was named for the allotment of ground. Every foot of space granted for the purpose by the Commissioners of Her Majesty's Woods and Forests was taken within a week, and every intending exhibitor received a ticket in the following form:—

FAIR IN HYDE PARK.

No. ____ Allotment of Ground.

The Bearer _____, of _____, _____, is hereby entitled to ____ feet frontage on the _____ side of the area for the purpose of erecting a _____.

__ June, 1838.

J. M. Mallalieu,

Supt.

Every ticket-holder was requested to fit up his show or stall in a becoming manner, and to display as illumination some device suitable to the occasion. The undertaking to this effect was adhered to in a commendable manner, and a very pretty effect was thus produced when the fair was opened, on the 28th of June, and the numerous shows, booths, and stalls were illuminated at night with so many thousands of coloured lamps. As the boom of the first gun announcing the departure of the Queen for Westminster Abbey was heard, Nelson Lee, standing on the parade of his theatre, struck the gong, and all the showmen unfurled their show-cloths, and the keepers of booths and stalls rolled up their canvas fronts, and commenced business.

The fair was a great success, the financial results being as satisfactory as its organisation and management. Many of the nobility visited it, and even patronised the amusements, as they had been wont to do at Bartholomew Fair in the seventeenth century, and the first half of the eighteenth. Johnson and Lee's theatre filled on the opening day in five minutes, and the time occupied by the performances was reduced to fifteen minutes. The drama was *The Mysterious Stranger*, which, thus contracted, became more mysterious than ever. All the principal avenues were crowded from noon till night, and the demand upon the resources of the refreshment booths was so great that Algar and other principal booth-keepers charged, and had no difficulty in obtaining, a shilling for a pot of beer, and sixpence for a lettuce or a penny loaf, other articles being sold at proportionate rates.

During the fair, the wife of a gingerbread vendor gave birth to a child, which, in commemoration of the occasion was registered by the name of Hyde Park. The stall was, in consequence of this event, allowed to remain several days after the time by which the promoters of the fair had undertaken to have the ground cleared, and it was visited by many ladies, who made presents to the child and its parents. Though the ground had been let at a low rate, a surplus of sixty pounds remained after defraying all expenses, and this sum was awarded to Johnson and Lee; but they did not apply for it, and it was divided among the constables who did police duty in the fair. The services of Johnson and Lee in promoting and organising the fair, and of Superintendent Mallalieu in supervising the arrangements and maintaining order, were so well appreciated by the showmen and the keepers of booths and stalls, that they joined in presenting each with a silver cup, at a dinner which took place at the Champion Tavern, Paddington.

At the ordinary fairs visited during the latter part of this year, Johnson and Lee exhibited a panorama of the coronation, painted by Marshall, which proved very attractive. Enfield Fair being spoiled by wet weather, application was made to the local magistrate for an extra day, which at Croydon was always conceded in such circumstances; but it was refused, the Enfield justice seeming to be of opinion that actors and acrobats were vagabonds who ought to be discouraged by every possible means. Resolved not to be disappointed, Johnson and Lee issued a bill in the name of Jones, a man who sold refreshments in the theatre, announcing that, in consequence of the wet weather having prevented him from clearing his stock of nuts, the proprietors had given him the use of the theatre for an extra day, when the usual performances would be given without charge, but prices ranging from a shilling to three shillings would be charged for nuts to be supplied to the persons admitted.

Haydon's theatre made its last appearance at Croydon Fair, where great exertions were made to render it as attractive as Johnson and Lee's, but it was not patronised to near the same extent as the latter; and Johnson and Lee's offer to purchase the concern being entertained by the proprietor, it from that time ceased to exist, being absorbed into the more popular establishment.

Croydon Fair used, at this time, to be visited by large numbers of persons, not only from the surrounding villages, but even from the metropolis. All the inhabitants of the town prepared for visitors, for everyone who had a relative or acquaintance in Croydon was sure to make the fair an occasion for a visit. Two time-honoured customs were connected with the October fair, everybody commencing fires in their sitting-rooms on the first day of the fair, and dining on roast pork or goose. The latter custom was observed even by those who, having no friends to visit, dined in a booth; and the number of geese and legs of pork to be seen roasting before glowing charcoal fires in grates of immense width, in the rear of the booths, was one of the sights of the fair.

There were two entrances to the fair from the town, one at the gate which gave access at ordinary times to the foot-path across the field, leading to Park Hill; and the other, made for the occasion, farther southward, for the accommodation of those who approached the field from the avenues on the east side of High Street. Each was bordered for a short distance by the standings of itinerant vendors of walnuts, oysters, and fried sausages, beyond which was a long street of gingerbread stalls, terminated, in the one case, by the shows of the exhibitors of wax-work, living curiosities, and pictorial representations of great historical events, and in the other by the smaller and less pretentious drinking-booths. At right angles to these canvas streets, and opening from them near their commencement, was a third, covered over with an awning, and composed of the stalls of the dealers in toys and fancy goods. This was called Bond Street.

Parallel with this avenue, and connecting the further ends of the two streets of gingerbread stalls, was one broader than the others, bordered on the side from which it was approached with gingerbread stalls, and on the further side with the principal shows and booths. First in order, on the latter side, stood Clarke's circus, with the proprietor on the steps, in a scarlet coat and white breeches, smacking a whip, and shouting, "This way for the riders! the riders!" Three or four spotted and cream-coloured horses, gaily caparisoned, stood on the platform, and a clown cracked his "wheeze" with a couple of young fellows in tights and trunks, in their intervals of repose from acrobatic feats of the ordinary character.

Next to the circus stood a portable theatre, usually Scowton's, in rivalry with the neighbouring show of the famous Richardson, which was always the largest, and was worked by the strongest company. On the exterior platforms of both, practical jokes were played upon the pantaloon by the harlequin and the clown; young ladies in short muslin skirts danced to the lively strains of the orchestra, and broad-sword combats were fought in the approved one! two! three! over and under style. Next to Richardson's show stood the menagerie of Wombwell or Atkins, where a broad array of pictorial canvas attracted a wondering crowd, and the brazen instruments of musicians, attired in uniforms copied from those of the royal "beef-eaters," brayed and blared from noon till night.

Then came the principal booths, wherein eating and drinking was the order of the day, and dancing that of the night. The largest and best appointed of these was the Crown and Anchor, well known to fair-goers for half a century, the name of Algar being "familiar in their mouths as household words," as that of an experienced caterer for their entertainment. There was a tolerable quadrille band in attendance from eve till midnight, and, in the best days of the fair, the sons and daughters of the shopkeepers of the town and the farmers of the surrounding neighbourhood mingled in the dance in the "assembly room" of Algar's booth without fear of scandal or loss of caste. There was dancing in the other booths, but they were smaller, the music and the lighting were inferior, and the company less select. Among those that stood in a line with Algar's were the Fives Court, kept by an ex-pugilist, and patronised chiefly by gentlemen of the "fancy;" and the gipsies' booth, which had no other sign than the ancient one of a green bough, and was resorted to for the novelty of being waited upon by dark-eyed and dusky-complexioned Romanies, wearing bright-coloured silk handkerchiefs over their shoulders, and long gold pendants in their ears.

Within the area enclosed by these avenues were swings and round-abouts, while the "knock 'em downs," the "three shies a penny" fellows, the predecessors of the Aunt Sallies of a later day, occupied the vacant spaces on the skirts of the pleasure fair, wherever the ground was not covered, on the first day, with horses, sheep, and cattle.

At midnight on the 1st the fair was opened by the ceremony of carrying an enormous key through it, and the booth-keepers were then allowed to serve any customers who might offer. By daylight next morning the roads leading to the fair-field were thronged with sheep and cattle, thousands of which, with scores of horses, changed owners before sunset. There was little movement in the long avenues of shows, booths, and stalls, until near noon, when nursery maids led their charges through Bond Street, and mothers took their younger children there to buy toys. About mid-day the showmen unfurled their pictures, which appealed so strongly to the imaginations of the spectators, the bands of the larger shows began to play, and clowns and acrobats, dancers and jugglers, appeared upon the exterior platforms. From this time till sunset the throng of visitors increased rapidly, and on fine days the crowd before the principal shows was so dense as to offer considerable impediment to locomotion.

When darkness began to descend upon the field, lamps flared and flickered on the fronts of the shows, smaller lights glimmered along the toy and gingerbread stalls, and thousands of tiny lamps, blue, and amber, and green, and ruby, arranged in the form of crowns, stars, anchors, feathers, etc., illuminated the booths. Then the showmen beat their gongs with redoubled vigour, and bawled through speaking-trumpets till they were hoarse; the bands brayed and blared louder than before; and the sounds of harps and violins showed that dancing had commenced in the booths.

In those days it sometimes happened that two circuses attended the fair, when the larger of the two was pitched in a field on the west side of the road, and bounded on the south side by Mint Walk, one of the avenues by which the fair was approached from High Street. In a circus thus located—I think it was Clarke's—Miss Woolford, afterwards the second wife of the great equestrian, Andrew Ducrow, exhibited her grace and agility on the tight-rope in a blaze of fireworks, in emulation of the celebrated Madame Saqui's performance at Vauxhall Gardens. The equestrian profession still numbers Ducrows in its ranks, two young men of that name belonging at the present time to Newsome's circus company; but I have not met with the name of Woolford since 1842, when a young lady of that name, and then about twelve or thirteen years of age, danced on the tight-rope in a small show pitched at the back of the town-hall at Croydon, during the July Fair.

The October fair at Croydon closed the season of the shows which confined their perambulations to a distance of fifty miles from the metropolis, where, or in the provincial towns possessing theatres, the actors, clowns, acrobats, etc., obtained engagements for the pantomime season. This year, the entire company of Johnson and Lee's theatre was engaged for the Marylebone.

In 1839, this theatre, with John Douglass and Paul Herring still in the company, stood next to Hilton's menagerie at Greenwich, where the season commenced with most of the shows which made London their winter quarters. It was about this time that James Lee, who was then manager of Hilton's menagerie, suggested the certain attractiveness of the exhibition by a young woman of the performances with lions and tigers which had been found so productive to the treasuries of the Sangers, Batty, and Howes and Cushing, when exhibited by a man. It was proposed to bring out as a "lion queen" the daughter of Hilton's brother Joseph, a circus proprietor; and the young lady, being familiar with her uncle's lions, did not shrink from the distinction. She made her first public appearance with the lions at Stepney Fair, and the performance proved so attractive that the example was contagious. Edmunds had at this time a fine group of lions, tigers, and leopards, and a young woman named Chapman (now Mrs. George Sanger) volunteered to perform with them, as a rival to Miss Hilton.

Miss Chapman, who had the honour of appearing before the royal family at Windsor Castle, had not long been before the public when a third "lion queen" appeared in Wombwell's menagerie in the person of Helen Blight, the daughter of a musician in the band. The career of this poor girl was as brief as its termination was shocking. She was performing with the animals at Greenwich Fair, when a tiger exhibited some sullenness or waywardness, for which she very imprudently struck it with a riding-whip which she carried. With a terrible roar, the infuriated beast sprang upon her, seized her by the throat, and killed her before she could be rescued. This melancholy affair led to the prohibition of such performances by women; but the leading menageries have continued to have "lion kings" attached to them to the present day.

It was in this year that the war against the shows was renewed by the authorities of the City of London, who doubled the charges hitherto made for space in Smithfield, Wombwell, for instance, having his rent raised from forty to eighty pounds, Clarke's from twenty-five to fifty, and others in the same proportion. After the fair, the London City Missions Society presented a memorial to the Corporation, praying for the suppression of the fair, and the City Lands Committee was instructed by the Court of Aldermen to consider whether, and by what means, its suppression could be legally accomplished. The committee referred the question to the solicitor of the City, who was requested to report to the Markets Committee "as to the right of the Corporation of London to suppress Bartholomew Fair, or otherwise to remove the nuisances and obstructions to trade to which it gives rise."

The solicitor accordingly examined the archives in the town-clerk's office, as well as books in the City Library and the British Museum, for the purpose of tracing the history of the fair, and of other fairs which formerly existed in the metropolis, and the right to hold which was likewise founded upon charters, and which had been abolished or fallen into disuse. His researches led him to the conclusion that "the right to hold both fairs having been granted for the purpose of promoting the interests of trade, it is quite clear that no prescriptive right can be set up to commit any nuisance incompatible with the purposes for which they were established; if, therefore, the Corporation should be satisfied that the interests of the public can be no otherwise protected than by confining the fair to its original objects and purposes, they may undoubtedly do so, and this would in fact, be equivalent to its entire suppression."

This course was, however, that which had been adopted, without success, in 1735, and the legal adviser of the Corporation could not avoid seeing that "it is at all times difficult, by law, to put down the ancient customs and practices of the multitude." Both May Fair and Lady Fair had been suppressed without the intervention of Parliament, however, and it seemed probable that "old Bartlemy" would be extinguished before long by natural decay, and that the best course would be to provide for its due regulation during its decline.

"When we consider," said the report, "the improved condition and conduct of the working classes in the metropolis, and reflect upon the irrefragable proofs continually before us, that the humbler orders are fast changing their habits, and substituting country excursions by railroad and steamboat, and other innocent recreations, for vicious amusements of the description which prevailed in Bartholomew Fair, it is, perhaps, not too much to conclude that it is unnecessary for the Corporation to apply to Parliament to abate the nuisance; but that, if they proceed to lay down and enforce the observance of judicious regulations in the fair, and to limit its duration and extent, it may be permitted to continue, in the confident belief that many years will not elapse ere the Corporation may omit to proclaim the fair, and thus suppress it altogether, without exciting any of those feelings of discontent and disapprobation with which its compulsory abolition would probably be now attended."

When this report was submitted to the Court of Common Council, in July, 1840, considerable diversity of opinion was found to prevail as to the course which should be adopted. The majority either adopted the view of the London City Missions Society, or the more moderate sentiments of the reporter, Mr. Charles Pearson; but the principles therein enunciated did not pass without challenge. Mr. Anderton was "decidedly opposed to the canting and Methodistical grounds for interfering with one of the only amusements now remaining to the poor inhabitants of London." Mr. Wells thought that the fair, under proper regulations for the prevention of disorder, would be innoxious, and that the gaming-houses of the metropolis were a fitter subject for suppression. Mr. Taylor regarded the objections to the fair as "the wild chimeras of fanaticism." But after a long discussion, the report was adopted by forty-three votes against fourteen. The Market Committee declined, however, to limit the fair to two days, or to exclude shows entirely, though they resolved to again raise the rents of the shows that were admitted, to permit no disturbance of the pavement, to continue the exclusion of swings and roundabouts, and to admit no theatres for dramatic performances.

The policy resolved upon was, therefore, simply one of vexation and annoyance, and contributed nothing to the promotion of morality and order. Johnson and Lee's theatre, Clarke's circus, Frazer's acrobatic entertainment, Laskey's giant and giantess, and Crockett's and Reader's exhibitions of living curiosities, were refused space in Smithfield; and the only shows admitted were the menageries of Wombwell, Hilton, and Wright, and Grove's theatre of arts. Why the performances of lions and tigers should be regarded with more favour than those of horses, Miss Clarke on the tight-rope be considered a more demoralising spectacle then Miss Hilton or Miss Chapman in a cage of wild beasts, and the serpents and crocodile in Crockett's caravan more suggestive of immoral ideas than the monkeys in the menageries, is a problem which does not admit of easy solution, and which only an aldermanic mind could have framed.

The suburban fairs were declining so much at this time that Johnson and Lee were deterred by their diminished receipts at Greenwich and Deptford from visiting Ealing, Camberwell, and Enfield; and, on being excluded from Smithfield, proceeded to Chatham, whence they moved to Croydon. The decadence was still more manifest in the following year, and at Enfield an attempt was made by the magistrate to prevent them from opening on the third day, the more officious than learned administrator of the law being ignorant of the fact that, though the fair had for many years been held on two days only, the charter by which it was held allowed three days. Lee had taken care to obtain a copy of the charter, and on the superintendent of police going to the theatre with the magistrate's order for its immediate removal, he positively refused obedience to the mandate, and produced the charter. The superintendent thereupon apologised, and returned to the magistrate with the news of his discomfiture.

At Bartholomew Fair, Wombwell's was the only show of any consequence. His collection had at this time grown to be, not only the largest and best travelling, but equal, and in some respects superior, to any in the world. He had twelve lions, besides lionesses and cubs, and eight tigers, a tigress, and cubs, in addition to a puma, a jaguar, a black tiger, several leopards, an ocelot, a serval, and a pair of genets. There were also striped and spotted hyenas, wolves, jackals, coati-mondies, racoons, a polar bear, a sloth bear, black and brown bears, a honey bear, and a couple of porcupines. The hoofed classes were represented by three elephants, a fine one-horned rhinoceros, a pair of gnus, a white antelope, a Brahmin cow, an axis deer, and three giraffes, which had lately been brought from Abyssinia by M. Riboulet, a French traveller, and were the first of their kind ever exhibited in the fair.

Croydon Fair was disturbed this year by a fight between the youths of the East India Company's military college at Addiscombe, about a mile from the town, and the members of Johnson and Lee's company. The *fracas* originated with an insulting remark made by one of the cadets, as they were generally called, to a young lady of the theatrical company, promenading at the time on the parade. The insult was promptly resented by a male member of the *troupe*, who hurled the offender down the steps. A dozen of his companions immediately rushed up the steps, and assailed the champion, who was supported by the rest of the company; and the consequence was a sharp scrimmage, ending in the arrival of several constables, and the removal to the station-house of as many of the cadets as could not escape by flight. Next morning they were taken before the magistrates, and, being proved to have been the aggressors, they were fined; and from that time the military aspirants of Addiscombe were forbidden to enter the town during the three days of the fair.

Charles Freer was the leading actor of the company at this time, and the principal lady was Mrs. Hugh Campbell, whom I remember seeing a year or two afterwards at the Gravesend theatre. She was subsequently engaged, as was Freer also, at the Pavilion. Her successor on the Richardsonian boards was Mrs. Yates, who was afterwards engaged at the Standard.

The harlequin was a nervous, eccentric, one-eyed young man named Charles Shaw, who was dismissed from the company towards the close of the season on account of his freaks reaching a pitch which at times raised a doubt as to his sanity, besides threatening detriment to the interests of the theatre. When the time approached at which the campaign of 1842 was to be commenced, it was found necessary to advertise for a harlequin; and the announcement of the want produced a response from Charles Wilson, who stated that he had been engaged through the preceding pantomime season at the Birmingham theatre. This gentleman seeming eligible, he was engaged, but was not seen by Lee, or any of the company, until he presented himself at the theatre on Easter Sunday, at Greenwich. Lee was immediately struck with the new harlequin's remarkable resemblance to the old one, which extended to every feature but the eyes; these were the same colour as Shaw's, but he had two, while Shaw had lost one. On the second day of the fair, however, it was discovered that the eye which had thus long puzzled every one as to his identity was a glass one; and on his being charged with being Shaw, he acknowledged the deception, observing that he had felt sure that he would not be re-engaged if he applied in his proper name. The deception was pardoned, and Shaw's subsequent freaks seem to have been fewer, and of a milder character.

The effects of the policy resolved upon by the City authorities in 1840 became more perceptible every year. In 1842, only one of the few shows that appeared in Smithfield issued a bill, which, as a curiosity, being the last ever issued for Bartholomew Fair, I subjoin:—

Extraordinary Phenomenon!!!
The greatest wonder in the world
Now Exhibiting Alive,
At the Globe Coffee House, No. 30, King Street,
Smithfield,
A Female Child with Two Perfect Heads,

Named Elizabeth Bedbury, Daughter of Daniel and Jane Bedbury, Born at Wandsworth, Surrey, April 17th, 1842. The public is respectfully informed that the Child is now Living; and hundreds of persons has been to see it, and declares that it is the most Wonderful Phenomenon of Nature they'd ever seen.

Admission 1*d.* Each.
No Deception; if dissatisfied, the Money Returned.

Nelson Lee played a trick at Croydon Fair this year which can only be defended on the principle that "all is fair at fair time." Finding that the Bosjesmans were being exhibited in the town, and were attracting great numbers of persons to their "receptions," he hung out, on the second day of the fair, a show-cloth with the announcement, in large black letters, "*Arrival of the Real Bosjesmen.*" to represent the strange specimens of humanity which had lately been discovered in South Africa, and their appearance on the parade in an antic dance produced a rush to witness the further representations of the manners and sports of savage life to be seen inside.

A startling event occurred on the following morning. One of Wombwell's elephants escaped from confinement, and at the early hour of three in the morning was seen, to the amazement and alarm of old Winter, the watchman, walking in a leisurely manner down High Street. He was in the habit of being taken every morning by his keeper to bathe in Scarbrook pond, a small piece of water skirted by a lane connecting the modern and now principal portion of the town with the Old Town; and on such occasions he was regaled with a bun at a confectioner's shop at the corner which he had to turn out of High Street, near the Green Dragon. While a constable ran to the George the Fourth, where some of Wombwell's *employés* were known to be located, the elephant reached the confectioner's shop, and, finding it closed, butted the shutters with his enormous head, and, amidst a crash of wood and glass, proceeded to help himself to the delicacies inside. On the arrival of his keeper, the docile beast submitted himself to his guidance, and was led back to his stable; but Wombwell had to pay the confectioner seven or eight pounds for the damage done to the shop window and shutters.

Johnson and Lee commenced the season of 1843 with several members of the Pavilion company in their fair *corps*; but they attended fewer fairs than in any previous year, and in 1844 their theatre appeared only at Greenwich, Enfield, and Croydon. In the following year, it was burned, while standing in a field at Dartford, and the proprietors, not being insured, suffered a loss of seventeen hundred pounds. Nothing was saved but the parade waggon, which was dragged away before the flames reached it, and, with the scene waggon and other effects which had been bought of Haydon in 1838, formed the nucleus of the new theatre with which the proprietors opened the fair campaign of 1847. Henry Howard joined the travelling company in that year at Ealing Fair, on the closing of the Standard.

During the latter part of their career as proprietors of a travelling theatre, the successors of Richardson found it more profitable to conduct their business on the system, since adopted by Newsome and Hengler with their circuses, of locating the theatre for two or three weeks at a time in some considerable town, than to wander from fair to fair, staying at each place only three or four days. At the present day, the circuses just named draw good houses, as a rule, for three months; but a quarter of a century ago this was not thought practicable, and in 1849, when Johnson and Lee erected their theatre at Croydon (in the Fair Field, but some time before the fair), they did not deem it expedient to extend their stay beyond three weeks. The company was drawn chiefly from the minor theatres of the metropolis, and included Leander Melville, Billington, Seaman, Phillips, Mrs. Barnett, Mrs. Campbell, and Miss Slater. *The Stranger* was selected for the first night, and drew a good audience, as it invariably does, wherever it is played. Under the able and judicious management of Nelson Lee, and with a change of performances every night, good business was done to the last. The experiment was repeated with equal success at Uxbridge and Reading.

Another step towards the extinction of Bartholomew Fair was taken this year by the exclusion from Smithfield of shows of every description; a step which would have been at least consistent, if the civic authorities had not made arrangements for the standing of shows of all kinds on a large piece of ground adjoining the New North Road, called Britannia Fields, near the site of the Britannia theatre. If the suppression of the fair had been sought on the ground of its interference with the trade and traffic of the city, this step would have been intelligible; but the moral grounds upon which it was urged served to cover with ridicule the removal of what was alleged to be a hot-bed of vice from Smithfield to Hoxton. What right had the corporation to demoralise the dwellers in one part of the metropolis, in order to preserve from further contamination the inhabitants of another part?

Bartholomew Fair was reduced by this step to a dozen stalls, and from that time may be considered as practically extinct. In Britannia Fields, what was called New Bartholomew Fair was attended by the shows which of late years had resorted to Smithfield and one or two others, among which was Reed's theatre, the prices of admission to which ranged from sixpence to two shillings. The performances consisted of *The Scottish Chieftain*, in which Saker played Ronald, the principal character, and a pantomime called *Harlequin Rambler*. Among the minor shows was that of Hales and his sister, the Norfolk giant and giantess, who issued a bill containing the following effusion of the Muse that inspired the poet of Mrs. Jarley's wax-work:—

"Miss Hales and her Brother are here to be seen,
O come let us visit the sweet lovely Queen;
Behold she is handsome—in manners polite—
Both she and her brother near eight feet in height!
I have seen all the tallest in towns far and near,
But never their equal to me did appear!
All England and Scotland, and Ireland declare,
Their like was ne'er seen yet in them anywhere.

"Here's the smallest of women creation can show,
Complete in proportion from top to the toe;
And a Lady of rank from New Zealand secured,
Escap'd from the murder her husband endured!
And a fine youthful female presented to sight,
All spangled and spotted with brown and with white;
Large Crocodiles here, and a Boa behold,

With a fine Anaconda all glistening with gold.

"Here's a silver-haired Lady, with skin white as snow,
Whose eyes are like rubies that roll to and fro!
You will find her a species different from all,
The black and the whites, or the low and the tall!
But to sing all her beauties I need not begin,
Nor the fine azure veins that appear through her skin;
For these, mind, no poet or painter can show,
But when you behold her, O then you may know!

"Exhibitions like this may to us be of use—
What a contrast of creatures this world can produce!
See the tallest and smallest before us in state.
What a prodigy rare and phenomena great!
From such wonders eccentric presented to view
We now may our study of nature pursue;
And philosophy truly may draw from it then,
That Temp'rance produces the tallest of men."

Hales made enough money by the exhibition of himself to purchase the lease and goodwill of a public-house in Drury Lane, where he lived several years. Many persons visited the house purposely to see him, but he never appeared in the bar before eleven o'clock, and was careful to avoid making himself too cheap. I saw him once, in crossing the street towards his house, stoop to raise in his arms a little girl, suggesting to my mind the giant and fairy of a pantomime.

In pursuance of the policy indicated in the report of 1840, Bartholomew Fair, now represented by a few stalls, was proclaimed in 1850 by deputy; and this course was followed until 1855, when not a single stall-keeper applied for space, and the ceremony of proclaiming the fair was omitted altogether. The new fair in Britannia Fields was held only two or three years, that concession to the showmen and to the fair-going portion of the public having been designed only for the purpose of facilitating the extinction of the old fair in Smithfield.

Greenwich Fair was the scene in 1850 of an outrageous and dastardly attack on Johnson and Lee's theatre by a body of soldiers from Woolwich. It seems to have originated in a practical joke played by a soldier upon a young man in the crowd before the theatre, and which, being resented, was followed by an assault. On the latter retreating up the steps of the parade waggon, followed by his assailant, Nelson Lee interposed for his protection, and was himself assaulted by the soldier, who was thereupon ejected. A number of soldiers, witnessing the discomfiture of their comrade, immediately rushed up the steps, and began an indiscriminate attack upon everybody on the parade. The company, finding themselves over-matched, took refuge in the interior, or jumped off the parade, and fled as if for their lives.

An actor named Chappell stood by Nelson Lee after the rest had fled, but he joined in the stampede ultimately, and the proprietor of the theatre was left alone, defending himself and property against a swarm of foes. The story told long afterwards of the harlequin of the company was, that he ran without pause to the railway station, and jumped into a train just starting for London. He then ran from London Bridge to Shoreditch, and rushing, exhausted and excited, into a public-house adjoining the City of London theatre, gasped, "Blood—soldiers—Mr. Lee—frightful affair—three pen'orth o' brandy!"

The soldiers, having driven their opponents off the field, began destroying the front of the theatre, and smashing the lamps, which, fortunately, were not lighted. If they had been burning, the result would probably have been a terrific conflagration, which might have swept the fair, and destroyed many thousands of pounds' worth of property. Nelson Lee, resisting with all his might the destruction of his property, had a rope made fast round his body, and was about to be hoisted to the top of the front, when a dozen constables arrived, and the assailants immediately abandoned the field, and, leaping off the parade, mixed with the crowd. Many of them were captured, however, and, being taken before a magistrate, were committed for trial at the ensuing Old Bailey sessions. Johnson and Lee withdrew from the prosecution, however, expecting that their forbearance would be rewarded by pecuniary compensation for the destruction of their property, which the Recorder had suggested should be given by the officers of the regiment to which the offenders belonged; but, on application being made to the officers, they informed Lee that there were *no regimental funds* available for the purpose, and I believe not a penny was ever received by Johnson and Lee by way of compensation.

During the Whitsuntide Fair, the soldiers were confined to their barracks; but, as many of them were in the habit of visiting the theatre with their friends, this measure diminished the receipts, and thus added loss to loss. Johnson and Lee attended no other fairs that year, but removed the theatre to Croydon, where they erected it in a field adjoining the Addiscombe Road, near the Brighton and South-Eastern railway stations. Henry Howard and Mrs. Campbell played the leading characters here, and afterwards at Hertford and Uxbridge.

Wombwell died this year in his living carriage at Richmond, at the age of seventy-three. He was buried in Highgate cemetery, his coffin being made of oak from the timbers of the *Royal George*, which sank off Spithead in 1782. As his executors were instructed by his will to have no nails used in its construction, it was put together on the dove-tailing system. The menagerie was divided in accordance with his will into three parts, which were bequeathed respectively to his widow, a niece named Edmunds, and another relative named Day.

The expectation of such results as attended the Hyde Park Fair of 1838 from the concourse of people flocking into the metropolis during the summer of 1851, when the first great international exhibition was held, caused arrangements to be made for a "world's fair" on a large scale, to be held during the same time at Bayswater. A committee was formed for its organisation and management, consisting of Johnson and Lee, Algar, Mussett, Mills, Trebeck, and Young. Algar was the proprietor of the Crown and Anchor refreshment and dancing booth, well-known to the frequenters of Greenwich and Croydon Fairs; Mussett and Mills were almost as well known as leading names among the stall-keepers attending the great fairs; Trebeck was a toy-dealer in Sun Street, Bishopsgate.

The undertaking was as complete a failure, however, as the fair of 1838 had been a success. The ground was in bad condition, and its softness was a difficulty at the commencement. Mrs. Wombwell's elephant waggon stuck in the mud, and had to be left there until the next day; and the elephant extricated himself with difficulty by lifting one leg at a time, and stepping upon trusses of straw laid down to give him a firm footing. Edmunds would not venture to the ground which he had taken for his menagerie, but arranged his caravans at the entrance of the field. The weather was cold and cheerless when the fair was opened, and the railway companies had not begun running trains at low fares. When the fine weather and the excursion trains did come, the fair had come to be regarded as a failure, and it never recovered from the chill and blight of its commencement.

Johnson and Lee's theatre appeared at Greenwich Fair for the last time in 1852, and proceeded thence to Uxbridge, where the company was joined by James Robson, afterwards so famous as a comedian at the Olympic. In the following year, the property was sold by auction, and, as a memorial of an event which has seldom occurred, and will never occur again, I subjoin the advertisement:—

"Notice.—To Carmen, Builders, Proprietors of Tea Gardens, Exhibitors, Van Proprietors, Travelling Equestrians, Providers of Illuminations, &c.—The Travelling Theatrical Property known as Richardson's Theatre, comprising Covered Vans and Parade Waggons, Scenery, Wings, Stage Front, Orchestra, with a double stock of beautiful scenery, waterproof covering, draperies, massive chandeliers, a great quantity of baize, flags, &c. Large coat of arms, variegated lamps and devices, eight capital 6-inch wheels, parade waggons, with two large flaps to each, two capital excursion vans, trucks, double stock of new scenery, shifting flies, fourteen long forms, large stock of book-cloths and baize of large dimensions, battened dancing-boards, erection of booths, handsome imitation stone front, two capital money-takers' boxes, with fittings up, handsome ornamental urns, large figures on pedestals, four guns and carriages, handsome pilasters, machinery, flooring throughout the building, with numerous scenery and stage devices, and every other article connected with the stage, a quantity of quartering, iron, old wheels, &c., &c., &c. Which will be sold by auction by Mr. Lloyd, on the premises, Richardson's Cottage, Horsemonger-lane, Boro'. May be viewed, and catalogues had on the premises, and of the Auctioneers, 5, Hatfield-street, Blackfriars-road."

The property was completely dispersed; the timber and wood-work being purchased by builders, the waggons by wheelwrights, the canvas and tilt-cloths by farmers, and the green baize, curtains, fittings, etc., by Jew dealers. There is not the shadow of a pretence, therefore, for the use of the name, "Richardson's theatre," by any showman of the present day.

The shows travelling after the sale and dispersion of Johnson and Lee's were, exclusive of menageries and exhibitions, Abbott's theatre, Jackman's theatre, and Fossett's circus. I am not sure that Reed's theatre was still in existence. Abbott's theatre was at the Easter fair at Greenwich in 1852, when Charlie Keith, since famous all over Europe as "the roving English clown," was fulfilling his first engagement in it as an acrobat. Robson, the comedian, was at the same time performing in Jackman's theatre, from which he transferred his services to Johnson and Lee's.

Fossett's circus was pitched that summer at Primrose Hill for a few days, when one of the irregular fairs which are occasionally held in the neighbourhood of London was held. It is a small concern, with only two or three horses. Miss Fossett, the proprietor's daughter, is a tight-rope performer, in which capacity she appeared a few years ago in Talliott's circus, when the company and stud appeared one winter in a temporary building at the rear of some small houses in New Street, Lambeth Walk. James Talliott, to whom the houses belong, was then well known to the frequenters of the London music-halls, and may be remembered as a trapeze performer in conjunction with Burnett, who called himself Burnetti, but was known among the professional fraternity as Bruiser. He afterwards performed singly at the Strand Music-hall, now the Gaiety Theatre, and other places of amusement in the metropolis, and has since owned a small circus, with which he travels during the summer within a circle of a dozen miles from London.

Hilton's menagerie had at this time passed into the possession of Manders, and the lion-tamer of the show was an Irishman named James Strand, who had formerly kept a gingerbread-stall, and had been engaged to perform with the beasts when those attractive exhibitions had been threatened with temporary suspension by the abruptness with which his predecessor, Newsome—a brother, I believe, to the circus-proprietor of that name—

had terminated his engagement. Strand's qualifications for the profession were not equal to his own estimate of them, however, and Manders had to look out for his successor.

One day, when the menagerie was at Greenwich Fair, a powerful-looking negro accosted one of the musicians, saying that he was a sailor just returned from a voyage, and would like a berth in the show. The musician communicated the man's wish to Manders, and the negro was invited to enter the show. His appearance and confident manner impressed the showman favourably, and, on his being allowed to enter the lion's cage, at his own request, he displayed so much address and ability to control the animals that he was engaged at once, and "the gingerbread king," as Strand was called, was informed that his services could, for the future, be dispensed with. This remarkable black man was the famous Macomo, who for several years afterwards travelled with the menagerie, exhibiting in his performances with lions and tigers as much daring as Van Amburgh, and as much coolness as Crockett.

One of the finest tigers ever imported into this country, and said to be the identical beast that escaped from Mr. Jamrach's premises in St. George's Street (better known by its old name of Ratcliffe Highway), and killed a boy before it was recaptured, was purchased by Manders, and placed in a cage with another tiger. The two beasts soon began fighting furiously, upon which Macomo entered the cage, armed only with a riding-whip, and attempted to separate them. His efforts caused both the tigers to turn their fury upon him, and they severely lacerated him; but, covered with blood as he was, he continued the struggle for supremacy until the beasts cowered before him, and he was able, with the assistance of the keepers, to separate them.

It is worthy of remark, in connection with the causes of accidents with lions and tigers, that Macomo, like Crockett, was a strictly sober man, never touching intoxicating liquors of any kind. "It's the drink," said the ex-lion king, who was interviewed by the special commissioner of a London morning journal two years ago; "It's the drink that plays the mischief with us fellows. There are plenty of people always ready to treat the daring fellow that plays with the lions as if they were kittens; and so he gets reckless, lets the dangerous animal—on which, if he were sober, he would know he must always keep his eye—get dodging round behind him; or hits a beast in which he ought to know that a blow rouses the sleeping devil; or makes a stagger, and goes down, and then they set upon him."

Macomo's fight with the two tigers was not the only occasion on which he received injuries, the scars of which he bore upon him to the day of his death, which, contrary to the expectation of every one who witnessed his performances, was a peaceful one. He died a natural death in 1870, when he was succeeded by an Irishman named Macarthy, who had previously been attached in a similar capacity to the circus of Messrs. Bell and Myers. While performing, in 1862, with the lions belonging to that establishment, he had had his left arm so severely mangled by one of the beasts that amputation became necessary. This circumstance seems to have added to the *éclat* of his performances; but he had neither the nerve of Macomo, nor his resolution to abstain from stimulants. Unlike his predecessor, he frequently turned his back upon the lions, though he had frequently been cautioned against the danger he thereby incurred; and it was believed that his disregard of the warning was one of the causes of the terrible encounter which terminated his existence.

Macarthy was bitten on two occasions while performing with Manders's lions, prior to the disaster at Bolton. The first time was while performing at Edinburgh, when one of the beasts made a snap at his remaining arm, but only slightly grazed it. The second occasion was a few days before the fatal accident occurred, when one of the Lions bit him slightly on the wrist. He lost his life in representing a so-called "lion hunt," an exhibition which was introduced by Macomo, and consists in chasing the animals about the cage, the performer being armed with a sword and pistols, and throwing into the mimic sport as much semblance of reality as the circumstances allow. The exhibition is acknowledged by lion-tamers themselves to be a dangerous one, and it should never be attempted with any but young animals. For their ordinary performances, most lion-tamers prefer full-grown animals, as being better trained; but a full-grown lion does not like to be driven and hustled about, as the animals are in the so-called "lion hunt," and when such are used for this exhibition they are frequently changed.

Macarthy was driving the animals from one end of the cage to the other when one of them ran against his legs, and threw him down. He soon regained his feet, however, and drove the animals into a corner. Whilst stamping his feet upon the floor, to make the animals run past him, one of them crept stealthily out from the group, and sprang upon him, seizing him by the right hip and throwing him down upon his side. For a moment the spectators imagined that this was part of the performance, but Macarthy's agonised features soon convinced them of the terrible reality of the scene before them. As he struggled to rise, three other lions sprang upon him, one of them seizing his arm, from which he immediately dropped the sword.

The keepers now hurried to the unfortunate man's assistance, some of them endeavouring to beat off the infuriated lions, while others inserted a partition between the bars of the cage, with a view to driving the animals behind it. This was a task of considerable difficulty, however, for as one beast was obliged to relinquish its hold of the unfortunate man, another rushed into its place. Heated irons were then brought, and by their aid, and the discharge of fire-arms, four of the lions were driven behind the partition. Macarthy was lying in the centre of the cage, still being torn by the lion that had first attacked him. A second partition was attempted to be inserted, but was found to be too large; and then one of the keepers drew the first one out a little, with the view of driving the fifth lion among the rest. More blank cartridges were fired, without effect, and it was not until the hot irons were applied to the nose of the infuriated brute that it loosed its hold, and ran behind the partition.

Even then, before the opening could be closed, the lion ran out again, seized the dead or dying man by one of his feet and dragged him into the corner, where four of the beasts again fell upon him with unsatiated thirst of blood. The terrible scene had now been going on for a quarter of an hour, and, even when all the animals were at length secured, it was found that they were next the entrance of the cage, the opposite end of which had to be broken open before the mangled corpse of the lion-tamer could be lifted out.

As lion-tamers are well paid, and this was only the second fatal accident in the course of half a century, it is not surprising that, as soon as the catastrophe became known, there were several candidates for the vacancy created by Macarthy's death. Mrs. Manders had resolved to discontinue the exhibition, however, and the applicants for the situation received an intimation to that effect.

Mrs. Wombwell retired from the menagerie business in 1866, and was succeeded in the proprietorship by Fairgrieve, who had married her niece.

Fairgrieve retired from the occupation in the spring of 1872, when his fine collection of animals was sold by auction at Edinburgh. As the public sale of a menagerie is a rare event, and Mr. Jamrach and Mr. Rice do not publish prices current, the reader may be glad to learn the prices realised.

The first lot was a racoon—"a very pleasant, playful pet," the auctioneer said—which was knocked down to the Earl of Roseberry for one pound. Mr. Bell Lamonby, another private collector, became the possessor of a pair of agoutis; which he was assured were "sharp, active little animals, and could sing like canaries," for an equally moderate sum. Then came a strange-looking and ferocious animal called the Tasmanian devil, of which there is a specimen in the gardens of the Zoological Society, and which the auctioneer assured his hearers was as strong in the jaw as a hyena, but not to be recommended for purchase as a domestic pet. Bids were slow, and even the prospect of purchasing the devil for three pounds did not render buyers enthusiastic; so that Mrs. Day bought the animal for five shillings more.

Then came the baboons and monkeys. The Diana monkey, a white and rose-breasted little animal, was purchased by Dr. Mackendrick for seven pounds; while the Capuchin monkey, full of intelligence, and belonging to a kind fancied by Italian organ-grinders, was knocked down to Mr. Rice for thirty shillings. Mr. Jamrach purchased the drill, "a playful little drawing-room pet, worth twenty pounds to put on the kitchen shelf to look at," for five guineas; and Mr. Rice paid thirty pounds for a male mandrill, five for a female of the same species, eighteen guineas for a pair of Anubis baboons, and fifteen pounds for five dog-faced baboons.

Passing on to the bird carriage, the first specimen submitted to competition was the black vulture, one of the largest birds of the species, and in excellent plumage. Mr. Rice bought this bird for three pounds ten shillings, and the condor, which had been forty years in the show, for fifteen pounds. Next came the emu, "a very suitable bird for a gentleman's park, and a nice show thing for the ladies in the morning, after breakfast," which Mrs. Day secured for her collection at seven pounds. Mr. Jamrach gave thirteen pounds for the pair of pelicans, bought at the sale of the Knowsley collection, and which had been trained to run races. The fine collection of parrots, macaws, and cockatoos was dispersed among a number of local fanciers of ornithological beauties.

Proceeding to the larger mammals, the auctioneer knocked down a male nylghau to Mr. Van Amburgh, the great American menagerist, for twenty-six pounds, and a female of the same species to the proprietor of the Manchester Zoological Gardens for ten guineas; while Mr. Jamrach secured a llama for fifteen pounds, and Mr. Rice a young kangaroo for twelve pounds. Professor Edwards, who had come over from Paris to pick up a few good specimens for the Jardin des Plantes, purchased the white bear, "young, healthy, and lively as a trout," for forty pounds, and a jackal for three pounds. A Thibet bear and three performing leopards were knocked down to Mr. Jamrach for five guineas and sixty pounds respectively. Another leopard, advanced in years, realised only six guineas. Mr. Van Amburgh secured the spotted hyena for fifteen pounds; while a performing striped hyena brought only five shillings above three pounds. Among objects of minor interest, a pair of wolves were sold for two guineas, an ocelot for six pounds ten shillings, three porcupines for ten pounds more, a wombat for seven pounds, a Malabar squirrel for five pounds, and a pair of boa constrictors for twelve pounds.

The large carnivora excited much attention, and fair prices were realised, though in some instances they were less than was expected. Mr. Rice gave a hundred and eighty-five pounds for the famous lion with which Signor Lorenzo used to represent the well-known story of Androcles, two other lions for a hundred and forty pounds each, two young ones for ninety pounds each, and a lioness for eighty pounds. A black-maned lion, said to be the largest and handsomest lion in Britain, was sold to Mr. Jackson, for the Bristol Zoological Gardens, for two hundred and seventy pounds; and his mate, in the interesting condition of approaching maternity, to Mr. Jennison, of the Belle Vue Gardens, Manchester, for a hundred guineas. Mr. Jamrach gave two hundred pounds for a fine lion, and a hundred and fifty-five pounds for the magnificent tigress that used to figure conspicuously in the performances of Signor Lorenzo.

Mr. Rice, who was the largest purchaser, bought the gnu for eighty-five pounds, and the zebra for fifty pounds. The camels and dromedaries, bought principally for travelling menageries, realised from fourteen to thirty pounds each, with the exception of a young one, bought by Dr. Mackendrick for nine pounds ten shillings. Menagerists restrict the word "camel" to the two-humped or Bactrian variety, and call the one-humped kind dromedaries; but the dromedary, according to naturalists, is a small variety of the Syrian camel, bearing the same relation to the latter as a pony does to a horse. The dromedaries of Mr. Fairgrieve's collection were, on the contrary, taller than the Bactrian camels.

There was a spirited competition for the two elephants, ending in the magnificent full-tusked male, seven feet six inches in height, being knocked down to Mr. Jennison for six hundred and eighty pounds, and the female, famous for her musical performances, to Mr. Rice for a hundred and forty-five pounds. The former animal was described as the largest and cleverest performing elephant ever exhibited. In stature he is exceeded, it is said, by the elephant kept by the Emperor of Russia at the gardens of Tsarski-Seloe; but, while the performances of that beast have been confined to the occasional killing of a keeper, the animal now in the Belle Vue Gardens at Manchester, besides performing many tricks evincing great docility and intelligence, was accustomed to draw the band carriage, would pull a loaded waggon up a hill, and had for the last eighteen months preceding the sale placed all the vans of the menagerie in position, with the assistance of a couple of men. The entire proceeds of the sale were a little under three thousand pounds.

I do not remember ever visiting a travelling menagerie that afforded me greater pleasure than one of the smaller class which I saw some thirty years ago at Mitcham Fair, and subsequently at Camberwell Fair. There were no lions or tigers in the collection, but it included four performing leopards, a tame hyena, and a wolf that seemed equally tame, if such an inference could be drawn from the presence of a lamb in its cage. The showman, who wore neither spangled trunks, nor a coat of chain-mail, but corduroy breeches and a sleeved vest of cat's skin, entered the leopard's cage, with a riding whip in one hand and a hoop in the other. The animals leaped over the whip, through the hoop, and over the man's back, exhibiting throughout the performance as much docility as dogs or cats. The whip was used merely as part of the "properties." The man afterwards entered the cage of the hyena, which rubbed its head against him, after the manner of a cat, and allowed him to open its mouth. The hyena has the reputation of being untameable; but, in addition to this instance to the contrary, Bishop Heber had a hyena at Calcutta which followed him about like a dog.

Tigers are little used as performing animals, partly perhaps from being less easily procured, but also, I believe, from greater distrust of them on the part of brute-tamers. There was a splendid tigress in Fairgrieve's menagerie, however, with which Signor Lorenzo used to do a wonderful performance; and I saw, some five-and-thirty years ago, in a show pitched upon a piece of waste ground at Norwood, a tiger that played a prominent part in a sensational drama, the interest of which was evolved from the hair-breadth escapes of a British traveller in the wilds of Africa. The author did not seem to have been aware that there are no tigers in that part of the world, the animals so called by the Cape colonists being leopards; but, as the old woman who took money replied to my remonstrance that one tiger could not, without an outrage upon Lindley Murray, be called performing *animals*, "what can you expect for a penny?"

The old showmen are now virtually extinct, and the London fairs have all ceased to exist. "Old Bartlemy" died hard, but its time must soon have come, in the natural order of things. Its extinction was followed closely by that of all the other fairs formerly held in the suburbs of the metropolis. Camberwell Fair was abolished in 1856, and the Greenwich Fairs in the following year. I cannot better express my opinion as to the causes which have led to the decline of fairs generally, but especially of those held within half an hour's journey from the metropolis, and the suppression of most of those formerly held within a shorter distance, than by quoting a brief dialogue between a showman and an acrobat in 'Bob Lumley's Secret,' a story which appeared anonymously a few years ago in a popular periodical:—

"'Fairs is nearly worked out, Joe,' said the red-faced individual, speaking between the whiffs of blue smoke from his *dhudeen*. 'Why, I can remember the time when my old man used to take more money away from this fair with the Russian giant, and the Polish dwarf, and the Circassian lady, than I can make now in a month. Them was the times, when old Adam Lee, the Romany, used to come to this fair with his coat buttons made of guineas, and his waistcoat buttons of seven-shilling pieces. Ah, you may laugh, Joey Alberto; but I have heard my old man speak of it many's the time.'

"'There's good fairs now down in the shires,' observed the younger man; 'but this town is too near the big village.'

"'That's it!' exclaimed the showman. 'It's all along o' them blessed railways. They brings down lots o' people, it is true; but, lor'! they don't spend half the money the yokels used to in former times.'

"'Besides which,' rejoined he of the spangled trunks, 'the people about here can run up to London and back for a shilling any day in the week, all the year round, and see all the living curiosities in the Zoo, and the stuffed ones in the Museum, and go in the evening to a theatre or a music-hall.'"

The fair referred to was the October fair at Croydon; and I may add that views similar to those which I have put into the mouths of the acrobat and the showman were expressed to me in 1846 by a showman named Gregory, who exhibited various natural curiosities and well-contrived mechanical representations of the falls of Niagara and a storm at sea. He had just received from the printer five thousand bills, which he carefully stowed away.

"This fair don't pay for bills," said he. "I want these for Canterbury Fair, where there's more money to be taken in one day than in this field in three."

"Which do you reckon the best fair in your circuit?" I inquired.

"Sandwich," he replied. "That's a good distance from London, you see, and though it's a smaller town than this, there's plenty of money in it. This is too near London, now the rail enables people to go there and back for a shilling, see all the sights and amusements, and get back home the same night."

The fairs within half an hour's journey from London which are still held are in a state of visible decadence. I walked through Kingston Fair last year, about three o'clock in the afternoon, at which time Croydon Fair would, even twenty or thirty years ago, have been crowded. The weather was unusually fine, the sun shining with unwonted brilliance for the season, and the ground in better condition for walking than I had ever seen the field at Croydon on the 2nd of October. Yet there were fewer people walking through the fair than I had seen in the market-place. The gingerbread vendors and other stall-keepers looked as if they were weary of soliciting custom in vain; the swings and the roundabouts stood idle; some of the showmen had not thought the aspect of the field sufficiently promising to be encouraged to unfurl their pictorial announcements, and those who had done so failed to attract visitors.

Day's menagerie was there, and was the principal show in the fair; but the few persons who paused to gaze at the pictures passed on without entering, and even the beasts within were so impressed with the pervading listlessness and inactivity that I did not hear a sound from the cages as I walked round to the rear of the show to observe its extent. There was no braying of brass bands, no beating of gongs or bawling through speaking-trumpets. One forlorn showman ground discordant sounds from a barrel-organ with an air of desperation, and another feebly clashed a pair of cymbals; but these were all the attempts made to attract attention, and they were made in vain.

This was on Saturday afternoon, too, when a large number of the working classes are liberated who could not formerly have attended the fair at that time without taking a holiday. There was a good attendance in the evening, I heard; but, however well the shows and stalls may be patronised after six o'clock, it is obvious that their receipts must be less than half what they amounted to in the days when they were thronged from noon till night.

Fairs are becoming extinct because, with the progress of the nation, they have ceased to possess any value in its social economy, either as marts of trade or a means of popular amusement. All the large towns now possess music-halls, and many of them have a theatre; the most populous have two or three. The circuses of Newsome and Hengler are located for three months at a time in permanent buildings in the larger towns, and the travelling circuses visit in turn every town in the kingdom. Bristol and Manchester have Zoological Gardens, and Brighton has its interesting Aquarium. The railways connect all the smaller towns, and most of the villages, with the larger ones, in which amusements may be found superior to any ever presented by the old showmen. What need, then, of fairs and shows? The nation has outgrown them, and fairs are as dead as the generations which they have delighted, and the last showman will soon be as great a curiosity as the dodo.